AMBER GARZA

WHERE

I LEFT

HER

mira

Recycling programs for this product may not exist in your area.

ISBN-13: 978-0-7783-3206-0

Where I Left Her

This edition published by arrangement with Harlequin Books S.A.

For questions and comments about the quality of this book, please contact us at CustomerService@Harlequin.com.

Mira
22 Adelaide St. West, 40th Floor
Toronto, Ontario M5H 4E3, Canada
BookClubbish.com

Printed in U.S.A.

Praise for the novels of Amber Garza

On *Where I Left Her*

"Garza taps into every parent's worst nightmare, a child gone missing, and worse, the discovery of a hidden internet world that shows they've been hiding a life from you. In this high-tension domestic drama, nothing is as it seems."
—J.T. Ellison, *USA TODAY* bestselling author of *Her Dark Lies*

"Amber Garza establishes herself once again as a master of domestic suspense... A teenager's disappearance forces a family's secrets to the light in this pitch-perfect thriller."
—Mindy Mejia, author of *Everything You Want Me to Be*

"*Where I Left Her* is a reminder of why thrillers are my favourite genre. This is a tale that's dark and twisted...secrets galore...shifting allegiances... And that ending! It'll blow your mind."
—Hannah Mary McKinnon, bestselling author of *Sister Dear*

On *When I Was You*

"*When I Was You* doles out twists and turns at the perfect pace, leading up to a fantastic conclusion... A gripping psychological barnburner."
—*Shelf Awareness*

"Fans of tricky tales of obsession and revenge will be well satisfied."
—*Publishers Weekly*

"Amber Garza has upped the game on the classic stalker novel! *When I Was You* is a fast-paced, beautifully plotted book that will keep you reading until the last page. You won't want to put this one down."
—Samantha Downing, *USA TODAY* bestselling author of *My Lovely Wife*

"Exhilarating, page-turning, shocking, this is one of those rare psychological thrillers that really is the whole package. An electric, raw, emotional story that will leave you breathless... *When I Was You* is a dark and twisty delight."
—Christina McDonald, *USA TODAY* bestselling author of *The Night Olivia Fell*

"A compulsive read about a friendship and maternal instincts gone awry, with a twist you won't want to miss."
—Karen Cleveland, *New York Times* bestselling author of *Need to Know*

"Garza's debut thriller packs a wallop of intrigue... The unpredictable twists and turns culminate in an explosive, shocking ending. A definite must-read!"
—Samantha M. Bailey, author of *Woman on the Edge*

Also by Amber Garza

When I Was You

To Kayleen, who was, thankfully, right where I left her

WHERE

I LEFT

HER

1

WHITNEY WANTED TO get rid of her daughter.

How awful is that?

Not forever, of course, but for the night. She was weary of the sixteen-year-old attitude. The rolling of eyes, stomping of feet, the judging glances and biting remarks.

That's why she wasn't paying as much attention as she should've been when dropping Amelia off at Lauren's. Her mind was back in their apartment, her butt planted on the couch, bare feet propped on the table, a pint of ice cream in her lap.

"The destination is on your right." She turned the steering wheel, following the instructions given by the disembodied voice of the GPS in her daughter's phone. Amelia held it up, giving the illusion that her palm was talking. The house in front of them was nondescript. A tract home, painted tan with beige trim, a cream door, two large windows overlooking the narrow front walkway. The only thing that set it apart from the others was the row of rosebushes lining the left perimeter of the yard, scarlet red petals and thorny, jagged stems.

Whitney pulled her car over, tires hugging the curb.

Amelia hopped out the minute her mother's foot pressed down on the brakes, as if she was desperate to be free of her.

"You sure this is her house?" Whitney asked.

Amelia shrugged, glancing down at her phone and then back up. "This is the address she gave me." Her tone was impatient, irritated. That's how she'd been lately. Distant and moody. Everything her mom said and did annoyed her.

Originally, she'd planned to walk Amelia up to the front door and meet Lauren's mom. But on the way over here, Amelia had begged her not to do that, pointing out that she was no longer a little girl.

As much as Whitney hated to admit it, she could see her point. Amelia *was* sixteen. As soon as she finished her driver's training and passed her test, she'd be driving on her own and then Whitney wouldn't even have the option of dropping her off at her friend's. It was time she learned to let go, loosen the death grip a little.

Instead of following her daughter, Whitney stayed inside the car, watching through the smudged glass of the passenger-side window. Amelia's dark hair swished down her spine as she sped to the front door. When she reached it, she readjusted the blue overnight bag that was secured on her shoulder while lifting her other hand to knock.

Lauren appeared in the doorway, flashing a smile at Amelia. She wore a pink headband that made her look much younger than seventeen. Amelia peered over her shoulder before stepping forward, her lips curling at the corners as she threw her mom another wave. It was the largest grin Whitney had gotten in days, and she welcomed it, grabbed hold of it and then gave it back.

After watching them both disappear inside, Whitney pulled away from the curb. Without even looking in the rearview mirror, she sped toward her night of freedom, dreaming of a couch to herself and a movie Amelia couldn't make fun of.

SATURDAY, 10:00 A.M.
SEVENTEEN HOURS
AFTER DROP-OFF

Whitney had been up for hours, and still hadn't heard from Amelia. Last night was restful. Quiet. Peaceful. All the things Whitney had wanted it to be. Much needed. But this morning she was suffering from a serious case of mom guilt. She missed her daughter. Was anxious for her to come home, attitude and all. Unlocking her phone, she shot her a quick text: Ready for me to pick you up?

Even after several minutes, no response came. Not that she was shocked. When Amelia had friends over, they stayed up all night giggling and talking. No matter how many times Whitney would remind them to keep it down, within minutes their muffled voices would return, drifting through the adjoining bedroom wall. Most likely, she'd done the same at Lauren's and they were both still asleep.

The house smelled like Saturday morning—coffee, creamer, maple syrup.

French toast had been a weekend tradition for years. When Amelia was little, she'd wake up early and bound into her mom's bedroom, eager for breakfast. But lately it seemed Whitney ate alone more often than not. Even when Amelia was home, there was no guarantee she'd join her. Amelia lived in her room, earbuds perpetually plugged in her ears, as if she'd grown another extremity. Still, Whitney couldn't bring herself to stop the tradition altogether. The French toast would get eaten, even if it took a couple of days. Whitney didn't mind leftovers, anyway. Not that she had many this morning. She'd gone for an extra-long jog and had been ravenous.

After cleaning up the kitchen, Whitney went back into her phone and clicked on the Snapchat app. Amelia may have been quiet around the house lately, but she had no problem sharing her life with the rest of the world. Whitney expected to be greeted by smiling selfies of her and Lauren, maybe some photos of the food they were eating, proof to all the other teenagers on social media that they were having a blast on their Friday night together. But nothing had been posted on her story in the last twenty-four hours.

With slick fingertips, Whitney closed out of Snapchat and checked Instagram. Nothing there either. A chill brushed over her neck, causing the hairs to stand on end. She shook the feeling away with an abrupt jerk of her head. Whitney had always been like this. Anxious. A worrier, especially when it came to Amelia. Perpetually thinking the worst. Amelia hated it. So had her ex-husband. It was one of the many things they fought about. And it was probably one of many reasons why Dan had ended up marrying that sunny, smiling, high-pitched preschool teacher. If Whitney had to take a guess, she'd say there were no skeletons in Miss Karen's closet. No past indiscretions she was afraid of coming to light. No monsters from her past lurking around the corner.

No secret buried inside, so deep the roots had become invisible.

When Dan married Karen, Whitney remembered thinking how he had succeeded in finding someone completely opposite from her, just like he said he would. It didn't take him long either. He'd met Karen less than a year after they'd split up. He and Karen were friends for a while, and then dated for several years before marrying.

That was how he always defended it.

We were friends first.

We took it slow.

But that was never the point. He should have made Amelia his priority. Whitney hadn't dated at all while Amelia was growing up—she'd only started within the last couple of years. Once Amelia hit high school and started having a life of her own, Whitney figured it was time she did too.

Leaning against the counter, she stared out the kitchen window. There wasn't a view. The window overlooked the apartment across the way. A man stood in his kitchen, his back to Whitney as he drank coffee. His build vaguely reminded Whitney of Jay, and it made her smile.

Going into her last text thread with him, she typed, I miss you.

Then she bit her lip. *Too forward? Too soon?*

They'd been dating for a couple of months, and he'd only been on an overnight business trip. He was returning later today. She didn't want to come on too strong.

Backspace. Delete. She tried again: Hope your trip was good. *Too formal?*

Whitney paused, thinking.

Why am I making this so hard?

She really liked Jay. That was the problem. He was the first guy in a long time she felt hopeful about. Usually by month two of dating someone, the red flags popped up and her interest waned. That hadn't happened yet with Jay.

Turns out, she didn't need to stress over what to text. Jay beat her to it.

Boarding the plane now. Will call you when I'm back, he texted.

Sounds good, she responded.

It was 10:30. There were a million things on the agenda today and waiting around for Amelia wasn't one of them.

After hitting the grocery store and Target, Whitney swung by Lauren's, using the memory of how they'd gotten there yesterday as her guide. It was a little tricky, since she hadn't paid enough attention to Amelia's directions yesterday, but after a few minutes of circling the neighborhood, she came upon a

familiar street and turned on it. A couple of houses in, she recognized the rosebushes.

It had been well over an hour since she'd sent the last text to
Amelia. Although there hadn't been any response yet, Whitney was sure she was up by now. Probably hoping to buy more
time with her friend.

Whitney had gotten Amelia a bag of gummy worms. She
pulled it out of one of the grocery bags. It crinkled as she set it
on the passenger seat. Amelia probably wouldn't even eat them.
Certainly, they didn't fit within the parameters of her latest diet,
but, still, Whitney couldn't resist. Whitney's habit of picking up
treats at the store had started back when Amelia was a toddler,
when she'd surprised her with a bag of cookies one afternoon
when picking her up from preschool. Whitney would never forget how wide Amelia's eyes got, how broad her smile became
as she clutched the little bag. A lot of things may have changed
between them over the past few years, but Whitney didn't want
that to be one of them.

After getting out of the car, she slipped the key ring around
her finger and walked up the front walkway, flip-flops slapping
on the pavement. It was a warm, spring day. Kids played outside
a few houses down. A lawnmower kicked on. A couple rode
their bikes past, bright neon helmets bouncing up and down like
beach balls bobbing in the waves. Amelia used to love to ride
bikes. For a while, it had been a weekend tradition. Whitney
couldn't remember the last time they'd hit the trails together,
but she made a note to ask her about it. Most likely her answer
would be a big resounding no, coupled with the same cringey,
horrified look she had whenever Whitney suggested they hang
out. Still, it was worth a shot. Sometimes Amelia surprised her
with a yes, reminding Whitney of the girl she used to be before
the teenage monster took over.

When Whitney reached the door, she lifted her hand to knock
the same way she'd watched Amelia do the day before. A min-

ute passed and no one answered. That funny feeling returned, but she shoved it down, feeling silly.

She knocked again, this time so hard it stung her knuckles. The girls were probably listening to music or something. Or maybe they were in the backyard. It was a nice day. Ears perked, she listened for the sound of her daughter's voice or of music playing inside. Hearing neither of those, she frowned.

Finally, Whitney caught the hint of footsteps inside.

The door creaked open, an older woman peering out, eyebrows raised. She looked to be in her late sixties, maybe early seventies.

Whitney was taken aback. She'd never met Lauren's mom, but there was no way this was her. Maybe Lauren's grandparents lived with them. Recently, Whitney had watched a news report about how the cost of living had gone up, causing multigenerational homes to become a growing trend. And Lauren had mentioned that her parents were divorced. Whitney knew firsthand how financially taxing it was to raise a child alone.

"Hi, I'm Whitney. Amelia's mom." Smiling, Whitney jutted out her hand.

But the elderly woman just stared at it, not saying a word. She glanced over her shoulder where a man around her same age stood. He furrowed his brows and stepped forward. Whitney's body tensed.

Maybe she's got dementia or Alzheimer's or something. Whitney caught the old man's eyes. "Hi, I'm Amelia's mom. She spent the night here."

"Nope. Not here." Shaking his head, he came closer. "You must have the wrong house. They all kinda look the same in this neighborhood."

Whitney glanced around. Hadn't she thought the same thing yesterday? She must've turned down the wrong street or something.

Face warming, she backed away from the door. "I'm so sorry to have bothered you."

"No bother at all," the man said, and the woman offered a kind smile.

Whitney turned on her heels and made her way back to the car. She turned on the ignition and pulled away from the curb. The couple had already disappeared inside. Whitney drove to the main street and turned right. When she came up on another street, she turned onto it. The man was right. There were lots of houses that looked like theirs. She pulled up in front of one, scanning the yard.

Nope. No roses.

That's what had set the other house apart. The one she dropped Amelia off at.

She moved farther down the street, carefully looking to the right and to the left, searching for a one-story house, roses lining the perimeter. Coming up empty, she swung the car around. Maybe her mistake had been turning right at the main street.

Backtracking, this time Whitney turned left.

This street was almost identical to the other two she'd just been down. Same tract homes. Manicured lawns. Shuttered windows. A sea of tan paint and beige trim. The odd red door or colorful lawn art. But, again, no roses. At least, not in the correct spot.

Turning onto another street, she finally found it. The simple house. The roses lining the side.

After parking in front, she leaped out and hurried to the front door. It was answered after only a couple of knocks.

She gasped, taking in the elderly man standing in the doorway. The same one she'd just spoken to a few moments ago.

Oh, my God.

She'd ended up right back where she'd started. As she backed away from the door, apologizing profusely, she took in the shuttered windows, the manicured lawn, the roses lining the perimeter of the yard. Peering back at her car, she envisioned Amelia in the front seat holding her phone, the voice of the GPS speaking in her palm.

There was almost no doubt in Whitney's mind—this was where she'd left her.

2

EIGHT WEEKS
BEFORE DROP-OFF

THE HIGH SCHOOL parking lot was packed. Whitney followed the slow line of cars, weaving through rows of vehicles and students walking in large groups. She tapped her fingers against the steering wheel with impatience. The million things she still needed to get done filled her mind. But Whitney was grateful to be able to pick Amelia up this afternoon. Lately, she'd been so busy with work she rarely was able to. She felt bad about how many days Amelia had to hitch a ride with a friend or take the bus.

Rounding the corner near the football field, Amelia's group of friends stood in a huddle on the grass, heads bent together, a kaleidoscope of colored hair. Becca was talking animatedly, her hands moving in sync with her lips. Amelia wasn't in the circle. When she appeared, walking out from behind a nearby building, Whitney pulled her car over to the pickup area. As Amelia passed by her friends, they glanced over but didn't say anything. She kept her head down, eyes averted. Becca shot her a glare before returning her attention back to the other girls.

Could they be shunning her?

Amelia swung the passenger door open and plunked down with a loud sigh. She tossed her backpack down by her feet.

"What's going on with you and Becca?" Whitney asked, pulling away from the pickup area and joining the slow line again.

Amelia shrugged, staring down at her hands. Her nails were painted black, chipped at the edges. Some of the skin was torn and red. "Nothing."

"It didn't look like nothing."

"I guess we're just not really hanging out that much anymore."

"Why? Did you get in a fight or something?"

"I don't know." She groaned, sinking lower in her seat.

"How can you not know? Haven't you talked to her at all?"

"God, Mom, why can't you just let it go? It's not that big a deal."

Amelia and Becca had been BFFs since the beginning of junior high. Becca practically lived at their house; she had become part of their family. Whitney had never known the girls to ignore each other.

Whitney was at a loss. Amelia had always been the happiest kid. Whitney joked that she came out smiling and talking. It never took much to get her to smile and laugh as an infant. Just one look could get her going. She'd started talking before she was even a year old, and she never stopped. When she was in elementary school, she would talk constantly from the time Whitney picked her up until she went to bed. Some days it gave Whitney a headache. Every once in a while, Whitney couldn't take it and she'd make her play the "quiet game" just to give her ears a rest.

But the last couple of months she'd changed into this quiet, sullen, angry girl.

Whitney had tried to have conversations with Amelia about it, but that only pushed her further away. It was like she had no idea how to communicate with her own child anymore. She'd asked her friend Natalie about this the other day, but she assured Whitney it was normal. Natalie had two kids—a boy and a girl. They were both adults now, and she had great relationships with them. She encouraged Whitney to take a lot of deep breaths during this time.

At this rate, Whitney was breathing so deeply she might hyperventilate.

It will get better, she'd been saying over and over in her head. A silent mantra. Some days it was the only thing that got her through.

But now Whitney wasn't so sure it would get better. It was one thing for Amelia to be weird at home. All kids went through that phase where they pushed their parents away in an effort to find their own identities. God knows, she'd done that with her own parents. But nobody had said anything about pushing best friends away too.

"Can my friend Lauren spend the night Friday?"

"Lauren?" Whitney repeated, grateful for any foray into conversation. "I don't think I've met her before."

"Yeah, she's a new friend."

A new friend? Since when did Amelia need new friends? She already had a friend group. And Whitney had put in all the necessary time and effort to feel comfortable with that friend group, getting to know all the kids and parents. Becca's mom she knew especially well. Whitney had taken great comfort in that over the years. And since Amelia was a junior, she'd assumed her friend group would stay intact until graduation. Her mind spun with all the things she had to do now. Get to know the new friend's parents. Look her up on social media. She could already feel the tiredness settling into her bones, thinking of the late nights she'd spend worrying about this new friend. If she was a good influence. If she was safe.

"Well, that's nice," she said, careful to keep her tone calm. "Is she new to the school? The area?"

Amelia's eyebrows rose, and Whitney knew then that she'd been too eager. Asked too many questions.

"Sure," Amelia said. It wasn't an answer.

"Okay. I guess as long as you clean up your room, she can come over." Whitney kept her voice nonchalant, masking the discomfort she felt.

"Thanks, Mom." Amelia smiled, before shoving her earbuds into her ears and staring out the window.

It wasn't much, but it was something. And Whitney would take anything she could get.

The tightness in her chest loosened a little. The girl she'd raised, the one with the sweet smile and a million words on her tongue, was in there. This was merely a phase. It wouldn't last forever. As Whitney drove, her shoulders relaxed, and she bobbed her head to the soft jazz that floated through the speakers. It clearly wasn't as loud as Amelia's pop music. Whitney could hear it almost as well as her own. Well enough to catch Ariana Grande's distinct tone.

At the stoplight, Amelia stared out the window. Whitney heard a little ping interrupt the music blasting through her earbuds and Amelia's head shot downward. Following her gaze, Whitney read the notification.

Phil Lopez sent you a Snapchat.

Amelia smothered the phone with her hand when she noticed Whitney looking. The traffic light changed. Before releasing her foot off the brake, Whitney gently bumped her daughter's knee with her hand. Craning her neck, Amelia popped out one earbud.

The music still played, a harsh muffled beat as it dangled off her shoulder.

"Who's Phil?"

"No one."

"No one, huh? He must be someone if he's snapchatting you."

A car honked behind them.

"God, Mom, go."

"Not until you answer me."

Another honk.

Amelia glanced desperately over her shoulder. "Oh, my God, Mom, you're so annoying. He's just a guy in one of my classes. He was asking about an assignment." She shoved the earbud back in.

Amelia had a tell. She bit the inside of her mouth when she lied.

She was doing it now.

But a third honk forced Whitney's foot off the brake. Her car moved forward while her mind spun with questions. Who was Phil? Amelia had never mentioned him. Actually, she never mentioned any boys. Probably because she wasn't allowed to date until she was sixteen.

Which was happening in a month...

Whitney's stomach twisted.

She planned to press Amelia on it when they got to the apartment, but Amelia hopped out the minute the car was parked, before Whitney even had time to shut off the car. Then she walked swiftly up the stairs, earbuds locked in place. Whitney did her best to keep up but by the time she made it inside, Amelia was in her bedroom with the door shut.

A bird chirped from inside Whitney's pocket. She yanked out her phone.

Natalie: Are the photos of the new line ready?

Crap. She should have had them done by now. Nat's Fancy Finds was an online boutique that Natalie started about five years ago. At first, she only sold jewelry and accessories. Back then, Whitney was working hard to get her photography business up and running. Her degree had been in business, but she didn't have a lot of real-world experience. While she and Dan were married, she'd stayed home with Amelia. That's when she'd taken up photography. It started as a way to capture pretty pictures of her daughter but it became apparent early on that she had a talent for it.

When she and Dan split up, Whitney took a part-time administrative job, which worked out perfectly since she was off right around the time Amelia got out of school. Money was tight, and she worried that even if she snagged a full-time job, she wouldn't be able to afford daycare. Dan probably would've helped pay for it, but she hated relying on him for everything. Hated giving him the ammunition. Something to lord over her. When Natalie first started her business, she hired Whitney to take some photos for her website.

They quickly became friends, and shortly after, when Natalie added clothing to her inventory, she brought Whitney on as a full-time marketing manager for the business. Whitney was able to work flexible hours, mostly from home, or occasionally at the warehouse where she was able to bring Amelia if need be.

Last week, Whitney had done a photoshoot of their new spring line. Some of those photos had been edited, but not all of them. Heading over to her desk in the corner of the family room, Whitney sank down onto the seat, the padding sighing beneath her. After logging on to the computer, she texted Natalie back: I'll have them to you soon.

For the next hour, she worked intently, only glancing up when she heard the click of Amelia's door opening. The sun had started to go down outside. The sky was a deep blue, almost purple with flecks of gold glittering the edges. Whitney rubbed her blurry, tired eyes.

"What's for dinner?" Amelia asked, stepping into the room. She was wearing a pair of leggings, a long T-shirt and fuzzy socks. Her hair was pulled up into a messy bun at the top of her head and her face had been scrubbed clean. The smell of her peppermint lotion was strong, even from across the room.

"I don't know." Squinting, Whitney glanced at the time on the bottom of the computer screen. "It's getting late. You wanna just grab takeout? We can order pizza or call that Chinese place you like."

Leaning her shoulder against the wall, Amelia frowned, her nose wrinkling. "Nah, I'm trying to eat healthy, remember? I'll probably just make a salad or something."

The last thing Amelia needed to worry about was her weight. She was already skinny. Too skinny, in Whitney's opinion, but try telling her that. She was adamant about losing a few pounds.

"Okay, well, I can help you." Whitney swiveled in her chair, planting her feet on the carpet.

"It's okay. I got it." Amelia waved away the suggestion, her gaze sliding past her mom's shoulder. "That's a good shot." Her head bobbed toward the picture open on Whitney's screen of a model wearing a long maxidress and a distressed jean jacket. "She's really pretty."

Whitney's stomach tightened as she took in the stick-thin model on the screen. Impossibly smooth skin, blond shiny hair, not one imperfection thanks to Whitney's photo-editing skills. Whitney always blamed social media for her daughter's distorted self-image, but she guessed her job sometimes contributed to it. "Not as pretty as you." Whitney smiled.

Whitney's compliment was rewarded by a dramatic rolling of the eyes before Amelia headed into the kitchen.

Whitney dragged the edited photos into her shared Dropbox with Natalie and then shot her a text alerting her to their arrival. As expected, Natalie immediately sent back a thank-you.

In the kitchen, Amelia loudly pulled things out of the fridge. It reminded Whitney of the nights she was angry with Dan when they were married. She'd slam things around, making as much noise as possible, so he'd know how upset she was.

But that wasn't what Amelia was doing right now. She was wearing her earbuds again, so she had no idea how loud she was being.

Whitney went into the kitchen, pulled out the cutting board and a knife. She snatched up a cucumber.

Amelia's head snapped up, and she yanked out her earbuds. "I said I got it. You can keep working."

"I'm done." Whitney brought the knife down, slicing the cucumber into little rings.

Amelia nodded, closed the fridge and then ducked down, dipping into the lower cabinet for a large salad bowl. As she tossed the lettuce into it, Whitney continued chopping the vegetables, glad their partnership in the kitchen was still intact. They worked well together. Always had.

It had been the two of them for many years.

"Is your friend coming home with you after school on Friday?" Whitney asked, palming a tomato. When the knife hit it, juice squirted out, landing on her cheek.

Amelia grinned. Whitney did, too, as she wiped it off with her finger.

"No, I think she'll just come over later in the afternoon," Amelia replied.

"Okay, good. Is her mom bringing her over?" Whitney raised her brows. Amelia always accused her of being the most overprotective mother on the planet. Anytime another mom behaved the same way, Whitney made sure to point it out. Becca's often did. That was one of the main reasons Whitney liked the girls hanging out.

"No. Lauren's driving herself."

Whitney's hand froze, the knife suspended over the tomato. "How old is she?"

"Seventeen."

"Seventeen, huh?"

"You say it like it's so old."

"It's older than you."

"Barely. I'm sixteen."

"You're not sixteen yet." Whitney nudged her in the side in a teasing way.

But Amelia didn't laugh. Instead, she moved out of reach. "I will be soon."

"I know." Whitney tossed the chopped veggies into the bowl and then went to the sink to wash her hands.

Sixteen already. It seemed unfathomable.

The baby wrapped in Whitney's arms, a blanket woven tightly around her tiny body, as she hurried down the hallway, her socked feet slipping on the linoleum.

Glancing up from the sink Whitney saw Amelia's blurry reflection floating in the glass window. For so many years, she had known her daughter better than anyone. Saw her with so much clarity. But lately, she'd been like this reflection—muddled, mysterious, out of reach. Whitney knew it was the natural order of things. Her daughter was getting older. Asserting her independence.

But in Whitney's heart, Amelia would always be her baby.

It was still Whitney's job to keep her safe.

3

SATURDAY, NOON
NINETEEN HOURS
AFTER DROP-OFF

"MA'AM, ARE YOU OKAY?" The man's voice was far away, echoey, like he was speaking from the other end of a tunnel.

Whitney's vision blurred at the edges, her knees softening. The woman approached, standing at the edge of the doorway, frowning. Her paper-thin skin gathered around her eyes like fabric being pinched between two fingers.

She was at the wrong house again. She'd been sucked into the suburban vortex and gotten lost. There was no other explanation.

"I'm so sorry to bother you again," Whitney said, her face flushing. "I guess...I just got turned around...or something."

"Easy to do around here," the man said, and Whitney was grateful for his understanding.

After throwing them one last apologetic half smile, she went back to her car and hopped inside. In the rearview mirror, she spotted the groceries. On the seat next to her sat the gummy worms, melting against the plastic wrapper. The couple remained in the doorway, watching Whitney with wary expressions. After sending Amelia another text, she threw the couple a wave and then turned on the car.

They hadn't left the doorway. Probably afraid she'd knock again.

After putting the car into Drive, she stepped on the gas. At the main street, she went right, but this time she passed the first street and eased into the second one.

Again, all the houses looked similar but none with roses lining the yard. Her palms were slick. She wiped them alternately on the thigh of her jeans.

She headed down to the next street. No roses there either.

She was certain they hadn't gone any farther than this yesterday. Making a U-turn, she headed back to the original street. Reaching over to the passenger seat where her phone sat faceup, she touched the screen. No text from Amelia.

The rule had always been that Amelia had to respond to her within the hour.

Whitney had been making an exception for her earlier because she thought she'd been sleeping. But now it was after noon.

She pulled over and scooped up her phone. Clicking into the Find My Friends app, Whitney was surprised she hadn't thought of it sooner. Tracking Amelia was something she did often. She couldn't help it; it always made her feel better seeing Amelia was safe at school, at Becca's, at home when Whitney wasn't. Whitney's chest expanded.

But the relief didn't last long.

Amelia's phone wasn't showing up. Her location had been turned off.

Whitney's body went cold.

With a trembling hand, she clicked on Amelia's name in her contacts, then held the phone to her ear. It only rang once before going to voice mail.

"Amelia, I don't know what's going on, but call me back right away. I'm getting worried," she blurted out in a rush of words after the beep.

As she lowered the phone she envisioned dropping Amelia off yesterday, the way she and Lauren waved at her from the doorway of that home. The one the elderly couple lived in. But it couldn't be the same house, right? It didn't make any sense.

The door open. Crib empty. Blanket gone.

A dark figure in the doorway.

"Where is she? My baby, she's gone."

She was startled by the phone ringing in her hand. Natalie's face popped up on the screen.

"Nat?" Whitney answered. "Have you heard from Amelia?"

"No," Natalie said, sounding startled. "Why? What's going on?"

There was a pause at the other end of the line when Whitney finished explaining, and she wondered if she'd lost her. But then Natalie spoke. "There has to be a logical explanation. I mean, you clearly went back to the wrong house. That's easy to do in those neighborhoods, especially if you don't remember the address. And maybe Amelia just shut off her phone when she went to bed last night and hasn't turned it back on yet."

"Yeah," she responded slowly, waiting for the words to sink in and give her peace. But they didn't. Something felt off about this whole thing. "That's probably it. Thanks."

"No problem. Call me when you find her. I only wanted to tell you—oh, never mind. The photos are up online and look great, that's all."

"Okay," Whitney said, barely listening. Tossing the phone onto the passenger seat, she drove around the neighborhood a couple more times looking for another house with rosebushes lining the yard. Coming up empty, she groaned in frustration.

Where was Amelia?

Lauren's seventeen. She drives.

Whitney's mind reeled back over all her conversations with

Amelia in the last few days, trying to remember if she ever specifically said she was picking her daughter up. Nope, she couldn't recall ever coming up with a plan for how Amelia was getting home today. Whitney had just assumed she was picking her up, since that's what she usually did.

But everything had changed lately.

Maybe Amelia was already home and Whitney was freaking out over nothing.

As she drove swiftly through the Sacramento streets, she pictured her daughter curled up in bed, fluffy white comforter wrapped around her body. Amelia often took a nap after a sleepover. That was the most likely reason she wasn't answering any texts. She was at home asleep.

Yes, that has to be it.

Whitney couldn't wait to get home and tell her what happened. Amelia would probably be mortified at first. But then she'd make fun of her, and they'd both have a good laugh before putting this entire weird day behind them.

When she reached their apartment complex, she quickly parked and hopped out. She was about to walk away from her car, when she remembered the groceries in the backseat. For a split second she contemplated grabbing one of the bags. But her need to see if Amelia was inside trumped anything else at this point. Groceries could wait. It wasn't like they were going anywhere.

She raced up the stairs, making it to their front door in record time.

"Amelia!" Whitney tore into the apartment, dropping her purse and keys on the ground. The scent of French toast and syrup lingered. "Amelia!"

After sprinting down the hallway, she flung open her daughter's bedroom door. Cold, stale air smacked her in the face. Amelia's bed was made in a haphazard way, half the comforter spilling over to one side, pillows askew on the top.

Your room has to be clean before I take you to Lauren's.

Amelia had groaned as she stared up at the ceiling as if complaining to God. *Fine*, she'd said, the *n* punctuated by an "uh" sound at the end, before slumping back into her room.

The pile of clothes that usually threatened to take over the floor of Amelia's room wasn't exactly gone, but at least she'd pushed it to one side. The desk in the corner was covered in jewelry and lotions. Whitney had no idea how she ever did her homework over there. Makeup lined the entire perimeter of her dresser. Sadly, it had been like pulling teeth to get her room looking this good.

Stomach sinking, Whitney ran around the rest of the apartment, checking all the other rooms.

Empty. Every single one.

Exhaling, she yanked her phone out and pressed on Amelia's contact information. Voice mail again. She tried the Find My Friends app but her location still wasn't showing up.

It was like she'd disappeared.

Vanished into thin air.

"Oh, my God. My baby!"

The phone rang. Her pulse spiked.

Natalie again. "Did you find her?"

"No, and I'm starting to worry a little bit."

"Where are you?" Natalie's voice was firm, authoritative. Whitney had heard her use that same voice in business meetings.

"Home."

"Okay. I'm on my way over."

"All right." She nodded as if Natalie could see her and then numbly hung up the phone. Silence was thick in the air, wrapping around her neck like two large hands strangling her.

My daughter's gone. Again.

4

WHEN I TELL YOU what happened, it will be easy to blame me. To say it was all my fault. My doing. But that's not fair. We all make our own choices, sure. But we don't live in a bubble. People influence us. Shape us into who we ultimately become. For me, that person was Millie.

I've often wondered where I would be now if we'd never met. Would I have made similar mistakes? Hurt as many people? Would it all have turned out differently?

The questions swirl in my mind, day and night.

It's futile, though. This line of thinking.

I can't change what happened.

Sometimes I go back to when it started. The day Millie literally crashed into my life. It was the first day at my new high school. I was walking down the hallway, eyes whipping from my schedule to the classroom doors, desperately trying to find my next class in time. I wasn't paying attention, and neither was she. That's why we collided.

When I replay this moment in my mind, I imagine walking away then. Keeping my head down. Ignoring her. But that's not what I did.

Instead, I brushed my hair from my face and looked up at the person I'd walked into. She had dark hair, pale skin, nervous energy.

She was pretty. Really pretty. I wished I could look like her.

Her gaze took in the schedule I held between my fingers, and she asked if I was new.

I said something sarcastic, like, "How can you tell?"

A group of girls walked past. Former friends of Millie's, as I'd learn later. They glared at her, and I watched her neck swell as she swallowed hard. But she recovered quickly, smiling at me and snatching the schedule from my hands.

Snaking her arm through the crook of my elbow as if we were two members of the gang from *The Wizard of Oz*, prancing down the yellow brick road, she offered to show me to my next class.

But she didn't stop there. She helped me find the rest of my classes that day.

And the next day we sat together at lunch in the school quad.

After that, we were inseparable.

It was like we'd met at the perfect moment. She was in need of a new friend, and I was in need of *any* friend.

But Millie wasn't just any friend. She was different from any person I'd ever met. I'd felt so lucky to have found her the way I did.

At least, I thought so then. Now, I'm not so sure.

It seems weird to describe Millie as my best friend. From the get-go, she was so much more than that to me. Sometimes we joked that we were more like sisters. Soul sisters. But even that phrase doesn't do our relationship justice.

Our friendship was intense and all-consuming from the beginning. The connection we felt to each other was strong. The first few times we had sleepovers, we played this game late at night, when everyone was asleep and the sky was pitch-black, dotted with shimmering stars. One of us would draw an image on the other one's back and that person would try to guess what it was. It was a game of focus. Of shutting everything else out. In order to guess correctly, I had to home in to every curve of her fingertip, every angle, every motion, every push and pull.

It was simply me and her. Our fingertips. Our breaths. Our beating hearts.

Nothing else.

Millie was good at the game. Much better than I was. Then again, I'd never claimed to be an artist.

The first time we played, I'd been so nervous. Mostly because I thought I'd have to pull up my shirt and she'd see my fat rolls. Millie was thin. I was afraid she'd make fun of me the way my former friends sometimes did. I didn't know her well enough then to know she'd never do that.

But, lucky for me, we drew over each other's shirts. No skin required. I can't tell you how relieved I was.

That night I drew simple, easy things—a sun, a tree, the wavy cresting lines of the ocean. Millie drew a cloud, a rope, a woman drowning. I didn't get close to guessing the last one.

That was the first inkling I had that there was more to Millie. There was a darkness in her.

At the time I had no idea how deep it went.

Probably because to me Millie didn't feel dark. When we met, she was the only bright spot in my life. Normally, I was so guarded with new friends. Suspicious. But something about her felt right. I'd liked her immediately and trusted her just as quickly. No reservations.

Looking back, I guess that was a mistake.

5

SATURDAY, 1:00 P.M.
TWENTY HOURS
AFTER DROP-OFF

"HELLO?" WHITNEY ANSWERED HER CELL.

"Hey," Jay said. "I'm back."

Where had he been? Whitney's mind reeled back. *Oh, right, the business trip.* Had that only been yesterday? It seemed like a million years ago. Whitney rolled out her tense shoulders. Her entire body ached, as if she'd just returned from a grueling uphill run.

"Whitney?"

"Yeah. I'm sorry. I'm here…it's just." She pinched the bridge of her nose and squinted. "Well, Amelia spent the night at Lauren's last night and she's still not back yet. And I can't get a hold of her."

There were footsteps on the stairs, a dog barking in the distance. Whitney's skin prickled.

"She probably just wants more time with her friend. Milkin' it, you know?"

Milking it. Yeah, that sounded like her daughter. She'd even used that exact phrase to describe Amelia's actions when she used to take her to the community pool. They went almost every weekend in the summer when Amelia was younger. Whitney always dreaded having to wrangle Amelia out of the water when it was time to leave. She'd stand at the edge, hollering at Amelia, who would dive underwater repeatedly, acting as if she couldn't hear her.

Was that what she was doing now? Ignoring Whitney's calls, pretending she didn't know it was time to leave Lauren's in the hopes of staying longer?

It was possible.

A knock on the door startled her. "Oh, I'm sorry, Jay, but Nat's here."

"Call me when Amelia comes home, okay?"

"Yeah. Okay." She hung up and opened the door.

"Is she back yet?" Natalie whisked into the room, wearing her usual yoga pants and T-shirt, her strawberry blond hair pulled back in a ponytail. Whitney often joked that it was Natalie's uniform. She always looked ready for the gym, although Whitney didn't think she even had a membership.

"No." Whitney closed the door firmly behind her. It was afternoon. The air outside was warm. Amelia should've been lying lazily across her bed, feet propped up on the wall as she scrolled her phone.

"I'm sure she's fine." Natalie reached out to pat Whitney's shoulder. "Teenagers do this all the time. I can't tell you how many times Kayla came home late from a friend's without calling or checking in. And don't even get me started on Marc."

Whitney knew that Marc was the more rebellious of the two. Natalie had told her many stories of his pot smoking and failing grades. But he'd turned it around. Grew up. Whitney and Amelia had attended his wedding a few months earlier. Even though Kayla had gotten pretty good grades, and, at least according to Natalie, had never used drugs, she had been caught sneaking out to see her boyfriend a couple of times in high school. Now she was in her first year of junior college, and still living at home, but Natalie often joked that she'd never know it based on how often she saw her.

Whitney nodded. There was a time when she would've scoffed at Natalie's remark, declaring that Amelia wasn't rebellious. That she was responsible, respectful. That she always called or texted, kept in contact with Whitney. Up until recently Whitney had believed that was true. Believed that her daughter wasn't like other teenagers.

But she didn't think that anymore.

She thought back over the past few months. To all the times Amelia wasn't where she said she'd be.

A couple of weeks ago, Whitney was working at the warehouse, counting inventory and taking some pictures. She'd lost track of time, working late into the evening. Before heading home, she'd checked Amelia's location, and was relieved to see she was at the apartment. But when she'd arrived at home, Amelia was nowhere to be found. She was about to call her when she breezed in through the front door nonchalantly.

When Whitney asked her where she'd been, she said she'd gone down to the pool. Any other time Whitney would've believed her. The pool was one of the main selling points for moving to this apartment complex. Amelia spent much of her time there. But that night she hadn't gone for a swim. She wasn't wet, she wasn't wearing her suit and she reeked like smoke.

Whitney called her on it, but Amelia said she'd just been sitting on the edge, with her feet in the pool, and that someone else had been smoking out there. It had probably just gotten on her clothes. No big deal. Then she rolled her eyes and headed back to her room.

It sounded plausible and maybe if it had been an isolated incident, Whitney would've bought it.

Now, Whitney felt stupid for freaking out and making Natalie come over when Amelia was simply being a rebellious teenager. Surely her anxiety was fueled by the fact that she'd gone back to the wrong house, and the fact that her relationship with Amelia had been so strained lately. She'd already been on edge, and this added to it.

"Yeah, you're probably right," she said. "Man, I really miss the days when she was little, and sweet and helpful." Maybe that was the real reason she missed Amelia's old friends. She'd known them when they were younger. Back when they still needed help with things. When they were around, she felt that old maternal instinct kick in, and still had the sense—regardless of how false it may have been—that she was in control.

"Tell me about it." Natalie smiled in a conspiratorial way. "Before Marc turned into the teenage-monster, he was the sweetest little boy, always giving hugs and kisses and helping me bring in the groceries and stuff."

"Oh, my God. The groceries," Whitney blurted out, Natalie's words reminding her. "I went to the store earlier, and the food's still in my car."

"Oh, okay. Well, I'll help you bring it up," Natalie offered without hesitation.

Whitney waved away her words. She'd already taken enough of her time. "It's all right. I got it. You can head home if you need."

"Nonsense." Natalie shook her head. "I'll stay with you until Amelia comes home." Without waiting for Whitney to respond, she moved toward the front door. "Let's go grab those groceries."

Smiling, Whitney grabbed her keys and followed her friend out the front door. Together, they bounded down the stairs and made their way to the parking lot.

In her haste, she'd left the car unlocked earlier. So, they both opened the back doors and grabbed out a bag. Whitney was about to lock the doors when she spotted the gummy worms in the front seat.

"Oh, hang on." She opened the door with her free hand and reached inside. Her fingers wrapped around the warm bag of now-melted candy as she plucked them off the seat. The plastic was slick, and it slipped from her fingers, falling to the floorboards. She set the grocery bag on the pavement and then bent down to fish around for the bag of gummy bears. When she was about to stand back up she noticed a receipt crumpled up under the front seat. She snatched it up and smoothed it out.

It took a minute for the words to register. None of it made any sense.

Victoria's Secret.

Sunrise Mall.

She didn't shop at Victoria's Secret. Maybe she should have. She'd thought about it lately, since she and Jay had started dating. Before that, she had no need for pretty bras and panties. She needed functional. Budget friendly. But even so, they lived right by Arden mall. There would be no reason to go to Sunrise. Her gaze shot to the top of the receipt. Amelia's card was used, not hers. It was from a couple of weeks ago. Thursday. Time-stamped at 3:30 p.m.

Whitney would've been at the warehouse that afternoon. Possibly running errands for Natalie. Amelia should have been at swim practice. Not traipsing around Sunrise Mall and certainly not buying lingerie.

Was that what she bought?

The item was listed in a generic way. It could've just as easily been a regular bra.

But why would Amelia need a bra from Victoria's Secret? And why wouldn't she tell Whitney?

"Everything okay?" Natalie asked, shielding her eyes from the sun as the other one held a bag of groceries.

"Uh." Whitney shook her head, shoved the receipt in her pocket. Then she reached down to the bag she'd abandoned. "Yeah. I just need to check something upstairs."

When they got back to the apartment, Natalie immediately went to work putting away the groceries.

Whitney knew she should help her friend, but impatience buzzed through her. She headed straight to the computer. Going into her favorites, Whitney clicked on the bank tab. Then she went into Amelia's account. She rarely checked it. Amelia was great at saving her money from her babysitting jobs and birthday cards from her grandparents.

That's why Whitney was shocked to see the balance so low today. Scrolling, she saw the Victoria's Secret purchase, along with several other purchases that day, including Starbucks and Chik-fil-A. Both totals were more than they would've been for one person. Amelia had clearly been treating someone else. Lauren, maybe?

But the transaction that surprised Whitney the most was one from earlier this week. Amelia had withdrawn three hundred dollars.

Whitney sat back in her chair.

What would Amelia need that much money for?

Heat snaked up her spine. There was only one thing that came to mind. Something Amelia could've done with all that money. She turned to her friend.

"Oh, my God. I think Amelia may have run away. And I think I know where she went."

6

SEVEN WEEKS
BEFORE DROP-OFF

IT WAS QUIET. Eerily so.

Whitney walked slowly down the hallway, listening intently. When she reached Amelia's bedroom door, it was open a sliver, enough for her to peek one eye through. Amelia and her new friend were sitting on the floor facing each other, legs crossed. When Lauren got here earlier, Amelia had barely taken the time to introduce her before the two scurried off and hid away in Amelia's room. They sat so close their bare toes were practically entwined. With heads bent inward, they talked in low, hushed tones. A chill pricked the back of Whitney's neck. It felt like she was encroaching on something private and intense. Usually, when Amelia had friends over, she'd find them in her room blasting music and dancing around. Amelia loved to dance. And be silly. This was new. Different. She swallowed hard and stepped back, the floor creaking beneath her feet.

Both of their heads snapped upward, their gazes shooting in Whitney's direction.

"Mom?" Amelia called out.

When Amelia was a little girl, the word *mom* rolled off her tongue with such affection, it made Whitney warm and fuzzy inside. Today it sounded like a curse word. Whitney's shoulders tensed.

Drawing in a breath, she pressed the door open all the way and stepped inside. "I was just checking to see if you girls wanted a snack or something."

"If we wanted a snack, we would've gotten one," Amelia said with annoyance.

"I'm good right now, but thank you for the offer," Lauren said, wearing an apologetic smile.

Why was a stranger treating her better than her own daughter?

Whitney's gaze shot to Amelia. She was on her phone, typing something with her thumbs.

On the ground near her knee was a smattering of papers. They appeared to be printed from a web page. Some of the words were highlighted.

"Are you guys doing homework?" Whitney asked, taking a step toward them. Amelia hadn't told her much about Lauren. She didn't even know what class they had together.

After lowering her phone, Amelia gathered up the papers. "It's...no, it's not homework."

Pink spots had appeared on Lauren's cheeks.

"What is it, then?" Whitney asked, curiosity piqued.

"Have you heard of the Enneagram?" Lauren adjusted the glasses on her nose. Whitney mused again at how different she seemed from Amelia's other friends. Quieter. More subdued. Serious.

"The what?"

Amelia blew out an irritated breath.

"The Enneagram," Lauren repeated, ignoring the exasperated look on Amelia's face. "It's kind of a personality test."

"Oh, like Myers-Briggs or something?" Whitney nodded,

remembering how she'd taken that test back in college when she and Dan were dating.

"No, it's not really like that," Amelia said, throwing her new friend a knowing look, as if to say, *You never should have involved my mom.*

It irked Whitney the way she acted like they were in cahoots. Amelia barely knew this girl. With Becca, Whitney never felt like the odd one out. She and Becca didn't used to hole up in Amelia's room, sit close and whisper. Whitney would take them to the mall, the movies, out to eat. Or they'd stay here and all watch TV together. Whitney was often included. Becca may have been Amelia's best friend, but Whitney was her mom. The person who knew Amelia better than anyone.

At least she thought she had.

"Same concept, though," Lauren said.

Whitney nodded, grateful for how gracious Amelia's new friend was being. Maybe she wasn't so bad, after all. Whitney had been skeptical. Honestly, she wasn't prepared to like her. She was still hoping this was all a passing phase and Becca would be back before she knew it.

"What class is it for?" Whitney asked.

"I already said it wasn't homework," Amelia said, her tone impatient.

Right. "Then why are you doing it?" Amelia usually hated stuff like this. Becca had once tried to get her to play some game on Facebook to see what kind of animal she would be, and she said that tests like that were silly. A waste of time. She even refused to see the career counselor when Whitney had suggested it. Said she could figure things out on her own.

"Everyone does it," Amelia said at the same time Lauren said, "To see how alike we are."

There was probably truth to both answers, but Lauren's rang the truest to Whitney.

Why would they be taking a test to see how alike they were?

"We flunked." Dan laughed.

"What?" Whitney peered over his shoulder at the relationship quiz they'd just finished. "Can you even flunk a compatibility test?"

"Apparently, you can because we did." His laughter increased.

She wanted to laugh along, but she didn't find it funny. Odd that Dan did.

"You're not worried?" she asked him.

He quieted down, his expression smoothing out. Wrapping his arms around her waist, he drew her close. "I don't need a test to tell me we're compatible."

"Well, that's good because it didn't," she joked, only it came out sounding more like a warning. Maybe it was.

"Hey." He kissed her forehead, the simple act causing some of her fears to dissipate. "We're different. I've known that since the moment we met. But we make it work. We're good together." She lifted her head, their eyes meeting. "Right?"

"Right."

Amelia and Lauren both stared at Whitney as if willing her to leave.

Taking the hint, she offered a small smile. "Just let me know if you two need anything," she said, backing out of the room. Before the door had even shut, they'd already scooted closer to each other again.

Was it possible that Lauren was more than a friend?

Whitney dipped the thick slice of bread into the egg batter and then tossed it onto the skillet. It sizzled, emitting a sweet buttery scent. That smell had the power to transport her back. Not only to all the mornings she'd made it for Amelia, but back to her own childhood.

Growing up, her dad was in charge of breakfast on Saturdays. He'd wake up early to go running while her mother slept in. He'd be back and showered by the time Whitney and her brother, Kevin, would shuffle out of their rooms in their pajamas, blankets fisted in their hands. Then they'd lie on the couch and watch Saturday morning cartoons while their dad whipped up eggs and French toast. Once their mom got up, they'd all gather around the kitchen table. It was Whitney's favorite time of the week.

That's why she'd gotten so angry when everything fell apart, when Kevin's illness stole the one time of the week her family was all together.

Kevin coughing, struggling for breath. Her parents gathered around him. Ingredients for the breakfast her dad was about to make were strewn all over the counters. Whitney knew it was only a matter of time before it would be put away and her parents would tell her to grab a bowl of cereal or something, to fend for herself.

She looked longingly at the table, fantasizing about them all sitting together, forks full of syrupy toast. Her dad regaling them with stories of his week, her mom smiling and laughing, encouraging him.

The blue flame caught her eye. It danced below the pan. Her dad must've left it on. She reached out, her fingers lighting on the knob. But then she stopped, a thought forming. Gathering up courage, she steeled herself for what was to come.

Carefully lifting her hand, she pressed her palm down against the inside of the pan, skin sizzling. She could only bear it a few seconds before screaming out in pain.

"Oh, my God. What happened?" Her dad spun around, eyes concerned, trained on her. Only her.

"I was only trying to make breakfast." Her little lip trembled. "I was just trying to help." From over her dad's shoulder, her gaze met her brother's.

Take that, Kevin.

Clearing her throat, she shook away the memories, flipped the bread.

Her cell sat faceup on the counter, black screen staring up at her. It had been a couple of weeks since she'd talked to her dad. Her mom called every Saturday. But her dad spent Saturdays out golfing, and in the evening was either grabbing a beer with his buddies or at home relaxing, too tired for a phone conversation. She made a mental note to call and try to catch him sometime this week.

For a time, she'd had the perfect childhood. Doting, attentive parents. Especially her dad. They were tight when she was little. He'd read her bedtime stories every night, often inserting their names into the text to make her laugh.

Dad was the strongest superhero in the world.

Princess Whitney was beautiful.

He taught her to ride her bike, took her on trips to the zoo and Fairytale Town in Land Park. She'd spend hours sliding down Mother Goose's slide, her dad catching her at the bottom, or running along the yellow brick road. And on Sundays, the two of them often took a walk to the doughnut shop around the corner. She'd always get a maple bar, though she was only able to eat half. But that was okay. Dad didn't mind finishing it off for her. In fact, Whitney was certain he looked forward to it.

But slowly all of that went away.

The trips to the zoo, the riding of the bikes, the doughnut shop walks and eventually even story time.

All gone.

For most of her life, she'd blamed her brother's illness for the demise of her family. But she knew that wasn't entirely fair. Whitney had made decisions that irrevocably changed things. And now it seemed the relationships were too broken to fix.

A burnt smell wafted under her nose.

Shit. She pulled the half-blackened piece of French toast off the skillet and tossed it onto the plate with the others.

As Whitney reached for another piece of bread, the hairs on the back of her neck stood at attention. She spun around. Lauren stood in the doorway of the kitchen wearing a T-shirt and pajama pants, her hair piled high on her head in a messy topknot. She was leaning against the doorframe, her eyes narrowed behind the lenses of her glasses.

Whitney shivered. How long had she been standing there?

"Good morning," Whitney said, clearing her throat.

"Good morning." Lauren smiled, pushing off the wall and stepping into the kitchen. "Can I help with anything?" Her face was shiny, eyes bright.

"Um…" Whitney glanced around. "Nope. I'm actually almost done. Can I get you anything to drink? Orange juice? Milk? Water?"

Her gaze drifted to the coffee maker, half-filled. "Do you mind if I have a cup of coffee?"

"Sure, I guess." After wiping her hands off on a nearby towel, Whitney took a mug out of the cabinet and moved over to the coffee maker. Whitney hadn't started drinking coffee until she had Amelia. Living off of three hours of sleep, caffeine was a must. *Oh, well, I'm not Lauren's mother.* Whitney poured hot coffee into the mug and then turned toward Lauren. "Would you like creamer or anything?"

"No, black is good."

"Ookay." Dan used to drink his coffee black, too, but Whitney put so much creamer in hers it was more of a tan color. She often joked that she'd like some coffee with her creamer.

As Lauren sipped on her cup of straight caffeine, Whitney went back to making the French toast.

"So, have you lived here long?" Whitney asked after a couple of minutes of silence.

"No. Not long."

"Where did you move from?"

"Oh." Lauren shrugged, both hands wrapped around her mug. "We've lived a lot of places."

Not really an answer. "Like where?"

"Sorry I slept so late." Amelia walked into the kitchen, red cheeks, her mouth open in a yawn, her hands high above her head. It reminded Whitney of when she was younger and she'd crawl in bed with her on Saturday mornings, sleep-drunk.

"Actually, you're right on time. Breakfast is made." Whitney slid the plate of French toast in front of Lauren.

"Mo-o-om," Amelia whined. "You know I'm trying to watch my carbs."

Is that what she was doing this week? Whitney couldn't keep up with her ever-changing dieting fads.

"Well, I'm gonna have one." Lauren reached out to grab the one on top. Her nails were painted the same dark color as Amelia's.

Amelia eyed her friend momentarily, then shrugged and plopped down next to her. "I guess one won't kill me."

Impressive. Lauren had the power of persuasion.

"Do you smoke?" A cocked eyebrow, a lit cigarette burning between two fingers.

Nope. Never. It was a disgusting habit Whitney never planned to partake in.

Eyes drinking her in, watching her every move, urging her to say yes.

"Sure. Of course. Always." Whitney took the cigarette and brought it to her lips.

Whitney ate her French toast while standing over the counter. She knew her presence at the table would put a damper on the lively conversation happening between the girls. It was the most animated she'd seen Amelia in over a month. They both ate their first piece of toast and then reached for another, passing the syrup between them. Becca usually stuck to one piece when she was over. It was nice to see Amelia actually eating.

Maybe Lauren was all right.

Once finished with her breakfast, Whitney ambled over to the coffeepot and poured herself a second cup of coffee, topping it off with a generous amount of creamer. The neighbor was in his kitchen again, wearing flannel pajamas and cooking something on his stove.

"Did you ask your mom yet?" Lauren asked in an overly loud whisper that was obviously meant to be overheard.

Keeping her back to the girls, she sipped her coffee and absently watched the guy across the way.

"Oh. Right." Amelia swallowed loudly. "Mom, do I have a passport?"

"A passport?" Whitney peered over her shoulder.

"Yeah." Amelia nodded.

Whitney set down her cup of coffee, thinking maybe she'd had enough for today. Her hands were slightly shaky, her nerves frayed. "Why do you need a passport?"

"I can't get to Amsterdam without one." Amelia laughed like Whitney was being daft.

About a year ago, Dan had gotten an offer to head up a project his construction company was starting overseas. Ever since her dad left, Amelia had been begging Whitney to let her visit him. Recently, Dan had called to say that he was taking a couple of weeks off this summer and that would probably be a good time for Amelia to come.

But Whitney wasn't so sure it was a good idea.

Amelia had never traveled at all, let alone to another country. The mere idea of it made Whitney nervous.

"No, you don't have a passport," Whitney said.

"You better start the process now, then. They can take a while. If you wait, the baby might come first." Lauren winked at Amelia over her plate of syrupy toast.

"Baby?" Whitney's heart pounded, her gaze reflexively shooting down to Amelia's stomach, hidden under the table. "What baby?"

Amelia's eyebrows shot up. "Dad didn't tell you? Karen's pregnant."

Her dejected tone caused Whitney to rein in the relief she felt at the fact that the baby wasn't Amelia's. But when her words registered, confusion filled her. "Really?"

"Yep." Bitterness tainted Amelia's tone.

Whitney had talked to Dan recently. Why hadn't he told her? "How far along?"

"I don't know. A couple of months, I think. He told me last week."

On the counter, Whitney's phone buzzed. Leaning over, she clicked on the screen.

It was a text from Jay.

Good morning.

Her lips curled upward at the corners as she typed back, stabbing at the screen of her phone with her index finger. She hadn't mastered the skill of typing with her thumbs, something Amelia teased her about incessantly.

Good morning back.

"Is that your boyfriend?" Amelia asked, a teasing lilt in her tone.

Was it that obvious? Heat rose to Whitney's skin. Looking up, she bit her lip. "He's not my boyfriend."

Amelia giggled, turning to her friend. "My mom's dating some guy she met at a bar."

Lauren's eyes widened.

Whitney bristled. "Not at a bar. Well, I mean, I was sitting at the bar, but it was in a restaurant."

It was girls' night. Whitney was sitting at the bar of the restaurant, waiting on Natalie, who'd been running a few minutes behind. She ordered a glass of zin and sipped it slowly, staring out the window. It had been raining that evening and the sky was a beautiful grayish blue, splatters of water creating a painting-like effect on the glass. Whitney had always loved stormy nights. Loved the edginess of the colors, the tension in the air, the crisp smell of the sky.

She'd been so lost in her thoughts, she hadn't heard him approach, take the seat next to hers.

"Scotch on the rocks." His voice was raspy and low, yet had a seductive quality to it. It piqued her curiosity, and she looked over. She was pleasantly surprised by what she saw. Strong jawline dotted with stubble, dark hair, a little unkempt and long, but not in slobby way. It was obvious that it had been intentionally styled like that. Dan had always kept his neatly shorn, no facial hair, except for on vacations when he'd let it grow out a bit. She remembered loving him like that. Made him look younger. More relaxed.

When the strange man smiled at her, she felt silly for staring.

"Scotch on the rocks," she said, nodding toward the drink in his hand. "That's always been my dad's drink of choice."

The corners of his mouth lifted. He propped an elbow on the bar. "Is that a good or bad thing?"

"I'm not sure yet," she said, surprising herself with the playful, flirtatious tone.

"What would make you sure?"

She shrugged. "Is it your usual drink?"

"No," he said. "I'll drink pretty much anything except for a dirty martini."

"Why's that?"

"Because that's my dad's drink of choice." He winked.

She liked him already.

"What about you? You always stick to red wine?"

"No, I'm like you. I'll drink most things, except for white zin."

"Let me guess, that's your mom's drink of choice."

"No." She shook her head. "It's just gross."

He laughed. Hard. She melted.

When Natalie arrived, Jay shocked Whitney by asking for her number. Natalie had given her a broad smile and a thumbs-up. By that point, she didn't need the endorsement, but she welcomed it.

Jay had already hooked her.

"Oh, yes, that's better. I'm sure serial killers never frequent bars in restaurants." Amelia laughed.

"He's not a serial killer," Whitney insisted, her phone buzzing again.

What are you up to today? his text read.

"How do you know?" Amelia asked.

Whitney glanced at his picture displayed at the top of their text thread. "I just know. He's a nice guy. Charming. Good-looking."

"That's what they said about Ted Bundy," Amelia pointed out, and her friend laughed.

"Okay, you watch way too much TV. Jay's a nice guy. He's not a serial killer."

"I sure hope not, since he totally knows where we live," Amelia said.

This time she wasn't laughing. "What's going on, Amelia? We've talked about this. I didn't think you had a problem with me dating Jay." She'd dated a few guys in the last couple of years and Amelia had never seemed suspicious of them.

"I don't." She shrugged.

"Then why were you saying he's a serial killer?"

"It wasn't really about Jay, I guess. I just wonder, you know, like how well do we really know anybody?" Amelia said, a faraway look on her face.

Lauren nodded in agreement.

Whitney's stomach knotted. Her daughter wasn't the philosophical type, and this new depth was not a welcome change.

"Lauren seems nice," Whitney said a few minutes after Lauren left.

"Yeah, she's cool." Amelia opened the fridge and pulled out a water. After unscrewing the top and taking a sip, she reached for her earbuds.

Inwardly, Whitney groaned. She was already losing her.

"You seem to really like her," Whitney blurted out loudly before she could get both earbuds in.

"Yeah, she's cool," Amelia repeated slowly as if Whitney was hard of hearing.

"No, I mean you really seem to *like* her." Whitney put emphasis on the word *like*, hoping Amelia would understand what she was getting at.

But she appeared more confused. "What's that supposed to mean?"

Smooth, Whit. Real smooth.

"Nothing. I've just never known you to spend all night working on a personality test with a friend."

"It's not that weird." Amelia bristled. "A lot of kids at my school are into the Enneagram."

Whitney tried a different tack. Leaning over the counter, she rested her elbows on top. "So, did you figure out how alike you were?"

"We actually weren't that similar at all," Amelia answered a little sullenly.

Maybe Whitney's instinct was right. She straightened up, tucking a strand of hair behind her ear. "Well, you know. Your dad and I took a compatibility test before we got married and we weren't alike at all either."

The look on Amelia's face told Whitney she had said the wrong thing.

Again.

"Why would you compare me and Lauren to you and Dad?" Her eyes widened. "Oh, my God. Do you think Lauren's my girlfriend?"

"I don't know," Whitney said. "Is she?"

Amelia shook her head. "I'm not gay, Mom."

"It would be okay with me if you were," she said quickly.

Amelia paused for a minute, studying her face. For the first time in weeks she didn't seem irritated. "Thanks. But I'm not."

"Okay." Whitney held on to the edge of the counter, feeling off balance.

"And no duh, you and Dad aren't alike. Did you really need a test to tell you that?" Amelia wore a teasing smile.

Whitney's lips tugged upward, and she let out a light laugh. "Well, it's like Paula Abdul says, 'Opposites Attract.'"

"Huh?" Amelia's nose scrunched up.

Whitney shook her head in a dismissive way. "It's a '90s song."

"Is that really why you and Dad were attracted to each other? Because you're opposite?"

"No, I was just joking. I actually don't think your dad and I are opposite. We're different, sure. Everyone is. But we're also alike in a lot of ways too."

Amelia snorted. "Yeah, right. You guys are totally different. Karen and him—now, they're alike."

Whitney's stomach coiled, remembering how Amelia was when Dan and Karen first started dating.

Dad's new girlfriend is so nice.

Dad's new girlfriend is so pretty.

Look what Dad's new girlfriend bought me.

Whitney was the only one who never bought into the perfect-Karen act. Everyone else did, Dan's parents included. Of course, they'd never approved of Dan's relationship with Whitney, so it made sense they'd like someone so wholesomely different.

But Whitney knew she was too good to be true. No adult was that sweet. That selfless. That smiley.

Whitney knew what a manipulator looked like. She saw right through Karen from the very beginning. And she'd been right. Karen quit her teaching job right after marrying Dan, confirming Whitney's gold-digging theory. And as much as Karen doted on Amelia when she and Dan were dating, Dan saw Amelia considerably less once he got married. Not only that, but a year into their marriage, Dan tried to get the amount of his child support lowered. As adamantly as he swore Karen wasn't the one who'd instigated that, Whitney knew better.

Unsure of how to respond to Amelia and certain she'd end up saying the wrong thing, Whitney kept her lips glued shut. Busying herself, she snatched up a sponge and wiped down the counter.

"I wonder what their kid'll be like," Amelia mused aloud. She said it in a nonchalant way, but the words felt charged, alive. "Anyway, I'm just glad I'll be visiting before the baby comes. Then I'll have Dad all to myself."

"I think you're getting a little ahead of yourself. Nothing's been decided."

"What do you mean?" Amelia cocked her head to the side. "Dad and I talked. He said I could come visit."

Whitney set down the sponge. "Honey, I'm sorry but I'm not sure if I'm comfortable with you traveling all the way to Amsterdam alone." It wasn't just the traveling either. Dan's parenting style was vastly different than Whitney's. When Amelia was with him, he let her do things Whitney never would. Amelia wouldn't be properly looked after. Who knew what kind of trouble she could get into, a naive girl in a foreign country? Dan didn't know Amelia the way Whitney did. She acted tough. Strong. But she was sheltered. Innocent. Not street-smart at all.

The perfect prey.

Amelia crossed her arms over her chest. "I don't care what you think. I'm going."

"Excuse me?"

"Dad said you might do this, but you can't keep me from going."

"Oh, yes, I can."

She shook her head. "Nope. Dad said it's in your divorce agreement. By law I get time with him. He can go to his attorney."

Was her own daughter threatening her with legal action?

It seemed unfathomable.

As she stared at the teenager standing in the middle of the kitchen, arms crossed, knees locked, eyes narrowed, she realized her own daughter had become a stranger to her.

7

I NEVER HAD a best friend before Millie.

I mean, yeah, sure I had friends. When I was young, I played with the kids my parents' friends would bring over. And later, I would go to the occasional sleepover. But, usually, I was the girl who got left out, no matter how hard I tried.

In middle school, I sat near a group of girls in English class. One day before the bell rang, they were all talking about their boyfriends. I didn't have a boyfriend, but I piped up anyway, telling them I was dating a boy in high school. They bought it and started drawing me into the conversations from then on. Our friendship didn't last past seventh grade, though.

But with Millie it was different. She was the first friend—maybe the first person in my entire life—who really saw me.

The real me.

I didn't have to put on an act or be someone I wasn't.

She thought I was amazing. Special. Unique. And when I was with her, I believed I was too.

One of my favorite things about Millie was how much she

loved to dance. When I picture her in my mind, that's what she's doing. Dancing. She was always doing it. It was like when she heard music, she was unable to keep her body from moving in sync with it. She'd dance in the store, on the street, in front of other people, she didn't care.

Whenever I was over, she'd blast music in her room and make me dance with her. I've never been much of a dancer. Seat-dancing, I can do. My arms aren't the problem. It's my legs that refuse to obey. But Millie never took no for an answer. She'd tug on my arms until I gave in. Although, in all honesty, it didn't take much coaxing.

Dancing with Millie made me feel weightless. Free. Beautiful.

She'd slide her fingers through mine and guide my movements to help me find the rhythm. The beat flowed from her.

I often danced with my eyes closed. Mostly because I was trying to concentrate, so I wouldn't step on her feet. But also, because then I couldn't see how clunky my movements were. In my mind, I could picture myself dancing gracefully.

One afternoon we were dancing in her room. My eyes were closed. Millie was guiding my movements, her fingers wrapped around mine, when all of the sudden one of her hands released mine and grazed my cheek. I opened my eyes to find her face so close I could feel the heat of her breath on my face, smell her fruity lip gloss that always sparkled intensely on her lips. She looked so serious, her eyes meeting mine. As she moved in closer, her hand sliding back toward my hair, I thought she was going to kiss me.

I've never been into girls. Not before or since. But in that moment, I wanted her to press her lips to mine.

Apparently, I'd read the entire situation wrong, though. She was just brushing a strand of hair off my cheek.

When she pulled back, I felt so many conflicting things. Disappointment. Relief. Confusion.

But one thing was clear: I would've done anything to be close to Millie.

Anything.

8

"DAN?" WHITNEY WAS grateful when he answered the phone. She'd been worried he might already be in bed, since it was eleven o'clock his time. He'd never been a night owl. *Early to bed, early to rise*, he used to say. Her fingers ached from the exertion of holding the phone tight to her ear. She perched on the edge of her bed, staring at the blank white wall in front of her.

"Whitney, hi." He didn't sound happy to hear from her. He also didn't sound like he was expecting her call.

But she held on to hope anyway. "Is Amelia there?"

"Of course not," he said as if it was a ridiculous question.

"Well, have you talked to her? Is she maybe on her way to see you?"

"No. Why would you even ask that?"

"Don't play dumb with me, Dan. I know you had been talking to her about visiting."

"Yes, but not today. This summer. And it wasn't a secret. I talked to you about it too."

"Yeah, and when I said I wasn't comfortable with it, you told Amelia you were going to your attorney."

Dan snorted. "Not exactly."

"Are you saying that Amelia lied to me?"

"No, I just…she was worried you wouldn't say yes, and I was just explaining to her that there are ways around that."

"So, is that what you did? You went around it? Helped her get a plane ticket. Told her to come see you, to hell with what I thought?" Her entire body was shaking now.

"No, I didn't. Geez. Calm down," Dan said in that patronizing tone Whitney hated. "Last time I talked to her she hadn't even gotten her passport yet."

Right. Her passport. Amelia didn't have one. There was no way she was on her way to Amsterdam. She exhaled, temporarily relieved. Then another thought hit. "What about your parents? Do you know if Amelia's been in contact with them?"

Amelia had always loved time with her paternal grandparents. They lived in the Santa Cruz area, so not that far. Every year they sent expensive gifts at Christmas and on her birthday. And the times when Amelia visited, they'd make her root beer floats and take her out for fast food.

Dan would sometimes take Amelia to see them in the summertime. She loved the beach. Swimming had been her favorite pastime since she was a toddler. Dan and Whitney used to call her their little fish.

"No, I actually just talked with Mom today. Dad's been pretty sick."

"Oh, I'm sorry to hear that," Whitney said, and it wasn't exactly a lie. She would never wish ill will on anyone. But there was certainly no love lost between her and Dr. Carter. There was a time when Dr. Carter was someone she trusted, confided in. He'd been her therapist when she was a teenager. That's how she'd met Dan in the first place.

Her first appointment with Dr. Carter, her mom dropped her off in front of a large two-story white house, a large porch wrapping around it.

"Are you sure this is right?" Whitney asked her mother.

She nodded. "Yeah, he said his office is in his home."

So Whitney hopped out of her mom's car and headed up the front porch stairs. Then she knocked on the door.

When it opened, a young man stood there. Whitney instantly noticed how good-looking he was. Brown hair, blue eyes, tanned skin, dimpled smile.

"Um…" she stammered, staring down at her tennis shoes. She wished she'd worn something cuter than the jeans and T-shirt she had on. At least she'd had the forethought to wear her hair down, put on some lip gloss. Smoothing down her hair, she forced a wobbly smile. "I'm…um… here to see Dr. Carter?" She hadn't meant it to come out like a question.

But the boy smiled, and her cheeks heated up. "Sure. I'll take you to his office."

Whitney took a step forward, but the boy stepped out and they bumped into one another. Giggling, she stepped back. So did he.

"My dad's office is actually back this way." He pointed toward the side yard.

"Oh." She bit her lip. "You're Dr. Carter's son?"

"Dan."

"Hi, Dan." She smiled, her cheeks warming. "I'm Whitney."

He guided her into the side yard and through the back to a guesthouse turned office, and he showed her how to access it the next time she came. She was a little bummed that he'd shown her. She'd been hoping to run into him next time.

"Mom didn't mention anything about Amelia," Dan said now.

"Okay." Whitney drew in a breath, her mind already reeling again with ideas. Possibilities.

"What's going on?"

Whitney explained the situation quickly—just the bare bones.

"And you think she might have run away?" he asked when she finished.

"I don't know," Whitney said honestly. "Everyone keeps saying she's probably just staying late at her friend's and she'll come home any minute, but I have a weird feeling in my gut."

"You and your weird feelings," he joked.

Despite herself, Whitney smiled. "It's just that she's been lying a lot lately. Sneaking around. And now I found out she's taken some money out of her account." Whitney bit her lip. "I honestly don't know what to think. It looks like she even skipped swim practice, and she never misses that."

"Swim practice? But she's not on swim team this year."

"What? Yes, she is."

"Have you been to a meet?"

"She's only had one and it was an away meet. She told me the first home meet isn't for a few more weeks."

"Well, that may be true, but Amelia's not on the team this year."

Stunned, Whitney stared at the wall. She thought back to the afternoons Amelia came home, hair wet from practice, dumping her swim bag by the door. To all the evenings when Whitney came home late from the warehouse, asking about practice, and Amelia replied that it went well.

"I don't...I don't understand. Are you sure?"

"One hundred percent," he said. "I paid her team dues over the summer for this upcoming season, but then I was refunded. When I called to ask her about it, she said she decided not to join this year. Studies were hard and she was worried about getting behind in classes."

"She never said anything to me. I thought she was getting good grades," Whitney said, this entire conversation leaving her dazed. "Why didn't you tell me?"

"I assumed you knew. Amelia said you did."

"I didn't," she mumbled. Her head spun. It didn't make any sense.

"Well, she couldn't keep it from you forever. You'd figure

it out soon enough when she wasn't competing in any of the meets."

Whitney nodded, forgetting Dan couldn't see her. She wondered when Amelia had planned to come clean. "Amelia loves swimming. What would make her quit the team?"

"Maybe she was telling the truth. Perhaps she is struggling in school and just didn't want to tell you."

"Maybe," Whitney said aloud, but she didn't think that was it. "But then, where has she been when she was supposed to be at practice?" She'd been so busy at work lately that she hadn't tried to track her while at practice. Didn't think there was a point, anyway. Now she wished she had.

"She did mention to me that she had a new group of friends."

"Group? I only know of one new friend."

"Oh." Dan paused. "I thought she'd said 'friends,' plural, but maybe not."

Natalie poked her head into the room, her eyebrows high, her eyes speaking to Whitney from across the room. She was familiar with that expression. Natalie had information.

"Look, Dan, I gotta go," Whitney said, her gaze never leaving Natalie's.

"Okay. Let me know when you find Amelia."

"I will." After hanging up, she tucked her phone into the back pocket of her jeans and stood.

"She's not with Dan?" Natalie asked.

Whitney shook her head. "What's going on?"

Natalie took a few steps forward, then held up her phone, the face turned toward Whitney. "Check this out. Kayla screenshotted this from Snapchat a few weeks ago."

Whitney squinted, moved closer. When she couldn't get a good look, she took the phone from Natalie, inspecting the photo on the screen. It was of a good-looking guy, late teens or early twenties—it was hard to tell. At first, Whitney couldn't figure out what this had to do with anything. But then her gaze slid over the cute guy's shoulder and she saw her. Amelia and a boy Whitney had never seen before. Sitting on a bench, heads close together, beers in their laps. Her stomach twisted.

"Where was this taken?"

Natalie shrugged. "Kayla doesn't know. One of her other friends posted it and Kayla screenshotted it because she thought the guy in the front of the picture was hot. Wanted to find out who he was." Natalie smirked. "Anyway, I called her a few minutes ago and told her what was going on. And she sent me this."

Whitney slid her thumb and forefinger apart on the screen to zoom in. "Does Kayla know who that guy is that Amelia's with?"

"No, I was hoping you'd know him. Do you think maybe that's why she stayed out late? 'Cause she's hanging out with this boy?"

"Maybe. I have no idea who he is."

"Okay. I'll text Kayla and have her ask around. See if she can get any information on this boy."

Something about the photo nagged at Whitney. Like a word on the tip of her tongue. There was a clue in here, but she couldn't pinpoint it.

"Thanks." She handed the phone back to Natalie so she could send Kayla the text. "I wonder if Amelia has any other pictures of this guy. Or maybe she follows him on social media."

Hurrying out of the room, she made her way to the computer, and wiggled the mouse. The screen lit up, roaring to life. Whitney opened up Facebook and went to Amelia's page. It had been months since she posted anything.

Facebook's for old people, Amelia repeatedly said.

Still, Whitney clicked on her friends list and typed "Lauren" in the search bar. No one came up. Her stomach sank. If only she knew a last name. Next, she tried "Phil," and then "Lopez." No luck there either.

She scrolled through Amelia's page, looking at all the comments, hoping to see Lauren's face. A couple of the comments turned her stomach. Rude, on the cusp of vulgar. Why did kids talk like that? Didn't they know their parents, employers, teachers, could see what they posted?

"You know you can block people," Amelia once told Whitney when *a guy she'd gone out on one date with wouldn't leave her alone.*

"You can?"

"Of course," she said. *"You can also hide your posts from certain people if you don't want to completely unfriend them."*

Amelia wouldn't hide her posts from her, would she? Whitney bit her lip, thinking about how distant her daughter had been lately. She wished she could get into Amelia's account, rather than only seeing it from hers. Sitting up straighter, she logged out of her account.

Using Amelia's email address as the username, she brainstormed several passcodes. In the past, Amelia always used her own name, the first letter of her last name and the number one: AmeliaC1. When that didn't work, she tried it with a lower case *c*. Still locked out, she attempted to use Amelia's birth date. But that wasn't it either. She only had one more chance. Tenting her fingers, she thought harder. Years ago, she'd helped Amelia set up an email for school. What had her password been back then?

Ah, yes.

Swimmergirl123

Great. Now she was locked out.

Blowing out a frustrated breath, Whitney signed back into her own account. That's when she saw Becca's picture, and felt a modicum of hope.

With a shaky hand, she pulled out her phone and clicked on Becca's contact information. It rang a few times before the familiar voice came on the line.

"Hello?"

"Becca, hi. It's Whitney…uh…Amelia's mom."

"Oh…hi." She paused. Whitney heard sounds in the background she couldn't decipher—chatter, shuffling, dishes clanging, maybe. "What's up?"

"Amelia's not with you, is she?" Whitney held her breath, willing her to say yes.

"No," she said. "Why?"

Whitney's heart dipped. She glanced at Natalie, who watched intently, gnawing on her nails, brows furrowed. "She went to Lauren's last night and hasn't come home. She's not answering her phone or texts." A thought struck. "Hey, you wouldn't happen to know Lauren's phone number, would you?"

"Lauren who?"

"Lauren...um..." God, did she really not know Lauren's last name? Why hadn't she ever asked for that information?

"I promise to always keep you safe." The baby's large eyes stared up at her, unblinking.

Swallowing hard, she said, "I...um...I don't know her last name. But Amelia's been hanging out with her a lot. She's in your grade, I think. Wait...no, probably not. She's seventeen, so maybe one grade up. Dark hair, pale skin."

God, that wasn't very descriptive. A dark haired, seventeen-year-old girl described a lot of people. Probably half their school. She knew that anything extra she could add would be helpful. "Um...she wears glasses, has a few freckles on her face. She doesn't wear very much makeup. Just sometimes a little mascara and lip gloss. Always wears her hair down."

"I don't know any Lauren like that at our school," Becca said.

"Well, surely, you've seen Amelia with her."

"No, I'm sorry. I haven't."

"Do you not see Amelia at school anymore? I mean...I know you don't hang out as much, but surely you see each other."

"Oh, yeah. I see her. I just haven't seen her with anyone like that."

"Don't you still follow her on Instagram and Snapchat?"

She hesitated a second before answering, and when she did it sounded like a question. "Yes?"

Whitney was most familiar with Facebook, but recently she'd been learning more about Instagram marketing for the business. She'd upped her postings for Nat's Fancy Finds account, and consequently, she'd seen the photos Amelia had been sharing lately. Most of them had been with Lauren.

"Then you've seen the pictures of her with Lauren, right?" Switching Becca to speakerphone, Whitney went into her Instagram app and searched for Amelia's account.

"I mean, I guess I've seen the pictures of her and some friend, but I didn't know who she was." There was a hint of bitterness and maybe jealousy in Becca's tone.

Amelia's page appeared, her pictures populating the screen. When they all finished loading, Whitney gasped. Every photo Amelia had posted with Lauren was gone. The last picture was of a smoothie Whitney had bought Amelia over two months ago.

"Becca, can you go into Amelia's Instagram account?"

"Sure. I can't get into her Finsta account, though."

"Her what?"

"Her Finsta," she repeated. "Um...her fake Insta. It's like where we post stuff we don't want like...our parents and stuff to see. Anyway, she blocked me from it."

Heat snaked up Whitney's spine as she stared down at Amelia's profile picture. "What kind of stuff do you guys post on these accounts?"

"I don't know. Just like random stuff."

"Random stuff you don't want your parents to see?"

"Uh...yeah."

"What's Amelia's other account called?"

"Um...I think it's her full name with her middle initial."

Whitney typed out Amelia L. Carter, and sure enough, there she was. Her daughter. She couldn't see anything beyond her profile picture because Becca was right, the account was private.

But knowing it existed gave her a bitter taste in her mouth. She swallowed hard.

"Oh, my God," Becca said. "Her last, like, two months of photos are missing."

"So, you're not seeing them either, huh?" Whitney sighed.

"Why would she delete them?" Becca spoke under her breath. It was exactly what Whitney was wondering. She had this sudden image of the three of them in Monterey last summer. Natalie had rented an Airbnb for the week, but her family could only stay for four days, so she offered the place to Whitney for the remaining three. Rarely did she allow Amelia to bring friends on vacations, mostly because Whitney couldn't afford it. But this time it was essentially free, so Whitney let Amelia bring Becca. She figured it would give Amelia someone to do stuff with when Whitney wanted to spend the day lying on the beach and reading. Amelia and Whitney had always differed that way. For Whitney, vacation was a chance to unwind, rest. For Amelia, vacation was theme parks, swimming in the ocean, running from activity to activity.

Whitney was content to let Becca try to keep up with her on the Monterey trip. Her only concern was that she would be alone most of the time. But, actually, she wasn't. The girls ended up spending most of each day at the beach with Whitney, only going off on their own a few times. The house was near Lover's Point, so most mornings they trekked it down to the sand, and set up their towels. They'd read, talk, dip in the cold water when they got too warm. Then they'd head up to the little hamburger stand, grab lunch. Later in the afternoon, they'd pack up. Head down the street for ice cream.

Whitney recalled that Amelia got a horrible sunburn on their last day there. It was on the cooler side that day, so Amelia had forgotten to reapply her sunscreen. Whitney's skin wasn't fair like Amelia's, so sometimes she'd forget to remind her. And usually, she didn't need to. Being on swim team and spending much of her time near a pool, Amelia was normally really responsible about it. Then again, it was a lot warmer in Sacramento. There was no way she wouldn't feel the warmth of the sun as it seeped into her skin.

None of them noticed Amelia's sunburn until they'd returned to the Airbnb in the evening. But that was how sunburns were. You didn't know you had one until it was too late. And then there was nothing you could do to fix it.

In Whitney's experience, relationships were the exact same way.

"What happened between the two of you?" she asked Becca now.

"You'd have to ask her."

Frustration burned through Whitney. "If I could do that, I wouldn't be calling you, would I?"

"Sorry," Becca mumbled. "It's just that I don't really know what happened with us. She just kinda pulled away from me. From our whole group, actually." It was hard to read her tone. Becca had always had a slight edge to her voice. But underneath that, she sounded sincere, truthful. It didn't make Whitney feel any better. She wanted a reason, and she wanted it to be Becca's fault.

"Surely something happened. Did you get in a fight or something?"

"I mean, I guess we argued sometimes, but nothing big."

It didn't make sense. What was Becca hiding?

Whitney thought about her teenage self. What had she and her best friend fought about back then?

Dark eyes.

Tousled hair.

Black jacket.

A wink. An outstretched hand. Lips curled upward on one side.

Whitney shivered, thinking back to the mysterious messages in Amelia's phone. "Do you know Phil Lopez?"

A pause, and then, "Isn't he, like, the lead singer of the Hard Knocks?"

"Huh? No, well, I have no idea." She didn't even know who the Hard Knocks were. "Maybe. But I mean, is there a guy at your school with that name?"

"Not that I know of."

"And you haven't seen Amelia hanging out with a guy?"

It was a moment before Becca spoke again. "No. I'm sorry."

"I have a picture of Amelia with some random guy drinking beers. If I text it to you, do you think you can let me know if he looks familiar?"

Another pause. "Sure."

"Thanks," Whitney said.

"Hey," Becca said suddenly. "Now that I think about it, there is one thing that might be helpful." Whitney sat forward, afraid to even breathe. "Right before Amelia and I stopped hanging out, she mentioned that she'd been talking to this older guy online."

"Older guy? Like how much older?"

"She never said. I kinda thought maybe like in college or something, but I don't know. They'd never met in real life, I don't think. But I know some of their conversations were like...well, you know. I don't wanna say they were sexting, but..." Whitney's stomach rolled, moisture filling her mouth at the thought. Becca cleared her throat. "Anyway, I remember teasing her, saying she better hope she's not being catfished or something."

Whitney thought about the picture of Amelia with that boy. He didn't look older, so she doubted it was the same person, but she supposed it was possible. "Do you happen to know the guy's name or anything?"

"Um...I feel like maybe it was like initials or something," she said, "but I'm not sure."

"Okay, well, if you think of it, can you let me know? And let me know if you recognize the guy in the picture."

"I will," Becca said. "And um…can you let me know if she comes home?"

"Sure."

"I hope you find her soon."

"Me too." While Whitney hung up, Natalie sat on the recliner, one eyebrow cocked. "Hey, can you send me that screenshot?" Whitney asked her. "I'm gonna shoot it off to Becca."

Natalie did as instructed, then Whitney sent the text.

"Have you ever heard of a Finsta account?" she asked Natalie.

"Yeah, Kayla had one of those. I think most kids do."

"Did she let you follow it?"

Natalie shook her head. "No, I think that would defeat the point of it."

"And it didn't bother you?"

"I mean, a little, I guess. But it is what it is."

Whitney had no idea how Natalie could be so nonchalant about this kind of stuff. Holding up the screen of her phone, she displayed Amelia's page. The one she was allowed to follow. "Check this out. All of her photos with Lauren are missing."

Natalie's eyebrows knit together. "That's weird."

"Really weird," Whitney agreed.

"Have you checked her Snapchat?"

"Earlier." Whitney went into it again. Still nothing new. "She hasn't posted anything in the last twenty-four hours." She paused. "At least, that I can see." Whitney was no longer sure what Amelia was sharing with others behind Whitney's back. "I don't think Becca's being honest. Says she's never seen Amelia with Lauren in real life. I mean, they've been attached at the hip for weeks. She also said she's never seen Amelia with a guy, but clearly, she's been hanging out with one."

Natalie's shoulders bobbed up and down. "Well, you know kids. They have a code. No one wants to be known as a snitch."

"True." Whitney knew better than anyone how easy it was

to lie. "But if I can't trust Amelia's friends, how am I gonna find her?"

"You won't need to. I'm telling you. She's going to walk in the door any minute."

Whitney glanced at the front door, willing Natalie's words to be true. "If that's true, then why did she shut off her phone?"

"Maybe she forgot her charger."

Whitney blinked. Amelia *was* forgetful. In first grade, she left her lunch at home so often that Whitney filled her account up with money and made her buy the rest of the year. And she almost flunked PE in middle school for neglecting to bring her uniform back to school after taking it home to be washed. The only thing she never forgot was her swim bag. Probably because swim team had always been a priority for her.

After going into her room, she did a quick scan of the floor, then eyed the outlets. Empty. Next, she went around to the side of the bed closest to the wall where she normally plugged in her phone. Not there either. Her heart pounded.

"Is it here?" Natalie appeared in the doorway.

Whitney shook her head. And that's when she noticed the bare spot on Amelia's desk. Her laptop was gone. Sinking down to the ground, she rifled through the pile of clothes. Not there either.

"Her laptop is gone too."

Bringing her hand up, her fingers caught on a lacy hot-pink push-up bra. One she never remembered buying Amelia. She drew her hand back like it was on fire and stared down at it. Her mind reeled with all the things she'd learned so far today.

The receipt.

The missing money.

The picture.

The older man.

She knew Amelia had been pulling away, asserting her independence, even lying occasionally. But she'd never expected all of this. Blowing out a breath, she dropped her neck back, her gaze skating up the wall, stopping at the poster of Ariana Grande she'd bought Amelia a few years ago at the concert. That was such a fun night. They'd both temporarily dyed their hair pink. At the concert, they danced and sang at the top of their lungs. And afterward, they went to In-N-Out to grab midnight burgers.

Whitney recalled Amelia saying how she was the "funnest" mom ever.

If only she felt that way now. Next to Ariana Grande, her gaze slid to the left, landing on a *Twilight* poster. Amelia had been obsessed with the series since she was in middle school. She'd seen the movies more times than Whitney could count. There were other movie posters too—Amelia loved movies. One time she even went to—

Oh, God.

"Can I see that picture again? The one of Amelia and that boy?"

Nodding, Natalie pulled it up and handed the phone to Whitney.

Her mouth dried out. "I know where they're sitting. I've been there before."

9

FOUR WEEKS
BEFORE DROP-OFF

"WHITE OR RED?" Jay asked from the kitchen.

"Red is fine." A window near Whitney was open, and cool air whisked over her skin. She shivered. Voices floated in from outside. Heated. A couple in a fight.

Whitney wasn't a snob, by any means. She'd lived in apartments much of her adult life. But even she had hesitated a moment when she'd first pulled into the parking lot of this one.

"Well, that's good because I think I'm out of white anyway," he called with a light laugh.

Whitney bit her lip, taking in her surroundings. Jay's apartment was nothing like she thought it would be. From what he'd told her, he had a great job in finance and made a sizable salary. He'd never said those exact words, but he'd alluded to it. This apartment reminded Whitney of the one she'd shared with Dan while they were in college, with its stained carpet and mismatched furniture. Not to mention that there were no photos anywhere, just a couple of framed movie posters, a mirror and a bookshelf which housed an array of items, but hardly any books. Plenty of DVDs, though. She thought of her own apartment, the paintings on the wall, and all the pictures of Amelia in various stages of life. Why didn't he have any personal pictures? Hugging herself, she exhaled slowly.

"A glass of red for the lady."

Jay wore that genuine, dimpled smile of his as he handed her a half-filled wineglass. His dark hair was tousled across his forehead, and his brown eyes sparkled under the dim lighting in the room. He wore khaki dress pants, a blue collared shirt. It hit her then why this place made her uncomfortable. It didn't match him. He exuded class, wealth, charm. His apartment didn't.

Maybe that's why he'd been hesitant to bring her here. He'd been to her place a few times. She'd entertained the idea that maybe he was married or something. It was why she'd pressed him about coming here. Now she wished she hadn't.

Jay motioned for her to sit on the couch with him, so she did. Their knees touched, and he flashed her his boyish grin.

When she took a sip of wine, her body began to warm, relax. Why did it matter if his apartment wasn't what she'd expected? He probably spent money on more important things. Or perhaps he was a saver. Her dad was like that.

"Fail to plan, plan to fail," he'd say.

"You okay?" Jay asked, his brows furrowing.

"Yeah." Whitney smiled, feeling silly about her mental freakout. It's not like they'd just started dating. She knew Jay. They'd been out countless times. There was no reason to be nervous. She glanced around. "Just admiring your decor."

He laughed at her joke. "Wish I could take credit for it."

"Don't tell me you hired a decorator."

Again, he laughed. "No. Somehow I think they would do a better job. Actually, this isn't my place." The discomfort she felt earlier returned. She shifted on the couch, and took another sip of wine, craving its calming effect. "I mean, I guess it is now.

I am paying rent, but my roommate is the one who should get the credit...or the blame—" he winked "—for the decor."

"You never mentioned a roommate."

"Yeah, it's not something a guy wants to bring up on a date." He shrugged. "Like, hey, my ex-wife really reamed me in the divorce, so I'm rooming with a friend until I can get back on my feet."

She felt bad for being so judgmental. Reaching out with her free hand, she touched his knee. "You could've brought it up. I get it. I'm divorced too, remember?"

"Yeah, but you seem to have gotten your shit together."

"I've had a lot more years than you."

His face moved a little closer, his lips twitching at the corners. "What you're saying is that it gets easier?"

"It does get easier," Whitney said emphatically. "And better. You'll see."

He abandoned his wine on the coffee table and lifted his hand to graze her face. "Oh, I'm already seeing that it gets better."

Whitney's heart flipped in her chest. She'd barely set her wine down on the coffee table when Jay's lips found hers. His hands moved to her hair, and she scooted closer to him, grasping his shoulders. A scratching sound caught her attention. She stiffened, tearing her lips away. "Your roommate isn't home right now, is he?"

"He's not supposed to be."

Biting her lip, she glanced over his shoulder. The noise seemed to have come from one of the bedrooms. "I think I heard something, though."

"I'll check, if it makes you feel better." He cocked his head to the side.

It was probably overkill, but she nodded. When he got up from the couch, she wondered if this would be their last date. Her anxiety wasn't her most attractive quality. She was one of those people who checked the doors multiple times to make sure they were locked before going to bed. Or walked through parking lots, eyes scanning the area around her, hands gripping her keys as if ready to use as a weapon if need be. Her mom used to say she had an overactive imagination. That might be true, but she couldn't help it. Still, she usually tried to keep it in check, hidden, until she'd been with a guy for more than a couple months.

But maybe it was okay that Jay was getting a glimpse of it. He would eventually, right?

"It was the cat." Jay sauntered back in the room wearing a grin.

"A cat?" He hadn't mentioned a cat, but that would explain the smell. Whitney peered down at the ground, her nose scrunching. And the hair.

"Yeah. Sorry. I sometimes forget about the little guy." After plunking down next to her, he drew her close. "But don't worry, he agreed to give us our privacy."

"Is that so?" She nestled in closer, their lips meeting once again. *Privacy.* An unexpected chill worked its way up her spine. It's what she wanted, right? To be alone with him. It's why she made him search the place. It's why she wanted to come back here for a nightcap. Whitney would've invited him to her apartment, but Amelia was home tonight.

Part of Whitney felt bad heading out for her date, leaving Amelia on the couch, a bowl of popcorn in her lap and the TV blaring. But a night away from the teenage attitude and eye rolling sounded amazing.

Now she just kind of wanted to go home.

"Everything okay?" Jay studied her face.

Whitney sighed, feeling like the biggest dud on the planet. "Yes, everything is great."

His eyes narrowed. "Funny, you're saying the right words, but your face is telling a different story."

"Sorry." She frowned. "I am honestly having a great time. I always do with you."

"But…" he prodded.

"But…Amelia's home by herself tonight, and…"

He sat back on the couch, releasing her. "She's a teenager. Surely, she can handle a night alone."

The comment stung. "Of course she can handle a night alone. It's just that we haven't been getting along that great…and I don't know…" Whitney wasn't even sure what she was trying to say, let alone how to convey it.

"I wouldn't worry about it." Jay moved in close again, wrapped one arm around her middle and tugged her toward him. "I'm sure she's fine."

His hand slid under Whitney's shirt and she shivered at his touch. She gave in to him then, allowing his mouth to cover hers, his hands to move over her skin, willing herself to be in the moment. As the kiss deepened, he guided her down on the couch. Her head hit the side. She drew her lips away from his, reaching up to rub the spot where her head met the couch.

"You okay?" he asked.

She was about to answer when the cat crawled into the room, meowing and staring up at her. Her flesh itched; she suddenly felt hyperaware of cat hair sticking to her skin. Wiping at it, she sat upright. From the half-open window she caught bits and pieces of the neighbors' heated conversation as it clearly escalated.

"Yeah," she said, looking away from the cat. "I'm sorry. I guess I'm just distracted tonight."

"I know." Lifting his hand, he touched her cheek, brushed back a strand of hair. "But I'm sure your daughter is fine. I used to live for the nights my parents went out when I was her age."

It was meant to make her feel better.

It succeeded in making her feel worse.

She readjusted her top, smoothed down her hair.

Jay sighed. Pulling back, he ran a hand through his hair. "Okay, I can take a hint."

She felt bad. He deserved better than this. He'd been so patient with her from the beginning.

"I'm sorry," she said again. "It's getting late, and I just really have to go."

He nodded. "I get it."

"Thanks for being so understanding." Reaching out, she put her hand over his. "And we'll do this again soon...I promise."

"Oh, I'll hold you to that." Leaning toward her, he gave her one last kiss.

10

SATURDAY, 3:30 P.M.
TWENTY-TWO AND A HALF
HOURS AFTER DROP-OFF

THERE IT WAS. The same bench.

Whitney held up her phone, picture displayed. "See, this is it. Right?"

"Looks the same," Natalie agreed. She pointed to the ground. "Even has the plant next to it."

Whitney glanced around at the grass surrounding them, a few picnic tables, barbecue pits and the pool a few feet away, enclosed in a fence. This complex was a good twenty minutes from where they lived. And Amelia had been here partying with people Whitney had never met. She swallowed hard. A warm breeze blew over them, leaves twitching on the branches of a nearby tree, a few falling to the ground.

"So, this is where Jay lives?" Natalie asked.

Whitney nodded. After she'd made the connection, she'd called him several times. He never answered. "Upstairs. But we'd passed this little picnic area on our way up. I remember commenting on how much cuter it was than our park area."

Natalie's shoulders bobbed up and down. "Could just be a coincidence."

"Yeah," Whitney agreed. "But I have to be sure." She thought about the receipts from Sunrise Mall, which happened to be right around the corner from here. "Come on." She walked forward, motioning for Natalie to follow.

They made their way up the stairs, passing a mom with her two young children in tow. Whitney's gaze lingered on them a beat too long. She noted the way the woman's hand rested on her daughter's back, the way she easily touched the top of her son's head. Neither child made any attempt to pull away. She longed for those days again.

When the mom caught Whitney staring, she averted her gaze and hurried up the remaining stairs.

The hallway was similar to Whitney's. She remembered thinking that when Jay brought her here too. Concrete floors, windows and doors facing the apartment across the way, the occasional flowerpot or chair as decoration. There was nothing in front of Jay's.

She knocked a few times and the door popped open. A woman who looked to be in her late twenties answered the door. Her hair was bleached a white blond, her roots dark, she had shimmery pink lipstick on her impossibly large lips and thick fake eyelashes that made it seem like it must be tough for her to keep her eyes open.

Her gaze fell to Whitney's empty hands and then her eyebrows shot up. "Oh, you're not DoorDash."

Whitney shook her head. "No, we're here to see Jay. Is he home?"

"Jay?" She frowned, crossing her arms over her chest. "No, he doesn't live here."

"Um…yeah, I mean, I know it's not his place, but he's been staying here." A toilet flushed from inside. "He brought me here like a month ago or so."

The woman's lip scrunched up in a sour way. "Sorry, but no. This is my boyfriend's place and he's the only one who lives here."

A clicking sound like a door popping open came from the hallway, and a man around the same age as the woman came around the corner. His eyes widened upon seeing Whitney and Natalie.

"What's going on?" He ran a hand over his hair.

The woman turned, her spiderlike eyelashes pointing toward the man. "I think this lady's, like, dating Jay and she thinks he lives here." She lowered her voice. "Sounds like he's brought her here before."

"What? Nah, man, that's not cool." The man approached, throwing Whitney an apologetic look. "Sorry, but Jay doesn't live here."

Whitney felt like she'd been slapped in the face, but she fought to keep her cool. "If you could just tell me how to find him. I think..." Whitney scrambled to find the right words "...my daughter might be with him...or at least may have been here before?" It ended up coming out like a question, Whitney's voice high and unsure. This whole thing had thrown her off-kilter. She didn't know what to think anymore.

"Your daughter?" The guy's eyes bugged out. "Nah. I'm not gettin' involved in this." He started to close the door.

Whitney threw her arm up to block it. "Wait. Please. If you could just—"

The door slammed in her face. Slumping over, Whitney pressed her forehead to the door, thinking of what to do next. That's when she realized she could faintly hear the man and woman arguing through the door.

"What the hell's...you." The man's voice was slightly muffled, and Whitney couldn't pick up on every word, but she got the gist. "Why did you...open...door for them?"

"I thought it was our DoorDash. And why ya mad at me?

Your brother's the one bringing girls back here." The woman's response was a shrill yell, and Whitney was grateful to be able to pick up on her words.

"I'll deal with Jay. You just keep your mouth shut, okay?" The man's voice was loud now too.

Whitney heard shuffling inside. Their feet moving away from the door.

The woman said something, but Whitney only picked up the tail end. "…what an asshole he was, anyway."

The man responded but their voices were even more muffled now, like they'd moved farther back into the apartment. Whitney couldn't make out anything anymore.

"What was the last thing she said?" Whitney asked Natalie, who had also been listening intently, ear to the door.

"Something to the effect of you already figuring out what an asshole Jay is."

A young man stepped into the hall, plastic bags dangling from his fingers.

"Must be their food," Whitney surmised.

Natalie grabbed her arm. "Okay, then we need to get outta here."

"Or, we could use him as a way to talk to them again," Whitney suggested.

Natalie shook her head firmly. "There's no way you're getting any more information out of those two."

You just keep your mouth shut, okay?

Keep her mouth shut about what? Whitney wondered as Natalie tugged her down the hall.

"Let's just go downstairs and regroup," Natalie said in her "boss" tone.

Nodding, Whitney allowed herself to be guided down the stairs. When they got to the little park area, Whitney leaned her back against the metal fence around the pool. The air smelled like chlorine, pulling her mind into the past. To summers. To swim meets. And all the way back to when Amelia was a toddler, running around the pool in her neon bathing suit. The way she'd push the little water wings up her scrawny arms, trying to secure them in place. How she'd have to chase Amelia around the pool, trying to slather sunblock on her between jumps into the water.

Natalie's phone rang. "Oh, it's Kayla," she said before answering. As Natalie spoke, she walked in a zigzaggy line across the grass. Natalie was never able to stand still while talking on the phone.

Whitney turned, staring into the water of the pool. It was warm today, but maybe not warm enough for a swim. The pool was empty, the surface still, sunshine shimmering on the top. She tried to picture Amelia here, drinking, partying. But instead she saw herself as a teenager, sitting with her best friend on a lounge chair sipping beers and talking about boys. Until recently, Amelia had been so different from how Whitney had been as a teenager. More responsible. Levelheaded. And Whitney had been lulled into the illusion that her daughter would never give her the grief she'd given her parents.

"Whit?"

She spun around to face Natalie. "Yeah?"

"So, Kayla asked around. And none of her friends knew the guy's name that Amelia was with. But her friend that took the picture is going to ask around too. Someone must've invited him to the party, so she's bound to find out something. She did say, though, that she overheard him talking, kinda bragging, I guess about…" She paused, swallowing. Whitney stepped closer. "Like how he could score drugs for them, and also something about being kicked out of his last school. She wasn't sure for what."

"Sounds like a winner," Whitney muttered under her breath. What was her daughter doing with a guy like that? Then again, it didn't sound like Whitney's radar was working very well either. Exhaling, she glanced around. Her head was spinning from all the information she'd received in the last few minutes. She pinched the bridge of her nose. "God, I just don't understand any of this. I have no idea what to think right now." Her gaze flickered to the stairs they'd just come down. "Jay seemed like such a genuine guy."

Natalie's shoulders softened, her lips lowering and her eyes crinkling in concern. "I'm sorry."

"Do you think he's the older guy Becca was talking about?"

Natalie bit her lip. "I mean, has he ever acted weird around her?"

The first time Jay came over was to pick Whitney up for a date. Whitney had been running late, on the last touches of her makeup, when she heard the knock on the door. Hollering down the hall, she asked if Amelia could answer.

While swiping on some lip gloss, Whitney heard Amelia and Jay talking in the family room. She should've paid more attention to what was being said, but she was more fixated on how she looked. It sounded like nothing more than small talk, but she couldn't be sure.

The second time he picked her up, Whitney had been ready early. Amelia came out of her room as they were leaving. All she said was goodbye and have fun or something like that. Whitney tried to remember if Jay acted oddly, stared at Amelia too long. Anything to indicate he was interested in her. But she came up empty.

Jay had always seemed focused on Whitney.

Even their conversations about Amelia revolved around him wanting more time with Whitney. Nothing to indicate he was up to anything shady regarding her daughter. The occasional times he'd been around Amelia their conversations were hi, bye. Nice to see you. Have a good afternoon. The kind of exchange she had in grocery stores with acquaintances.

"Not that I can recall," Whitney said now.

"Then I think our best bet is finding the guy in the picture,"

Natalie said. "I mean, she was here with him, not Jay. And, actually, Jay doesn't technically live here."

"I know. Seriously, what's that about?"

"I honestly don't know." Natalie shook her head. "But I feel like you're grasping at straws here. I honestly don't think Jay has anything to do with Amelia. She may have been chatting with some older guy online, but it seems like a stretch to think it's Jay."

Her words seemed logical. But Natalie hardly knew Jay. She'd only met him a couple of times. Why was she so quick to defend him? Thinking back, Whitney realized that she'd met Jay while waiting for Natalie at a restaurant. And it was Natalie who ultimately talked her into going on their first date.

"Are you excited about your big date tonight?" Natalie came toward Whitney, wiggling her shoulders, a smile stretching across her face. They were at the warehouse, going through inventory. It was cold and drafty, and smelled like damp wood.

Whitney pulled her sweater tighter around her body. "Actually, I think I'm going to cancel."

"What?" Natalie's head whipped in her direction. The shirt she'd been holding fluttered to the ground. "Why?"

Whitney's fingers wove around the fuzzy fabric of a nearby sweater. She nervously rolled it between her fingertips. In the distance she heard tires on asphalt, the breeze whisking over the outer walls of the warehouse. A chill brushed down her back. "I don't know. I just feel like it's not a good idea."

"Why not?" Natalie picked the shirt back up and added it to her pile.

Natalie would never understand. She'd married her high school sweetheart more than twenty years ago. She had no idea what the dating world was like. Or the issues a single mom faced while dating.

"I don't know…I mean, I don't know anything about this guy. I even googled him and couldn't find anything, but a private Facebook page."

"Well, he's not famous, is he?"

"Clearly not." Whitney chuckled. "It's just usually when I date a guy it's someone I already know. This guy sorta came out of nowhere."

"Uh-oh. Have you been watching crime dramas again?"

Natalie always teased Whitney about her overactive imagination, telling her she needed to stick to watching comedies or romances, not scary shows.

Whitney laughed, cocked a brow. "Maybe."

"That night you met Jay, you could not stop smiling. The whole dinner all you did was talk about how hot he was, and how nice he was," Natalie reminded her. "I think you should go for it. But if you're really worried, I can come hang out in the restaurant, keep an eye on you."

"Like as my bodyguard?"

Natalie laughed. "Incognito, of course."

Whitney pictured Natalie in sunglasses and a black hat, sitting at the bar, watching them on their date. Laughing along, she shook her head. "No, I'll be fine."

She looked at her friend. Wondered. Was Natalie behind her meeting Jay? Had she known him before?

"I think it's time to call the police, Whit," Natalie said.

Whitney glanced at her watch, reading the time. "Don't you have to wait twenty-four hours to report someone missing?"

"I've heard that, but I'm pretty sure it's a myth."

Whitney's mouth dried out. The idea of calling the police made this seem too real, as if she was admitting that something terrible had happened. She wasn't ready to do that. Surely, Amelia hadn't taken off or met with foul play. *She'd be back soon, right?* "First, I need to talk to Becca again. I get the feeling she knows more than she's sharing."

"Has she called back yet?" Natalie asked.

Taking out her phone, she checked her messages. Nothing. "No."

"Call her then. Find out what she knows and then we'll take it from there."

Nodding, Whitney turned away from Natalie. She was grateful her friend couldn't read her thoughts. How could she ever think Natalie would manipulate her? And for what purpose? Natalie was as genuine as they came. But old habits die hard. And Whitney wasn't used to trusting people. But Natalie had never given her any reason not to.

As the phone rang, she stared into the soothing, turquoise water of the pool.

11

FIVE WEEKS
BEFORE DROP-OFF

THE EMAIL CAME in the early afternoon. It was from Amelia's principal. A kid had come to school that morning with a knife. He'd been detained, his weapon confiscated. The school felt confident the threat had been taken care of.

Whitney wasn't so sure.

Images from news reports she'd watched over the years of kids running from their schools, hands over their heads, played like a montage in her mind.

Her skin crawled. Her body buzzed.

She was at the warehouse, shooting photos, but she couldn't concentrate. Amelia only had a couple hours left in her school day, and she was getting good grades. What would it hurt to skip out a little early? Besides, they'd hardly spent any time together lately.

Abandoning work, she drove to the high school. It wasn't far from the warehouse. Only about fifteen minutes. After parking, she made her way into the office and headed toward the attendance clerk. The scent of paper, pencil shavings and musty carpet brought her back to when she was in high school.

Mrs. Pruitt glanced up, frowning. "Ms. Carter?" She said it like a question. Like she was surprised to see her.

"Hi, Mrs. Pruitt," Whitney said. "I need to pull Amelia out of class, please."

Her eyebrows furrowed. "But…Amelia's not here."

Heat snaked up Whitney's back. "What do you mean?"

"She never came to school today."

"Are you sure?"

Mrs. Pruitt drew her lips to one side as if in thought. Then she typed something on her keyboard, her gaze scanning her computer screen. "Yep. She hasn't been to any of her classes. You called her out sick this morning."

Whitney's head spun. She thought back to this morning. It had been hectic. She'd overslept and then her favorite pants were dirty, so she had to figure out something else to wear. Usually, on the mornings when Amelia had to take the bus, Whitney would peek in on her before leaving. But she'd been running late for an early morning meeting. She hadn't even had time to grab breakfast before tearing out the front door.

But she was positive she didn't call Amelia out.

"I gotta go." Whitney whirled around and hurried out of the building.

As she headed out into the parking lot, she remembered Amelia complaining about a sore throat last night. Amelia probably stayed home because she wasn't feeling well. But did she call herself out? In an effort to ease her mind, Whitney pulled up the Find My Friends app after sliding into the driver's seat. It took a couple of minutes to locate Amelia. She was at a park a couple of miles away. So, she wasn't at home sick, then. What would she be doing at a park in the middle of the day?

"Here. Your turn." An arm outstretched. A joint burning between two fingers.

Whitney taking hold of it, bringing it to her lips. Allowing the smoke to fill her mouth, her lungs.

Her tires squealed when she raced out of the school parking lot. A couple of teachers stood near the sidewalk talking. Their heads jolted in Whitney's direction. Her face flushed, as she eased her foot slightly off the gas.

When she pulled into the park, it was filled with parents and little kids. As she walked through the damp grass, green blades sticking to the soles of her shoes, she remembered taking Amelia to the park all the time when she was younger. Her favorite thing in the world was being pushed on the swing. Often, Whitney would beg Amelia to run around or go down the slide. Anything to give her achy arms a break. But no, Amelia would insist on the swing, screaming and crying until Whitney gave in. Whitney's arms would be all numb and jellylike by the time they left.

What she wouldn't give to go back in time now, though.

She wouldn't complain about pushing her in the swing. Not for one second. She'd push her until her arms no longer worked. Until she fell over from exhaustion.

"What do you want to do, Amelia?" Whitney asked, while three-year-old Amelia tugged on her arm, pulling her toward the playground.

"Swings." Amelia pointed, her chubby cheeks squishing upward as she smiled, her pigtails bouncing with each boisterous step.

Whitney didn't know why she'd even bothered asking. Amelia never said anything different. But a mom could dream.

They hit the edge of the playground when Amelia stopped abruptly, her face stern.

"My swing," she said under her breath, pointing.

Following her gaze, Whitney saw a little boy around Amelia's same age sitting on the swing she usually occupied, spinning around in circles, the metal chain coiling around him. A little girl was being pushed by her mom on the neighboring swing.

"That's all right," Whitney said in a singsong, overly cheery voice.

"We'll just go on the slide until they're finished. That will be fun, right?"

"No." Amelia stepped forward, stomping over the bark in her pink tennis shoes. *"Mine,"* she hollered at the boy, and before Whitney could stop her, she'd slammed her palms into his knees trying to shove him off the swing. He was so wrapped up in the swing, he barely moved. *"Mine!"* Amelia hollered again.

Whitney ran after her, grabbing her by the hand. "Amelia, stop it. You can't behave that way." If Whitney had acted like this at her age, she would've gotten a spanking. But Whitney couldn't bring herself to spank Amelia. Time-outs were about as far as she went. Mostly she found that keeping Amelia close kept her out of trouble. Holding tightly to her hand, she led her to the slide.

"I don't wanna slide. I want swings!" Amelia stuck out her bottom lip in a pout.

Whitney lowered down onto her knees, looked her daughter in the eyes. "I know, honey, but someone else is on it right now, and we have to share."

Amelia turned to look at the swing-stealing boy, throwing him her best evil face. Despite herself, Whitney's lips twitched at the corners. It was hard for Amelia to grasp the concept of sharing since she didn't have a sibling. Sometimes Whitney wondered if she and Dan should try again, but never brought it up. Their marriage was rocky enough. Another child wouldn't fix it. Besides, Amelia was enough for her.

She was all Whitney needed.

Passing by the playground, Whitney scanned the large grassy area. Where would a teenage girl be? Her gaze connected with the bathrooms, and she walked toward them. Hushed voices reached her ears the closer she got.

"Amelia?" Whitney stopped abruptly before running right into a little boy with his mom. The mom's forehead knit together as she drew her child closer to her body.

"Sorry," Whitney mumbled. "I'm just looking for my daughter."

"Oh." The mom's eyes widened, and she relaxed her grip on

the boy. Her gaze darted around. "I haven't seen anyone. Want me to help you look?"

Whitney shook her head, spotting a cluster of trees near the back of the park. Two teenagers barely visible behind it.

Lazily, she stared up at the sky through the branches. Leaves fluttered in the breeze. Fingers tangled through hers. The earth seemed to spin beneath her as if she was floating above it all, her head high up in the clouds, among the birds and planes.

"It's okay. I think I found her. Thanks." Whitney moved swiftly past them.

The scent of cigarette smoke reached her before she even got to the trees. A guy laughed, coughed. A girl giggled. Angrily, Whitney stormed up to them. Their backs were to her. His arm was draped around her shoulder and plumes of smoke rose from their heads.

"Amelia!" Whitney snapped.

She turned, mouth agape. Only it wasn't Amelia.

"What the hell?" the girl said.

The boy peered over his shoulder, eyebrows raised.

Sighing, Whitney whirled around, gaze taking in the park once again. Where could she be?

Stepping away from the young couple, Whitney pulled out her phone and clicked on the Find My Friends app again. This time it showed Amelia at home.

When Whitney got to their apartment, she went straight to Amelia's room. Her door was closed, so she knocked softly. No response. Whitney opened the door. The room was empty.

"Amelia!" she called out.

Huh.

She checked the location app again, and it still showed Amelia at home. It was quiet. The humming of the fridge and the ticking of the clock on the kitchen wall, the only background noises. The apartment was a thousand square feet. She didn't need to search it to know Amelia wasn't here.

Whitney was about to call her phone when the front door popped open. Amelia breezed inside, wearing a tank top, cut-off shorts that were way too short and flip-flops. She gasped, clutching her chest.

"Oh, my God, Mom, you scared the shit outta me."

"What were you doing in the park today, and why weren't you at school?"

"The park? I was never at the park today."

"Don't lie to me, Amelia."

"I'm not lying."

"Then why did it show you at the park on the Find My Friends app?"

Amelia frowned, blowing a breath out her nose. "We've talked about this before, Mom. You have to refresh it or it will glitch and show you like the last place you were or something." She reached out. "Hand me your phone." Whitney did as she was told. Amelia clicked on the screen and then held it up. "See? It's showing you in the park right now." She glared at her mom. "Why? Were you there looking for me?"

Whitney's skin flushed. She didn't bother answering.

Amelia rolled her eyes. After stabbing at the screen with her finger, she showed the phone to Whitney again. "And now you're home."

"Oh." Whitney bit her lip. "But why would it show you in the park in the first place? When were you there?"

"I always cut through that park when I take the bus. So, I don't know. Maybe the last time you tracked me was yesterday, and it froze there or something. I don't own the app. I don't know everything about it."

It was a phrase Whitney used to use all the time when Amelia was younger. Amelia was the queen of questions and sometimes it was wearying.

"Mom, why is the TV station doing this?"

"I don't know. I don't work for channel ten."

"Right," Whitney responded now. Her eye twitched and she

closed it for a second until the sensation vanished. "But why weren't you at school?"

"I told you last night I wasn't feeling well."

"Yeah, but you didn't ask to stay home. Mrs. Pruitt said I called you out, but that's not true."

"Wait." Amelia held up her hand. "Mrs. Pruitt? You went to my school? Oh, my God, Mom. Why?"

"No." Whitney held her ground. She was the mom here. She had every right to check on her daughter at school. Amelia was the one who screwed up. Not her. "You're not turning this around on me. You skipped school and I wanna know why."

"I didn't skip school. I told you. I don't feel well," Amelia said. "I called myself out, okay? I didn't want to bother you. You've been really stressed."

It was true. Whitney had been stressed. But no, that wasn't a good excuse for lying. "Next time, you need to get permission *before* you can stay home. And no more calling yourself out, okay?"

"Fine." Amelia kicked off her flip-flops near the door.

"Where were you today? How come you're not in bed if you're sick?"

"I was earlier, but then I decided to go down to the pool for a little while. Lay out. Figured some vitamin D would do me good." She smiled. "And it did."

Whitney nodded, believing her easily. She always liked the feeling of the sun on her skin when she was sick too. When Amelia passed by on her way to her room, she expected to get a whiff of chlorine, outside air. Instead, Amelia smelled like something Whitney couldn't place. Kind of like a spice she recognized. Cinnamon? Cloves?

Whatever it was, it was foreign. Unfamiliar. Weird that it was coming from her daughter.

12

THE THIRD TIME I spent the night at Millie's, we snuck out to go to a party. She wore this black leather jacket with fringe all along the sleeves. Her hair was wild and loose with large curls, and her lip gloss was a deep berry color. She looked amazing. I had on a sundress, and my hair was pulled back in a ponytail. She lent me a pair of combat boots that were way too narrow, but I shoved my feet into them anyway. Then she talked me into letting my hair down, and she swiped a coat of the same dark lip gloss over my lips. I still didn't look as good as she did, but it was an improvement.

I'd never been to a party before, so I had no idea what to expect. My only frame of reference was from watching sitcoms. With that in mind, I'd been expecting bumping music and wall-to-wall kids dancing and making out.

That's not at all what this party was like.

This party was at an apartment downstairs from Millie's where these two college-aged boys lived. And it literally consisted of them and a couple of their friends. We were the only girls.

It was clear right off the bat that the apartment belonged to two guys. There were no decorative touches at all. Just a ratty couch, torn fabric, dirty yellow stuffing poking out. There were two dinner trays on either side of it, which I assumed were supposed to be end tables. They were covered in ashtrays and books of matches. In the kitchen, a little card table was set up. On the counter was a box of Coors Light, ripped open in the wrong spot, and a half-empty bottle of vodka.

There was no music playing and the room was dimly lit by only one lamp.

I remember reaching for Millie's hand, wishing we could leave. She squeezed my fingers and tugged me forward. The smile she wore kept my protests locked inside. No way would I do anything to wipe that smile off her face.

She was happy. Ready to have fun.

Who was I to spoil that for her?

I'd never even taken a sip of beer before, but when one of the guys held out two cans, Millie took one and immediately popped the top, so I did the same. It tasted so much nastier than I thought it would. Way too bitter.

Millie talked the guys into putting on some music. The minute the beat swelled around the room, her body started swaying. She reached for me. Giggling, I joined her, trying not to care who was watching. We spun in circles and swayed our hips back and forth. Beer kept sloshing out of my can, but no one seemed to notice.

They all noticed Millie, though.

The guys kept glancing over at her appreciatively.

She was clueless. Her attention was fixed on me. It made me all warm and fuzzy inside. The beer helped with that too. Made me feel all warm and loose, my limbs moving with more ease than usual.

That's why I took a second beer when the guys offered.

Millie lit up a cigarette. It crackled as she brought it to her sparkly lips. Drawing the cigarette away, she blew out a plume of smoke. Then she held it out to me, asking if I smoked. I never had, but I lied and said yes. Then I took it in between my fingers. The edge was stained in deep berry.

It was kind of embarrassing how much I coughed after attempting to take a drag. I think everyone knew then that I'd never smoked before. I heard a few chuckles from the guys. But Millie didn't make fun of me at all. She made some comment about there being a first time for everything, and then she told me to try again.

Millie was so persistent that I didn't have the heart to tell her no. But the truth is I hated it. Hated the way it coated my teeth in a nasty ash taste, hated the way it made my head pound and my mouth feel cottony.

After a few more tries, my stomach got all crampy and shaky, so I hurried to the bathroom. Trying not to touch the sides of the stained toilet seat, I hovered over it. Saliva filled my mouth. I gagged, coughed, tried to puke. But nothing came up. Eventually, the nausea subsided. I splashed some cold water on my face and took a few deep breaths before emerging from the bathroom.

When I returned to the living room, I found Millie sitting cross-legged on the ground with a couple of the guys, smoking. From the hallway, it looked like a cigarette. But as I got closer, the overwhelming scent of pot was undeniable. The guys huddled around her were leaned back, eyes red and glazed over, tiny slits.

Millie offered me a hit when I sat down next to her. She held the joint out toward my face, pinched between her thumb and forefinger. It glowed red on the end, emitting its pungent aroma.

I'd vowed to myself back in eighth that I'd never use drugs after watching a disturbing video in health class. Kids were convulsing, acting erratically, crazy-like, as if they could no longer manage their own bodies, control their own impulses. I hated feeling out of control. I couldn't figure out why anyone would do that to themselves voluntarily.

I doubted pot would cause me to act like that, but I'd overheard a girl at school saying she smoked pot once and unbeknownst to her it was laced with acid and she totally tripped out. I shook my head at the joint being offered. It was the first time since we'd met that I said no to Millie, but she was cool about it. Didn't make me feel bad at all. And in that moment, I liked her even more.

As I sat so close our thighs touched, I thought nothing could ever tear us apart.

I thought we'd be friends forever.

13

"HI, MS. CARTER," Becca answered.

Whitney didn't bother with pleasantries this time. "Becca, did you get the picture I sent?"

A pause. "Yes, I got it."

"And?"

"I um…yes…I think I know who that guy is."

"Oh? 'Cause you never texted back."

"I know. I just…I was trying to get a hold of Amelia first."

Whitney's pulse jumpstarted. She looked away from the pool. At the trees, the green grass, a group of boys walking by in the distance, their voices carried on the wind. "Did you?"

"No. She never answered her phone." A sigh. "I know we're not really hanging out right now, but she's been my best friend for a long time…and I just…I don't wanna, like, tell on her or whatever."

Whitney gripped the edge of the fence. "I understand, Becca, but if you care about Amelia, then telling me what you know is the right thing to do."

"Yeah, I know. It's just that Amelia would kill me if she knew what I was about to say."

"Amelia may be in trouble. And what you have to say might help her. I think she'd understand."

"Okay. Yeah, you're right." She started sounding more like herself. More self-assured. "Do you remember the last night we had a sleepover and Amelia got sick?"

Something fluttered low in Whitney's gut. She'd always known there was more to this story.

Voices spoke in the distance, at first nothing more than a soundtrack to Whitney's slumber. Then the timbre changed, yanking her from sleep.

"Oh, my God." Becca's voice rang out.

A door flying open. Footsteps pounding.

"You okay?"

Whitney shot out of bed, heart pounding. Amelia! Practically falling, she blindly stumbled out of the room and into the hall. Amelia's bedroom door was open, but no one was inside.

Coughing, sputtering and retching came from inside the bathroom.

"Amelia?" Whitney attempted to open the bathroom door, but it was locked. She hit it with her palm. "Amelia."

"Mom?" Amelia's voice was thick, pained.

"You okay?"

"She's fine," Becca answered. "Just not feeling great. I think maybe it's food poisoning."

Food poisoning? Ugh. Thank God Whitney hadn't eaten fast food with the girls.

"Are you sick too, Becca?" she asked.

"No." Becca answered through the door. Whitney heard Amelia retch again. "But I didn't have the salad."

Whitney nodded. Yeah, it was the produce that usually did it. "Do you need some Pepto Bismol? I think we've got some."

"We have it," Becca answered.

"Okay."

"It's all right, Mom," Amelia said. "Go back to bed."

"Are you sure I can't bring you something?" Whitney leaned her

head against the door, the coolness of the wood seeping into the warmth of her cheek. She imagined Amelia hunched over the toilet, Becca comforting her. It should've been Whitney. It had always been Whitney. "A cool washcloth? Some water?" What if she was getting dehydrated? "Or I could run to the store. Get some coconut water or Gatorade. You need some electrolytes."

The toilet flushed. "Oh, my God, Mom." Amelia groaned. The faucet turned on. "I'm fine. Just ate something bad. Go back to bed."

"Uh-huh," she said now, anxious to finally find out the truth. Even when she'd pressed Amelia about it days afterward, she had maintained her food poisoning story.

"Well, earlier that day we'd run into some boys who lived in your apartment complex. Apparently, Amelia had talked to one of them before. Mike, I think. Or Michael? I don't know. Something with an *M*, I think. Or maybe an *N*? I honestly have no idea. I was too busy texting Alec all night. We had kinda had a fight and he—"

"Becca," Whitney urged, knowing how easily Becca went off on tangents.

"Right. Sorry. Anyway, they invited us to hang out later in the night. So, after you went to bed, we went and met them down by that little park area. You know, where the slide and jungle gym are? They had alcohol. Beer. A bottle of rum, and some kind of sweet stuff. It was actually really nasty. I only had a couple of sips, but Amelia straight downed it. Anyway, that's why she was throwing up and stuff. And, afterward, Amelia kept seeing that guy. Michael, I'm pretty sure is his name. Anyway, he's the guy in the picture with her."

"Do you happen to know what apartment number he lives in?"

"Um…no. I never went into an apartment."

Whitney stared at the picture of Amelia on a bench with Michael—or whatever his name was.

"The older guy that Amelia was texting with—his name wasn't Jay, was it?" she asked.

"I mean, maybe?" It came out like a question. "I feel like maybe it was two letters, though. JT, maybe."

Jay Thomas.

A shiver worked its way up Whitney's spine.

"Okay, thanks," Whitney said.

"Also," Becca said suddenly, "I guess I wasn't completely honest earlier." Whitney tightened her hold on the phone. "I do know why Amelia and I aren't really hanging out anymore. It's because of that guy. Michael or whatever. He's not a good guy. He, like, parties all the time and brags about doing some pretty bad stuff. Anyway, ever since Amelia started hanging out with him and his friends she's not been herself anymore."

Yeah, Whitney knew firsthand how much Amelia had changed.

Was this why?

"Do you know the names of any of his other friends?"

"Um…there was another guy named like Carey or Craig or something. Oh, God. I honestly wasn't paying that much attention. I was so worried about—"

"Alec. Yeah, I know," she said, disappointed in Becca. Weren't girls supposed to look out for each other? Have each other's backs? Wasn't it some sort of code?

She'd always thought Becca was such a good friend to Amelia. Now she wasn't so sure.

But she was appreciative that at least she'd come clean now. "Thanks, Becca."

After hanging up, she turned to Natalie, whose eyebrows were raised in question. "Apparently, that boy is someone named Michael who lives in our apartment complex and Amelia has been seeing him behind my back."

Natalie touched my arm. "Oh, God, I'm sorry."

Tears pricked Whitney's eyes, but she blinked them back.

"There's so much I don't know about. So much she's been keeping from me." Tucking her phone into her pocket, she looked up at her friend. "I can't believe this is happening. I really thought she'd be back by now."

"Maybe she is. Let's go back to your place and check," Natalie said, but her tone lacked the conviction it had had earlier.

When they returned to the apartment, there was still no sign of Amelia. Whitney couldn't waste any more time. She called the police and reported her daughter missing. The woman she spoke with said she'd send an officer out to her apartment within the hour.

Whitney's weekly call from her mom came a few minutes after she'd hung up. Whitney stared at her phone, hesitating. Could she even handle a conversation with her mom today? It was always shallow. One-sided. Whitney often joked that it was nothing more than a box for her mom to check every week. A way for her to pat herself on the back, to feel like a good parent.

"You should answer," Natalie pressed. "She might know something."

Whitney doubted her mom knew anything about Amelia, but decided it was worth a shot. Anything was at this point.

At the sound of her mom's voice Whitney's spine instinctively straightened, her shoulders tensing.

Sit tall.

Spine straight.

Smooth your skirt.

Stop fidgeting.

Quiet down.

After clearing her throat, she responded to her mom's greeting, "Hi, Mom. How are you?"

Natalie left Whitney alone in the kitchen, ambling into the family room. She leaned her back against the counter and stared out the window. Across the way, the guy's kitchen was dark.

Empty. She focused in on the plant he had in the window. The green, curving leaves, the bright blue planter.

"Good. How about you?" She could picture her mom standing elegantly over the kitchen counter, elbow rested on top, phone to her ear. Her platinum bob was no doubt brushed neatly, not a strand out of place. And even though she'd probably only gone to the store today, she was most likely dressed formally, full makeup on. Her mom had never known how to have a scrounge day.

Whitney could keep this up. Say she was fine. Answer a few questions about her work, Amelia's schooling, possibly the weather, or her mom might share a tidbit about one of her neighbors, a person Whitney had never even met. Then her mom would say it was nice talking to her and hang up. It was a script Whitney had memorized. They rarely veered from it. Today would seem like the day to go off-book, but Whitney wasn't even sure how to do that.

What would her mom do if she told her about Amelia?

Would she empathize? Try to help? Or would she criticize? Accuse? Make Whitney feel worse?

Whitney wasn't sure. That was the problem.

Their relationship had been strained all of Whitney's life. She'd seen pictures from when she was an infant and a toddler, heard stories from others about that time period, and it appeared that her mom had been an attentive, loving parent back then. Maybe if her brother hadn't been born with cystic fibrosis, that would've continued. But from the time Kevin came into this world when Whitney was five, her mother's whole existence was about him—his breathing treatments, medications, hospital stays. Her parents' main focus in life was keeping him well. The logical part of her understood. Her brother was ill. He needed constant care. That wasn't his fault. She'd often felt sorry for him. Felt bad that he'd been dealt such a shitty card in life. But her empathy toward him had always been overshadowed by her jealousy. By her longing for a relationship with her parents that only he had.

He hoarded them, hearts and all, and deep down she hated him for it.

She'd watched her mom care for Kevin for years. Comfort him. Meet his every need. Perhaps, she was being too hard on her mom. Maybe if she knew about Amelia she'd rise to the challenge. Be here for Whitney.

Either way, Whitney didn't have it in her to stick to the script today. She was weary. Scared. If ever she needed a mother, it was now.

Clearing her throat, Whitney instinctively raised her chin. "I'm actually not that great, Mom."

"Why? What's going on?"

"Um…I don't really know. Amelia went to a friend's last night and hasn't come back yet."

"I see." By her tone, Whitney knew what she was thinking. *Like mother, like daughter.*

Whitney regretted opening her mouth. "But I'm sure she's fine. Probably on her way home now," she backtracked. Clearly, Amelia wasn't with her mom, so it wasn't like she could help. "Maybe it's just a case of getting our wires crossed. A miscommunication." She was rambling now. God, why did she always allow her mom to have this effect on her.

When she was younger, her mom would constantly criticize.

Be nicer to your brother.

Play with your brother.

Include your brother.

But when she'd give in, do what her mom wanted, her mom would nag at her.

Be careful with your brother.

Don't be so rough with your brother.

Look what you did. You got your brother too excited.

There was no winning.

Whitney had often fantasized about being older. Wiser. More mature. And she'd longed for that time when she could stand her ground. Say her piece. Be herself. But now here she was, in her midforties and she was still kowtowing to her mom.

"Yes, that's probably it. Amelia's such a sweet girl," her mom agreed. "I talked with her last week and she sounded like she was doing great. Just made a new friend, and she was really excited about visiting her dad in Amsterdam."

"She told you she was going to visit her dad?"

"Yeah. Said she was just working on the paperwork for her passport."

"There's no way she could move forward with the passport. I never signed anything."

"I think Dan was helping her with it," her mom said. "He's such a good dad."

"Yeah." Whitney was used to comments like this. Her mom always liked to remind her of the mistake she'd made letting Dan get away.

"Oh, Whitney," her mom said. "Dad's here. He wants to say hi a minute."

"Hi, Whitney." Her dad's voice came on the line, a soothing balm. As a child, she loved when he sang to her or read her bedtime stories. There was nothing quite like her dad's voice. It was smooth and rich, like one of those voice-over actors. "How is everything going?"

"It's okay."

"Why just okay?" His concerned tone caused her bottom lip to tremble.

"I don't know. Just stuff isn't great with Amelia. She's been acting out a little. Being rebellious."

"Well, you know how teenagers are. She'll grow up and figure it out," he said. "You did."

Tears rushed to her eyes. It may not have seemed like a huge compliment but coming from her dad it was high praise. A man of few words, each one was weighty.

"Thanks, Dad." All Whitney had ever wanted was for her dad to see her. Notice her. Like he did on those occasional nights when he would sing her to sleep. It only happened when Kevin stayed overnight at the hospital, her mother no doubt by his side. But when the hospital stays became more frequent, they would take turns staying with her brother, or both would go and they'd hire a babysitter for Whitney. Pretty soon, the singing and tucking in vanished altogether.

"Daddy, look!"

"Not right now. Daddy's busy."

You're always busy, Whitney thought bitterly, wishing for the man with the happy eyes and large smile. Ever since Kevin was born, his eyes were drawn, droopy, and his lips were always frowning.

"Look, Daddy, look. I can do a handstand." She placed her palms on the ground and threw her legs up over her body. Her hair fell over her face, smelling of apples and damp air.

Kevin started coughing.

"Hang on a second," her dad said.

More coughing. Wheezing.

Her dad hollered for her mom, who immediately came rushing out, her gaze trained on Kevin, never once even glancing at Whitney. Lowering her legs, Whitney sat in the grass, the reeds itching the back of her bare legs. Pretty soon, they'd all be back inside, leaving Whitney out here in the backyard alone. She just wanted one afternoon with her dad. Was that so much to ask?

If only she were the sick one.

Then she'd have their undivided attention.

Their backs were to her as they guided Kevin inside. It was like she was invisible.

Like they'd already forgotten her.

Her mom and Kevin were already through the doorway. Her dad wasn't far behind. Anger burned through her. She couldn't let them leave her alone. Again.

Without thinking it through, she flung herself on the ground, hitting her head hard on the nearest rock. Pain shot through her skull.

"Daddy!" she hollered. "Help. I fell down!"

She didn't have to fake the tears. The minute she felt blood trickling from her scalp, her insides trembled and so did her lower lip. Hot tears streamed her face.

"Oh, my God. Whitney." Her dad rushed to her, scooping her up into his arms. He smelled like leather and cigars, and she inhaled the comfort of it.

Pressing her face into his chest, she savored the feel of his arms around her.

After hanging up with her parents, she turned toward the family room. Natalie was hunched over, and she could only see the top of her head from behind the couch. Probably on her phone.

Without saying anything to her, Whitney dialed Dan.

His voice was groggy and garbled when he answered.

"Did I wake you?" she asked, glancing at the clock on the wall and attempting to do quick math.

"It is the middle of the night."

"Right. Sorry. I'm surprised you answered," she muttered.

"I assumed it was important."

"It is," she assured him. "I just found out that you've been helping Amelia get her passport."

A heavy breath. "So she could come visit me this summer, yes."

"But you said earlier that she doesn't have a passport."

"The last time we talked she didn't have it yet," he said. "I just signed the paperwork for her."

"Doesn't she need both of us to sign?"

"Not now that she's sixteen."

"I can't believe you went behind my back and did this."

"Whitney, it's the middle of the night. Can we not do this right now?"

"She's not back yet, Dan."

"Oh." There was rustling. A creaking sound like mattress springs shifting. "I guess I assumed you knew about the passport from her."

"No. My mom, oddly enough."

Another "Oh."

"She took several hundred dollars out of her bank account last week. You're sure she's not coming to you?"

"I think she'd need more than a few hundred dollars to get here," he said.

"I'm getting worried, Dan," Whitney confessed. "I've found out all this weird stuff about her today."

"Like what?"

"Like that she's been talking to some older guy online and seeing a different guy behind my back."

"I know she had mentioned wanting to date someone."

"She did? What else did she say to you about it?"

"Just that you told her she couldn't."

"I was trying to protect her."

"Hey, I get it. I don't want her dating until she's thirty."

Under different circumstances, Whitney would have laughed. Finally, something they could agree on.

"How long has it been since you heard from her?" Dan asked.

"Twenty-four hours."

"Do you think it's time to call the police?"

"I already did," she said, more defensively than she meant to. "They're on their way."

"Okay. Well, that's good," he said. "Keep me posted."

"I will," Whitney replied.

14

FOUR WEEKS
BEFORE DROP-OFF

IT WAS A Tuesday night. Business as usual. Whitney sat on the couch scrolling through Netflix, while Amelia holed up in her room, earbuds in her ears. After several minutes of not finding anything she felt like watching, Whitney left Netflix and clicked into Xfinity to see what shows she had saved.

The first one that came up was *The Bachelor*, her and Amelia's guilty pleasure.

Last season they had Bachelor Night every Monday, where they ate snacks and made predictions about who would win. A couple of times Becca joined them; once Natalie did. But for the most part, it was something they did just the two of them.

Whitney glanced over her shoulder toward the hallway. Amelia was probably sitting cross-legged on her bed, hunched over her phone, earbuds in her ears. She'd told Whitney earlier not to bother her. That she had "hella homework." But Whitney knew better. That was just Amelia's way of getting out of chores or spending time with her lately.

It was hard for Whitney to reconcile. It hadn't been that long ago that Amelia enjoyed spending time with her. But every time Whitney complained to Natalie about it, or anyone else who had had teenagers for that matter, they laughed, saying this was totally normal. According to them, a teenager not wanting to spend time with their mom was normal.

Normal or not, Whitney still longed for what they used to have.

Sighing, she clicked on the season premiere and sat back against the couch cushions. She'd gotten about five minutes in when she heard Amelia's bedroom door pop open. Footsteps made their way down the hallway.

"Are you watching *The Bachelor*?" Amelia asked, more surprised than accusatory.

"Yeah," Whitney said, keeping her eyes on the screen. "Wanna join me?" She didn't turn around because she knew Amelia would see the desire written on her face. For some reason that was something that repelled her daughter lately.

Amelia hesitated a moment. But then the new bachelor entered the scene and Whitney knew she wouldn't be able to resist. Plunking down on the couch next to Whitney, Amelia said, "So I've seen some spoilers online already about this season, but don't worry I won't say anything. Seriously, though, I think this is gonna be the best season yet."

Whitney smiled. "Want me to grab us some snacks?"

Amelia started to shake her head, but then stopped. "Maybe just some Skinny Pop and an apple."

"You sure?" Whitney raised a brow. "I think I have some gummy bears in the pantry."

"I probably shouldn't." She screwed up her face.

"Oh, come on. You look amazing. You don't need to diet."

Her mouth lowered. "You have to say that. You're my mom."

"It's the truth." Whitney stood up. "Anyway, I'll bring 'em out just in case." In the kitchen, she rounded up a bunch of snacks, then carried them into the family room and dumped them on the coffee table.

Amelia snatched up the bag of Skinny Pop and scooped out a handful. Unpausing the show, the mansion came into view, a car pulling up.

"Oh, her dress is really pretty," Amelia said through a mouthful.

"Really pretty," Whitney agreed. It looked faintly like Amelia's homecoming dress from last fall, glittery and purple.

"I don't think she's gonna last, though. Look at his expression."

Whitney laughed. "Yeah, he doesn't seem too into her."

"That was awkward."

Whitney nodded in agreement as the girl made her way into the mansion. They watched for a few more minutes in silence. When the commercials returned, Amelia picked up the remote to fast-forward.

"Did you finish all your homework?" Whitney asked as the people on screen moved at lightning speed.

Amelia didn't answer. Her head was down, her thumbs moving over the screen of her phone, the remote already abandoned, lying on top of her thigh.

Whitney scooted closer, tried to peek over her shoulder.

Amelia noticed, turned her phone away. Looking up, she noticed the show had returned and hit Play, tucking her phone facedown under her leg.

"Who was that?" Whitney asked.

"No one," Amelia said with a hint of impatience while staring at the TV.

Whitney decided to try a different angle. "Is it the same person you were talking to on the phone last night?" Whitney had heard hushed voices from their adjoining wall as she was trying to fall asleep. Getting out of bed, she hurried to Amelia's room and peeked in. Amelia gave Whitney a sharp shake of the head and shooed her with her one free hand. The other held the cell phone to her ear. It felt like a slap in the face.

When Whitney was younger, most of her nights were spent on the phone in long conversations with her best friend. But now she couldn't remember the last time she'd actually seen Amelia talking on the phone, not texting. She had no idea who Amelia had been talking to. Ever since it happened, Whitney had been waiting for the right moment to bring it up.

She hated that this was what their relationship had become. Searching for right moments. Walking on eggshells. Skirting around issues. Hoping not to aggravate the teenage monster.

It was getting old.

Hand shooting out to grab the remote, Whitney paused the TV.

"It wasn't no one," she said. "Who were you talking to?"

Annoyed, Amelia crossed her arms over her chest. "A friend, okay? God." After drawing out the word *god* and ending it with a hard *d*, she groaned. "Can we please just watch the show now?"

"Not until you tell me."

Amelia's eyes darkened, her lips melting into a hard line. "Why does it even matter to you? It's my phone. I can talk to whoever I want."

This wasn't okay. It wasn't how Amelia talked to her. She'd always told Whitney everything. Over the years other moms would comment about how jealous they were of the close relationship between them.

What had happened?

Whatever it was, Whitney wouldn't allow it to continue.

She reached for Amelia's phone, her fingertips latching on to the edge that peeked out from under Amelia's leg.

"It's not your phone. It's mine. I pay for it," she said, her tone firm.

"Stop. What are you doing?" Amelia pushed her leg down harder, cementing the phone in place.

Whitney yanked harder, and the phone came loose. She folded her hand around it.

"No." Amelia lunged for it. "Give it back."

"You're grounded from it." Whitney held it tight to her body, shielding it with her arms.

"Just 'cause I wouldn't tell you who I was talking to? Why is it your business, anyway?"

"I'm your mom, Amelia. Everything about you is my business."

"God, you are so annoying." Grunting, she stood up and stormed down the hallway. "I wish you'd just get your own friends and leave me the hell alone." Her bedroom door slammed loudly, the entire apartment rattling.

Usually, Whitney would leave Amelia alone. Give her a few minutes to cool off before going in. But tonight, she was too angry to wait. Leaving the cell phone on the couch, she popped up and raced after her daughter. Adrenaline pumping, she flung open Amelia's door with more force than she meant to.

"How dare you talk to me like that," she snapped. "You may think you're becoming an adult, but you don't own this place, Amelia."

"Oh, trust me. I know," she said, bitterness in her tone. "You've always been the one in control."

Whitney paused. "What's going on with you? Why are you talking to me like this?"

"I'm just so tired of you running my life, Mom. You won't let me have anything that's just mine."

"You can have whatever you want that's just yours if you pay for it," Whitney snorted. "Do you have a job?"

The minute the words left her mouth, she knew they were the wrong ones.

Amelia's eyes narrowed to mere slits on her face. "No, because you won't let me get one."

It was the truth, but only because Whitney wanted her to

focus on school. She was a child. She didn't need to work. Still, they'd had a huge fight over the weekend about Amelia wanting to apply to work at some clothing store in the mall. Whitney couldn't remember the name of it. One of those places that smelled like way too much cologne, where everything was overpriced. Whitney thought she was doing Amelia a favor by not letting her work there. Once Amelia was an adult, she'd have to work the rest of her life. Why did she need to start so early?

"You won't let me do anything that doesn't include you," Amelia continued.

"That's not true."

"Name one thing." Amelia cocked an eyebrow.

"You go to school." Amelia's brow rose further, and Whitney realized that was a stupid one, so she moved on. "You hang out with friends."

"Only here," she said, "where you always are."

Whitney hated the way she emphasized the word "always." Whitney worked from home to be near Amelia. It wasn't a curse. It was a blessing. Amelia would see that one day. She'd appreciate all the sacrifices Whitney made for her. To give her a good life.

To keep her safe.

Instead of saying all of this, she added, "You have swim team."

"Seriously?" Amelia scowled, placing a hand on her hip. "I joined swim team because of you."

Whitney frowned. "You love swim team."

"No," she said emphatically. "I love swimming. Same as you love running. You're the one who wanted me to compete. You're the one who signed me up for the team when I was little, and then every year after that without even consulting me." Amelia placed a hand on her hip. "I overheard you talking to Natalie about it once. Said it kept me out of trouble."

Whitney opened her mouth to defend herself, but couldn't come up with anything. She felt blindsided. This was the first she was hearing of any of this. She'd always thought Amelia loved being on swim team.

"Just admit it," Amelia said. "You don't want me to have anything in my life that doesn't include you," Amelia said, her voice rising. "It's why you won't let me date."

Whitney sucked in a breath. A cold chill worked its way up her back. "So, that's what this is about. Dating?"

"No," Amelia said quickly. "It's about you controlling my whole entire life, and I'm sick of it."

Whitney thought about the late-night phone call. "Have you been talking to a boy?"

"Oh, my God, you have a one-track mind," Amelia said, clearly deflecting.

"Answer the question," Whitney demanded.

Staring hard at the ground, Amelia kept her lips pressed together.

"I can go through your phone, you know," she declared, unsure if that was true.

Amelia's head popped up, and she opened her mouth as if she planned to respond, but then she closed it.

After a few seconds, she finally said, "Fine. Yeah. I've been talking to a boy."

"One you know in real life, right? Not someone you met online, because you know there are people out there called catfishes and they—"

"Oh, my God, Mom. Yes, I know all about that. I'm not stupid. He's someone I know in real life," she said. "He's really nice...and um..." She bit her lower lip. "He wants to take me out."

"Like on a date?"

Nodding, Amelia's cheeks turned pink.

"I don't know."

"What if we had him over for dinner? He's totally cool with meeting you," Amelia's words got faster, more desperate.

It made Whitney uncomfortable. "I don't think so. Let's table this for now."

Amelia's face fell. "But I'm sixteen now. Wasn't that the rule?"

Whitney sighed. Yeah, that was the rule. God, why hadn't she made it seventeen? "Just give me time, okay? I need to think on it."

Amelia shook her head, her eyes shining. "I can't even believe you."

"I'm sorry, honey. It's just that you barely turned sixteen. Maybe just give me a minute to get used to it?" Whitney lifted her arm, reaching out to touch Amelia's shoulder. "Let's go finish *The Bachelor*."

Amelia drew back. "Nah, I'm good."

"Come on." Whitney waggled her eyebrows. "You know you wanna watch it."

But Amelia didn't soften at all. Her face remained stoic, resolute.

"I'm only trying to protect you, Amelia," she said in a gentle voice. "That's my job as your mom, and it's not always easy. But you've gotta trust me. I know the world better than you do."

"Oh, here we go." Amelia rolled her eyes.

"What?"

"Just because you were a bad kid who got involved with the wrong guy doesn't mean I'm going to do the same thing," she said. "I'm a good kid, Mom. I'm not like you. Why can't you see that?"

"I know you are. I do see that." Whitney blew out a breath. "But good kids get taken advantage of all the time."

"He's not going to take advantage of me."

"You don't know that," Whitney said.

"I do—"

"Amelia," she cut her off, wearying of this back-and-forth. All she wanted was to go back to their fun evening with snacks and *The Bachelor*. This boy was already causing damage. Getting between her and Amelia. "I don't want to talk about it any more tonight. I said I would think about it, and we can discuss it later, okay?" She headed toward the doorway, lingering for a beat. "You sure you don't want to join me for more *Bachelor*?"

"And watch other girls get to go on dates? Yeah, I'm sure I don't," she said in a clipped tone, the finality of it unmistakable.

The second Whitney got into the hallway, Amelia slammed the door behind her, missing her back by mere inches. When Whitney returned to the couch, Amelia's cell phone stared up at her. After a few attempts to get into it, she set it down on the coffee table with frustration.

After watching the rest of the show, Whitney headed to bed, exhausted from her long day. By the time she got up the next morning, the phone was gone. She figured Amelia had retrieved it. Whitney decided not to fight her on it.

She figured they'd already done enough of that.

15

SATURDAY, 6 P.M.
TWENTY-FIVE HOURS
AFTER DROP-OFF

"WHAT TIME AGAIN did you say you dropped her off?" Officer McAvoy asked, staring at Whitney with his disproportionately large wide-set eyes. He sort of resembled an insect with his balding head, pointy ears and round middle, but she instinctively liked him. Maybe it was his scent—a mixture of coffee and cigars—which reminded Whitney of how her grandpa had always smelled.

The second officer, Sandavol, walked around the family room, carefully studying everything. Sandavol was attractive with tanned skin, black hair, and a thick fringe of eyelashes framing her normal-sized eyes. She wasn't as friendly as McAvoy, but Whitney could tell she was the type of woman to get the job done. From the minute she walked in she'd exuded confidence.

"Around five," Whitney answered.

"And you don't remember the exact location or the last name of the friend she was with?"

Whitney frowned. Officer Sandavol picked up a framed picture of Amelia that sat on Whitney's desk and inspected it.

"No…" she replied distractedly, then blinked. "Sorry, I mean, yes."

"So now you do remember?"

"No, I just meant…I mean, no, I don't know Lauren's last name…but I do know where I dropped Amelia off." Whitney sighed. "Or at least I thought I did…" She looked to Natalie for help.

"Amelia's sixteen years old," Natalie said. "She's been really asserting her independence lately. Whitney's a great mom, but you can't expect her to know every detail of her daughter's life at all times. Trust me, I didn't know all of my daughter's friends when she was Amelia's age, and I rarely knew where she was at." She laughed, but the officers didn't, so she stopped and threw Whitney an apologetic look.

Whitney knew Natalie was trying to help, but her words only made her feel worse. She should've known Lauren's last name and she should have paid more attention to where she dropped Amelia off. Whitney wasn't like Natalie. She knew every detail of Amelia's life. She'd been trying to back off, give her space, but that had been a mistake.

"Does Amelia drive?" McAvoy asked.

"Not yet," Whitney answered. Amelia had wanted to get her license the minute she turned sixteen. It was Whitney's fault it had been delayed, a fact Amelia never let her forget. Whitney had waited too long to get her signed up for behind-the-wheel training, and the classes were full for months after Whitney called.

"Is this a recent picture of Amelia?" Officer Sandavol held up Amelia's sophomore class photo.

Whitney nodded.

"Can we use it?"

Again, she nodded, keeping her lips pressed together, fearful that if she spoke, she'd cry. Having the police here in her home made everything feel so real. All day Whitney had been expecting Amelia to walk in the door any minute. Natalie rested a hand on Whitney's arm. Whitney breathed out through her nose, her bottom lip quivering.

"You said that she'd been asserting her independence lately." Officer McAvoy turned to Natalie. "What did you mean by that?"

"She's been kind of pushing Whitney away a little, trying to make her own decisions. You know, like all sixteen-year-olds."

Officer McAvoy nodded, turning his attention to Whitney. "Is it possible that Amelia ran away?"

A few months ago, she would've offered an emphatic no. But now she wasn't sure. It had been her own first guess, after all. "I honestly don't know. She's been different lately."

"Different how?" Sandavol jumped in.

"For starters, she stopped hanging out with the friend group she's had for years."

"Would you mind making me a list of those friends?" Sandavol thrust a pad of paper in Whitney's direction.

"Sure." Her hand shook so badly it was difficult to write legibly. The words kept coming out like slashes, as if she was ripping the paper, rather than writing on it.

"Thanks," Sandavol said when Whitney handed it back to her. The officer scanned it, then lifted her head.

"What about Amelia's dad? Is he in the picture?" One of Sandavol's eyebrows cocked.

"Yeah. He used to see her a couple of weekends a month. But a year ago, he went to live in Amsterdam for a work project. He and his new wife. They're expecting, actually." She clamped her mouth shut, wondering why she was rambling. Calming herself, she continued, "I talked to him a couple hours ago. She's not there."

"And he hasn't heard from her?"

"Not in the last few days. I thought maybe she would go to him, but I don't think she has her passport, yet." She paused, drew in a breath. "She did pull a chunk of money out of her bank account recently, though."

"We'll need you to provide Dan's information, as well."

Whitney nodded.

"Does Amelia have a job?" McAvoy asked.

"No, but she babysits from time to time."

"What about hobbies?" His eyebrows raised slightly.

"She dabbles in a lot of things. Drawing. Fashion. She loves music. Movies. She sometimes helps Natalie with the designs for the business. But her biggest hobby has always been swimming," Whitney said. "She's competed on swim team since she was seven."

For years, Amelia's skin perpetually smelled like chlorine, her hair crunchy with a greenish tint and her nose was freckled from too many sunburns. Most Saturday mornings were spent at the pool, Whitney in the stands with the other parents and Amelia with her team, playing cards and eating snacks while waiting for her heats to be called. Sometimes Whitney hated it, waking up at the crack of dawn and then sitting in the retched hot sun all day. In Sacramento, most summer days were well over a hundred degrees. And she'd be out in it all day, waiting for the few heats Amelia would swim in.

"Rec league or at school?" McAvoy asked.

"Both," Whitney said. "But I guess not this year. I thought she was signed up, but her dad informed me today that she dropped the school team."

A look passed between McAvoy and Sandavol that made Whitney's stomach twist.

"Why?" McAvoy asked.

Whitney shrugged. Looked at Natalie. "She told her dad it was because she's overwhelmed with schoolwork. I don't know if that's true."

"Do you think it's possible that she's depressed?"

The question threw her. She knew what depression looked

like, and she'd never once considered that Amelia was. "I don't think so."

"Any other recreational activities? Choir? Drama?"

"No." Whitney shook her head.

"What about a boyfriend?"

"I don't know if I'd call Jay my boyfriend," Whitney answered, twisting her hands in front of her. "Especially after what I learned today."

Sandavol's expression didn't change. "I was actually asking if Amelia had a boyfriend but tell me about Jay." *Right.*

The back of Whitney's neck itched, and she reached back to scratch it. "He's just a guy I met at a bar...err...a restaurant... and we started dating. He seemed really great, but today I found out he lied to me about where he lived."

"Any idea why he did that?" McAvoy asked.

Whitney shook her head. "I can't even get a hold of him now." With shaky fingers, she took her phone out of her pocket and pulled up the picture of Amelia and the strange boy. Holding it up, she told them about her conversation with Becca. About the older man Amelia had been talking to online, and the boy she'd been seeing behind Whitney's back.

When she finished, Sandavol handed Whitney back the pad of paper. "If you could add Jay's and Michael's details to the list that would be helpful."

As she wrote their names, her stomach soured.

"And if you know of any other boys she'd been talking to, you can add their names."

Whitney added the name Phil Lopez to the list, then handed it back to Sandavol.

"What about drug use?" McAvoy asked.

"No, I don't think Amelia does drugs," she said. "Then again, I didn't know she drank either."

"Okay." McAvoy scribbled something down. "Amelia's phone is still off, but we'll continue to ping it every forty-five minutes." Whitney's body swayed back and forth, like a balloon in the grip of a toddler. Any minute the child would let go and she'd leave earth completely. "Can you access her social media accounts for us, please?"

Nodding, Whitney made her way to the computer. She heard a noise outside, and her head turned. She wondered again about what Sandavol was up to. Time was blurred at the edges. Gray and hazy, slow-moving.

Numb, Whitney wiggled the mouse back and forth until her computer came to life. "I don't know any of Amelia's passwords, but I can go into her Facebook and IG account from mine."

"Does Amelia have her own computer?" McAvoy asked.

"Yeah. A laptop. But it's not here. She must've taken it with her to Lauren's."

"Do you mind if we take a look around her room?" McAvoy asked.

Whitney nodded. Then wordlessly guided them down the hallway. Amelia's room looked exactly like she'd left it. Not quite dirty, not quite clean. As McAvoy and Sandavol brushed past her, crowding the small space, Whitney leaned against the doorframe. There was a patch of worn carpet in the center of the room. She pictured Amelia dancing there, arms high above her head, hips swaying, head upturned, a smile on her lips.

On her nightstand sat a picture of the three of them—she, Dan and Amelia—back when Amelia was a toddler. Whitney moved toward it and picked it up. She'd given it to Amelia right after she and Dan split. It had always been one of Amelia's favorite pictures of them, and she thought it would give her comfort. It must have because she'd kept it displayed ever since. Whitney took in Amelia's big smile, mouth open around a giggle. Dan had his arm around Amelia as she nestled in his lap. Whitney leaned into Dan, her cheek resting on his shoulder. Behind them was a stark white backdrop, bringing out the brightness of their matching blue sweaters. Blue. Dan's favorite color.

A fact he had shared with her in one of their first conversations.

"Sorry," he said, appearing flustered as he ran a hand over his hair. "I just can't stop staring at your eyes. They remind me of the blue-blue water."

Up until that moment, he'd always seemed so scholarly. Articulate. And I'd never known him to stutter. "The what?"

He smiled. "When I was a kid, my parents took me to Universal Studios and we watched this one show that took place on a stage in front of all this water. And the water was this bright blue, almost turquoise color. Unlike any natural color I'd seen before. So the only way I could think of to describe it was by calling it blue-blue water."

Now I was the one feeling flustered. My cheeks heated up. I looked at the ground. "You know our eyes are the same color." I could hear my mom's voice in my head: Just take the compliment. Say thank you.

But it was too late. I'd already screwed up.

"Nah." He shook his head. "Sure, mine are blue. But yours are blue-blue."

I giggled, bobbed my head up to look at him. Blue-blue. I like it.

Amelia's had been blue as well, when she was an infant. But when she was about nine months old they started to change, morphing into a deep, chocolate brown. Whitney thought they were beautiful.

Dan thought they were suspicious.

"How did she end up with brown eyes when we both have blue? Isn't that an impossibility?"

"Pretty sure that's a myth, Dan."

Quiet a moment, he scratched his chin. "He has brown eyes, right?"

"Who?"

"You know who," he said, pursing his lips like he'd eaten something sour.

Whitney blew out a breath. "Yeah, so? He has nothing to do with Amelia."

"I saw you leaving his place that morning, right before you got pregnant. I know what happened."

"I told you it wasn't like that. When are you gonna let this go?"

"You okay?" Natalie sidled up to her, yanking her thoughts back to the present. With a shaky hand, she set the picture back down and smiled at her friend. When Whitney first met Natalie, she never imagined they'd become this close. Natalie was a client that eventually turned into her boss, and Whitney didn't expect their relationship to become anything more. As a single parent, Whitney didn't have a lot of time for friends. Mostly, she'd had acquaintances. But as she worked closely with Natalie a friendship evolved. Natalie had so many qualities Whitney liked—her fierce protectiveness and loyalty being right there at the top. Whitney knew she was the kind of person she wanted in her corner.

"I just can't believe this is happening," Whitney said, raking her fingers through her hair.

"We'll find her," Natalie said firmly.

Sandavol stood over Amelia's desk while McAvoy studied a picture on Amelia's dresser. He picked it up, nodded toward Whitney. "This you?"

Whitney was already bobbing her head before making it over to him, her mouth already forming the letter *Y.* She knew the photo well. It was one of her favorites of her and Amelia. But when she reached McAvoy, her stomach dropped, her mouth suspended around the word *yes* that was now wedged in her throat, unable to launch.

It wasn't the photo she'd been expecting. The one Amelia had had on her dresser for years.

McAvoy must have registered her shock, because he said, "Everything okay?"

She felt Sandavol straighten up behind her. Calming herself, Whitney forced a smile. "Um, yes, that's me." And she wasn't lying. It was her in the photo. But the person with her wasn't Amelia.

How had Amelia even gotten this photo? And why would she ever put it in her room?

"Who is the person with you?" McAvoy asked.

"Um…just an old friend." She swallowed hard. "A…a family friend." That part was a lie, but there was no way she could explain any of this. She didn't even understand it herself.

Rattled, she backed out of the room. Natalie trailed her.

"Want me to make some tea? Maybe that'll help," she offered.

Whitney nodded.

Natalie glided into Whitney's kitchen, opening drawers and pulling things out as if it were her place. They'd spent a lot of time at each other's respective homes. She figured she'd know her way just as easily around Natalie's kitchen. As Natalie filled the teakettle with water, Whitney's phone buzzed in her pocket.

She yanked the phone out so hard the edge of her jean pocket painted a white stripe on her finger, stinging. She rubbed it swiftly.

"It's Dan," she told Natalie. The officers' voices traveled from down the hallway as she answered.

"Did you call the police yet?" Dan asked, his voice tired, still groggy like earlier. Clearly, he wasn't able to get any sleep since they'd talked.

"Yeah, they're here now."

"Good. Do they have any ideas on what might've happened?"

"I get the feeling they think she ran away," Whitney said.

It was silent a moment. "Remember when she was like four and she got mad at us and packed a bag and said she was running away?"

"Yeah, and then she snuck out and we found her sitting on the neighbor's front lawn, playing with a baby doll?" Whitney laughed, finishing the story. After a few seconds the laughter died on her lips. "If only it were that simple this time, huh?"

"Hey, I don't know if it helps at all, but the last time Amelia and I talked she was asking a lot of questions about when we met."

"But she already knows the story of how we met."

"She didn't want to know *how* we met," Dan explained now. "She wanted to know more about your life back then. Like stuff about your ex-boyfriend and former friends."

"Why?" Nervously, she paced back and forth in the living room. The teakettle whistled from the kitchen. Cups clinked together.

"I don't know. At the time I just assumed she was trying to figure out why you were being so strict. You had just told her she wasn't allowed to date."

That would've made sense if Whitney hadn't just seen that photo from her past displayed in Amelia's room. Clearly, Amelia had been doing a lot of digging into Whitney's earlier years.

But why?

"What did you say?" Whitney asked.

"I just told her what I knew about your ex and how he treated you, you know?" His tone was tender. He was skating around it, the way he always did with this subject.

"She knows about him. I've told her already. I wonder why she felt the need to ask you."

"Maybe trying to get a different perspective," Dan added thoughtfully. "Probably has nothing to do with anything, but she was also asking questions about her birth and stuff."

Whitney froze. "What do you mean, questions about her birth?"

"I guess you'd never told her the story, about my layover and all the drama with that," he said. "It was a crazy time."

"Yeah, it really was." Whitney knew she hadn't shared much about that time with Amelia. Dan worked long hours, missing so much of Amelia's early days. And she'd gone through horrible post-partum depression. Honestly, she tried hard to push that whole time period to the back of her mind.

Whitney stumbled out of bed, body tight, eyes bleary. The light was dim, but not dark, sunlight streaming in through the closed blinds. Disoriented, she looked at the alarm clock. It was 3 p.m. She'd put Amelia down for a nap around noon. Was she still asleep? Wow, that's a long nap.

Too long, actually.

She was probably hungry.

Yawning, she ran a hand down her face, and ambled over to the bassinet.

Amelia wasn't in there.

The bassinet was empty.

Amelia's blanket in a pile near the bottom.

Exhaling, she rubbed her eyes. She'd been doing this lately. Hallucinating. But when she opened them, there was still no baby.

Gathering herself, she left her bedroom and headed into Amelia's room. She hadn't remembered putting her down in her crib, but she must have. Usually, she liked having her close, but Dan had been encouraging Whitney to acclimate Amelia to her crib. So sometimes she put her down in there.

Amelia's room was bright. Decorated in bold pink and sunny yellows. The kind of room she would've loved as a child. The blinds were pulled all the way up, and the window was open. Sunlight spilled into the room. A breeze blew in, bringing with it the scent of grass, damp earth, honeysuckles. The air was cool, and goose bumps rose on Whitney's flesh. She hoped Amelia was covered up.

Why hadn't she closed the window when she put her down?

She passed the large pink flowers hanging on the wall to reach Amelia's crib. Her heart sank.

Empty.

Oh, my God. It was happening again.

She couldn't lose another baby.

Her gaze shot to the open window, then back to the empty crib. A figure appeared in the doorway.

"Where is she?" she cried out, putting her head in her hands. "My baby. She's gone."

Footsteps neared her. "Whitney."

Her head popped up. "Dan," she breathed out.

His hands wrapped around her shoulders, his gaze blazing into her. "You've gotta stop this. Our baby is fine."

"She is."

"Yeah, I'll show you." Placing his hand on her back he ushered her forward. Out of the room, down the hallway. "I really think you should talk to someone, Whit."

"No way. I'm not talking to your dad. He already thinks I'm crazy."

"He does not," he said. "But I wasn't talking about him anyway. We'll find you a different therapist."

"No, I'm fine," she said. "I don't need one."

They rounded the corner, into the family room. There was a blanket on the floor. Her baby was lying on top on her stomach, facing the opposite wall. Her tiny hands were fisted, her feet suspended in the air.

"See? She's fine." Dan beamed.

Exhaling with relief, Whitney rushed forward and fell to her knees in front of her daughter. When the baby lifted her tiny head, Whitney's breath caught in her throat, and tears filled her eyes.

"This isn't her," she whispered. "This isn't my baby."

Out of the corner of her eye, she saw the officers emerging from Amelia's room. "Can I call you back, Dan?"

"Of course," he said.

Tucking her phone into the pocket of her jeans, she faced the officers. McAvoy approached, handing her a business card. "Here is my number. Call me right away if Amelia comes home or contacts you, okay?"

"You think she will?"

"In many runaway cases, the child eventually gets in touch."

"You think she ran away?"

"It fits when you look at the big picture. She took a chunk of money out of her account, she took off with a new friend, she's been seeing and talking to boys behind your back." When he rattled off the facts, counting them on his fingers, it sounded rational. The logical explanation.

"But what about all the other stuff? The boy she's been seeing—Michael. Or the fact that she's been talking to an older man online? Oh…oh, and I forgot to mention that all of her pictures of her and Lauren disappeared from her Instagram. I mean, that's weird, right?" Oh, God, what else had she forgotten to tell them? What if something bad had happened to Amelia and the cops dismissed it, too busy assuming she ran away?

"We'll look into all of those things," McAvoy promised her. "We'll also check the local hospitals, shelters, airports."

Whitney's skin flamed. She hadn't even thought to check those places.

"And like we said earlier," Sandavol interjected, "we'll ping her phone every forty-five minutes, so we'll know immediately when she turns it on."

"We'll be in touch every hour," McAvoy explained. "And you be sure to call us if you hear anything."

Whitney nodded like a robot. Once the officers were gone, she joined Natalie in the kitchen, where she was handed a piping hot cup of tea that she would probably never drink. Amelia and Natalie liked tea. Whitney preferred coffee but knew that would be a bad idea right now. So she held on to the mug, allowing it to warm her cold, shaky hands.

16

"WHEN WAS THE last time you ate?" Natalie came up behind Whitney, who flinched, not having heard her approach. She'd been staring out the window, willing Amelia to walk up to the front door. Since the cops left, she'd checked Amelia's location at least a dozen times. Still nothing.

In many runaway cases, the child eventually gets in touch.

God, she wanted to believe Amelia had simply run away, some stupid rebellious adventure that would be over as soon as she got bored or missed home. But that nagging feeling was back in the pit of her stomach. That sensation that something wasn't right.

"I don't know," she answered distractedly, glancing toward the kitchen. "I think breakfast, maybe…"

"That's not good." Natalie clucked her tongue. "I'll make you something."

"No, really. I'm not hungry." Shoulders slumping, Whitney walked with dragging feet to the couch and spilled into it, like a glass of dirty water toppling over. "I'm just tired."

"Probably because you haven't eaten anything. You need to keep your strength up. You're not doing Amelia any favors by wasting away."

There was no arguing with her when she got like this, so Whitney didn't even try. Her eyes burned, her entire body aching. Was this what shock felt like? Or had she surpassed that and was now moving on to grief?

No, grief would be giving in.

And Whitney wasn't doing that.

Cabinet doors opened and closed, Natalie's feet shuffling on the floor. Whitney heard the suction of the refrigerator seal being broken, followed by the sound of contents hitting the counter. She was lulled by the comfort of it, her eyelids fluttering closed, her body relaxing. As she drifted into the place where her bones turned to jelly and her mind went blank, an insistent buzzing aroused her attention. *Just ignore it*, her body protested and there was a relief in listening to it. Then she remembered Amelia and painstakingly forced her eyelids to open.

But it was only Dan, checking in. She gave him an update, and then Natalie set a plate with a sandwich in her lap.

"Thanks, Nat." Picking up the plate, she stood. "I'm gonna take this into Amelia's room, look around." Ever since she'd seen that picture, she'd been curious about what else Amelia had in there that she'd never noticed before.

Things the cops wouldn't have known to look for. Spots filled Whitney's vision as she walked down the hallway. A headache pricked behind her eyes. She really did need to eat. Stepping into Amelia's room, she reached for one half of the sandwich. It tasted like sandpaper and she struggled to chew and swallow. She was sure that under any other circumstance she'd enjoy it. But at this moment, nothing would taste good. After forcing down a few more bites, she set the plate down on Amelia's dresser. Then Whitney picked up the photograph from earlier, studying it. It still didn't make any sense. Where did Amelia even find it?

The picture did nothing but remind her of a past she'd tried for years to forget. Shuddering, she put it facedown on the dresser. Choking down another bite of her sandwich, she leaned her back against the dresser, her gaze scouring the room.

When it landed on the bed, comforter messy on top, a memory popped into her mind.

"Mom, can I ask you a hypothical question?" an eleven-year-old Amelia asked, eyes wide and bright.

"Do you mean a hypothetical question?" Whitney laughed.

"Yeah." She nodded. "Anyway, can I ask one?"

"Sure."

"What if hypothically—"

"Hypothetically," Whitney interjected.

"Hypothetically," she parroted, "I had a boyfriend."

"What? At eleven?"

"It's just hypothetical."

Whitney smiled. Amelia had gotten it right that time. "Right. Sure it is," Whitney said with sarcasm. Did Amelia think she was born yesterday?

"It is," Amelia insisted, and her tone bordered on whiny.

"Okay, well, then hypothetically, I'd have to forbid you from seeing this boy because you're not old enough to date. The rule is sixteen, remember?"

She nodded, her face serious.

"Amelia? Do you have a boyfriend?"

"No. It was hypothetical."

"But what made you think of it?"

"Oh, just 'cause a friend of mine at school has a secret admirer and it made me curious what would happen if I did."

It actually sounded plausible. Too bad she was biting the inside of her cheek so hard she was probably drawing blood.

Later that night, when Whitney went in her room to say good-night, she caught Amelia stuffing a piece of paper under her mattress. Whitney pretended not to notice, and Amelia must have thought she'd been sly

enough to get away with it. While she was at school the next day, Whit-
ney found several notes tucked under her mattress from a secret admirer.

After swallowing down her latest bite, Whitney pushed off
the dresser and headed toward Amelia's bed. She swept her hand
under the mattress, working her way from one side to the other,
scooting on her knees, carpet scraping against her skin.

On the right side, almost to the pillow, Whitney's fingertip
grazed a sharp, pointy edge. She pushed her hand in farther, her
palm sliding over what felt like the slick cover of a notebook.
Folding her hand around it, she yanked it out.

It was a small notebook with a black, crinkled cover. Whitney flipped through the pages quickly, a perfunctory glance.
Many of them were filled with blue ink, Amelia's cursive. From
the kitchen, Whitney heard cabinet doors opening and closing,
dishes clanging. Natalie was clearly keeping herself busy.

Hoisting herself up off the floor, Whitney sat on top of Amelia's bed, and opened the notebook. Poetry covered the pages.
Beautifully written, she noted. But dark and sad. As Whitney
skimmed through them, she started to wonder if Amelia actually was depressed.

When she reached one called "The Boy in 204," Whitney sat
up taller. Her eyes shot to words like *bruise, blood* and *ache.* Was
Amelia being hurt? Abused? Or was this symbolism? The other
poems all had macabre lines, as well. Things Whitney knew had
never happened. It seemed all of her poetry was morbid and dark.

But then Whitney thought about her talk with Dan. How
Amelia had been asking about Whitney's past relationships. Was
it because Amelia thought that history was repeating itself? That
she was following in her mom's footsteps? Whitney had spent
Amelia's entire life trying to stop that exact thing from happening. It was why she'd been so overprotective. So strict.

Clutching the notebook to her chest, she raced out to the
family room. Natalie was pouring another cup of tea. Steam
rose from it, circling her face.

"I think I know which apartment that boy lives in. The one from the picture." She held up the notebook. "This thing is filled with poems and one of them is called 'THE BOY IN 204.'"

"And you think it's about him?"

"Yeah, I mean, it sounds like it's about someone she's seeing or at least likes. But it also sounds like maybe he hurts her?"

"What?" Natalie wiped her hand on a towel and came around the kitchen island to where Whitney stood. "Let me see." Whitney set the notebook in her hands. Natalie stared down at the page for a few minutes and then looked up. "It's poetry, so you can't really take it literally. I mean, it's clearly a relationship of some kind, and it's probably complicated."

Her friend's words propelled her toward the front door. A pair of Amelia's flip-flops were discarded by the wall. Any other day it would've irritated her.

Does this look like a decorative item to you? she would've asked her, holding one up.

Today the flip-flop had the power to undo her. Swallowing down the unwanted emotions, Whitney shoved her feet into the flip-flops and reached for the doorknob.

"Where are you going?" Natalie was beside her in a matter of seconds.

"Apartment 204."

"Don't you think you should call McAvoy and tell him about it? Let him decide if it's something to pursue?"

Whitney waved away her suggestion with a flick of her wrist. "Who knows where they are? This'll be faster. I'm just gonna pop downstairs and see if he's the guy. No big deal." Before Natalie could stop her, she flung open the front door and burst outside. Cold air smacked her in the face. It had been so warm and stuffy inside that she hadn't realized how much the temperatures had dropped out here. Hugging herself, she clambered down the stairs, Natalie at her heels.

She made it to the bottom and turned right, heading toward

the park area—the place Becca had said they'd met up with the boys and partied together. They hadn't lived here when Amelia was small enough to enjoy the green space. She'd always thought it was a stretch to call it a park—it was one picnic table, a slide and a tiny play structure—but she could see how teenagers and young adults might use it as a party spot. It wasn't nearly as nice as the one at the apartment complex she'd thought was Jay's. She still didn't know what the deal was with him, but she couldn't imagine him being the older guy Becca had referenced. It may have crossed her mind for a minute, but it couldn't be him. Whitney couldn't be that bad a judge of character, could she? He'd seemed so nice. So genuine. To be honest, it was the couple at that apartment that seemed shady. Rude. Not anyone she would ever trust. They could be lying, for all she knew.

Then why isn't he answering your phone calls or texts? She ignored the question that sailed through her mind.

Focused on finding the boy from the picture and the poem. This was a more concrete lead.

She scanned the numbers on the doors across the way: 198, 200, 202. Aha. 204.

"There it is!" She shot forward, and within seconds was pounding on the door.

"What are you gonna say if he answers?" Natalie asked, catching up to her.

Whitney shrugged. "I'm gonna ask him if he knows where Amelia is." She smiled, a thought occurring. "What if she's here?"

"Okay." Natalie frowned. "Don't get your hopes up. It might not even be him."

Natalie was always practical. Logical. Usually, right. But this time, Whitney hoped she was wrong.

She knocked a few more times. Waited. Cool night air whipped around her. Cars buzzed in the distance. The apartment was quiet. No movement inside.

"Nobody's here." Whitney felt herself withering, crumpling like a deflated balloon. Like she might sink to the ground and never get back up.

"I'm sorry, Whit," Natalie said. "Let's go back upstairs and you can call the police and let them know what you found. Maybe they'll have better luck tracking this boy down."

Whitney peered up at the black night sky splattered with twinkly stars that reminded her of those little LED lights Amelia sometimes liked to string over her bed frame. "I just really wish she would've come home by now."

"I know, honey." Natalie's hand rested on her arm. "I know." Her pocket rang. Throwing Whitney an apologetic look she pulled out her cell and answered. "Hey, Bruce." She turned away from Whitney, phone pressed to her ear. Whitney stared at the door to apartment 204.

I'm not like you, Mom.

Whitney was starting to think Amelia was more like her than she thought.

"Sorry about that." Natalie joined her. "It was just Bruce checking in."

"It's okay," Whitney said. "You know that if you need to leave, you can."

Natalie shook her head. "No way. I'm not leaving you. Bruce is just gonna swing by and drop off some of my stuff."

"Really, you don't have to stay," Whitney said, but her words were weak and unconvincing even to her own ears. She couldn't imagine being alone all night. It was getting darker. Later. The dreamlike quality the day had had was clearing out like fog when the sun broke through. Stark reality stared her in the face, grotesque and scary. Her hope that Amelia would come home any minute, her tail between her legs and an apology on her lips, had completely vanished.

"Let's go back upstairs." Natalie's hand landed on her back.

Whitney glanced one last time at apartment 204, a chill running through her.

"Come on," Natalie pressed. "You can call McAvoy, or what was the other detective's name?"

"Sandavol," Whitney said as they bounded up the stairs.

"Right. Sandavol. Well, you can call one of them and tell them about the poem."

Whitney nodded as they entered the apartment. It was startling how much it smelled like Amelia. It was natural to grow accustomed to scents. They became like white noise, something she didn't even think about. But today, they jumped out at her. Grabbed her by the throat and squeezed. Amelia's peppermint lotion. Her vanilla shampoo. The floral hand soap Whitney had put in her bathroom. They all came at her in a rush, weighty and strong, a forceful wave. She had to choke back the emotions they carried with them, like algae sticking to her skin long after the wave receded. As Whitney walked farther inside, she struggled to catch her breath.

"Okay, you sit down and call the police. I'll just make myself useful." Natalie went directly to straightening things, picking up.

"My mom is like you," Whitney mused, watching her friend. "She's like this strong, take-charge kind of person. I've never been like that. Maybe that's part of the problem."

Natalie paused, eyeing her. "Part of what problem?"

"Why this happened." She was speaking but it almost felt like the words were coming from someone else. Somewhere outside of her body. "Like if I'd been a stronger mom, a wiser mom, Amelia would still be here."

"Whitney, stop," Natalie said firmly. "You're a good mom and this isn't your fault."

"But—"

"No." Natalie shook her head. "Thinking like this is futile, and you know it."

"Now you really sound like my mom." Whitney smiled, and

in that moment, she wondered if that was what had drawn her to Natalie in the first place. She was the version of her mom Whitney had longed for. A take-charge, no-nonsense woman who was also there for her. She was the best of both worlds.

She acquiesced. "Okay, fine. I'll sit." Sinking down into the couch, she got out her cell phone, deciding to try Amelia before calling McAvoy. Still not answering, and still nothing on Find My Friends.

We'll ping her phone every forty-five minutes.

Whitney reminded herself that if it got turned back on, the police would be notified. Silently, she prayed that it would be soon.

There was a text from Dan asking for an update.

Nothing new, Whitney typed.

Picking up the card McAvoy gave her, she dialed his number and pressed the phone to her ear.

When he answered she told him about the poem, about her suspicions that this might be Michael.

He thanked her and then hung up, his voice giving nothing away. Frustrated, she lowered her phone to the couch cushion near her thigh. This was exactly why she'd gone down to apartment 204 in the first place. As much as she wanted the police to be right, she worried that they might not be. And if they were wrong, what then? If they were fixated on the fact that Amelia ran away were they even taking this very seriously?

Leaning her head back against the cushions, she stared up at the ceiling, at the crack that ran along the edge of it. The one the apartment manager had said would be fixed months ago. And this was actually the nicest apartment she and Amelia had lived in together.

When she and Dan were married, they had a nice home. Spacious. Clean. Great neighborhood. No cracks in the ceiling. After they'd split up, Whitney's biggest fear had been that she wouldn't be able to care for Amelia as a single mom. That she wouldn't be able to juggle everything on her own. But, surprisingly, she had been able to.

At least, she thought she had.

Now she was realizing that even with how strict she was, how overbearing, there was still so much she didn't know. So much Amelia had been able to get away with. Whitney couldn't be home with her every second. She had a demanding job. A social life.

She thought of a crime drama she'd watched a few months back where a girl had been sold into sex trafficking by some guy she'd been talking to. Not even a creepy older guy online. But a guy she thought was her age whom she'd met through a friend. Apparently, he was a decoy.

As she watched the show, Whitney had thought about how lucky she was to have a daughter who was smart enough not to get involved in something like that. But was she? According to Becca, she'd been talking to two guys behind Whitney's back— one of them an older man she'd met online. Not to mention the Snapchat Whitney had seen from Phil Lopez. That would make it three guys. Unless he was the older one?

Sitting up straight, Whitney reached for her phone. Behind her she heard Natalie shuffle down the hallway, close the bathroom door.

Thinking about Becca's response to who Phil Lopez was, she googled the name. Yep. Becca was right. Phil Lopez was the name of the lead singer of the Hard Knocks. Whitney clicked on their website and then wrinkled her nose. Amelia had never been a fan of rock bands, so Whitney doubted that she listened to them.

And Phil Lopez was probably a common name.

Natalie came back into the room, stood behind the couch, peering over Whitney's shoulder. "Whatcha looking at?"

"About a month ago, Amelia got a Snapchat from a boy named Phil Lopez." Whitney pointed at the screen. "This guy is also

Phil Lopez, but clearly, not the same guy that was messaging my daughter."

Natalie leaned over the couch. "You know that Snapchat handles aren't usually a kid's real name. Maybe it's just the person's favorite band or something."

Whitney scrolled through the band pictures, the lead singer shirtless and often holding a beer in one hand and a cigarette in the other. Her stomach twisted as she tried to picture the kind of boy who would make this singer his Snapchat handle.

An image appeared in her mind, and she realized she'd once known that boy.

17

SIX WEEKS
BEFORE DROP-OFF

WHITNEY HAD WANTED to throw a party for Amelia's sixteenth birthday. She'd been imagining it for months, pinning fun ideas to her Pinterest account—mason jars filled with colorful candy, pink fizzy punch drinks in champagne flutes with bows on the stems, a fancy charcuterie board, an array of healthy salads. Whitney had even secured use of the pool at their apartment for the Saturday after Amelia's birthday, thinking it would be the perfect spot to celebrate.

When she brought it up to Amelia, she assumed she'd be elated. Instead, she immediately shot down the idea.

"Mom, I'm not turning six. I don't want a pool party."

Whitney was surprised, and honestly, a little embarrassed. She hadn't considered that maybe a pool party would be childish. "Well, I mean, you don't have to swim. I thought we could make it fancy." She proceeded to share her Pinterest ideas with Amelia, who wrinkled her nose in response.

"Candy and punch by the pool? You're right, Mom. That doesn't sound childish at all."

Well, when you put it that way.

"Okay," Whitney said, seeing the error of her ways. "We don't have to have it by the pool. We can maybe do it at the warehouse. I'm sure Natalie won't mind. I can move our inventory to the side, decorate it real cool. It's an awesome space."

Amelia shook her head. "I don't want to have it at your work."

"I guess we could rent out space at a restaurant," Whitney spoke slowly, in her mind already calculating the cost.

"Or we could just have dinner at a restaurant."

"You mean, no party?"

"Yeah." Amelia nodded. "I'm just not really feeling a party this year."

A few weeks before Amelia turned eight, Whitney received a call from a parent of a girl in Amelia's class, saying she was RSVPing for Amelia's birthday party. Since Whitney hadn't planned a birthday party for Amelia, she was confused.

Apparently, Amelia had made and passed out her own invitations. All without Whitney being privy to it.

As more RSVPs flooded in, Whitney realized she had no choice but to throw the party, even if she would have to scramble to have it ready in time.

Amelia's birthday was something she generally looked forward to all year, and in Whitney's experience, she had always been "feeling" a party. What had changed?

"Is this because of what happened with you and Becca?" she asked her daughter.

Amelia groaned. "No. God, can't I just do what I want on my own birthday?"

"Of course," Whitney answered swiftly, not wanting this to turn into an argument. "Where would you like to go?"

"Mikuni's?"

Whitney should have guessed. It had been Amelia's favorite

the past couple of years. "Sure. That sounds like fun." And, actually, it did. A night out having sushi with her daughter seemed like a lot more fun than facilitating a party with all of Amelia's friends. "Want to do it on your actual birthday or that weekend?" The wheels were turning now. If they did it on the weekend, Whitney was thinking they could make a day of it. Maybe get mani-pedis and do some shopping before dinner.

"Um...let me check with Lauren."

Whitney was taken aback. "Why would you need to do that?"

"To see what night works best for her," Amelia stated like it was obvious. Whitney's face must've registered her confusion, because Amelia said, "I can invite her, right?"

"Of course." She pushed her lips up into a painful smile. It was silly for her to feel let down, anyway. She'd always assumed she'd have to share Amelia on her birthday. It was only disappointing after believing they might get a night out, just the two of them.

And that's how Whitney found herself sitting in a booth at Mikuni's alone on the night of Amelia's birthday. Lauren and Amelia were in the bathroom. Again. They'd gone in there together no less than five times. At one point, Whitney went in there to check on them and caught them taking mirror selfies. She felt like a third wheel on someone else's date.

Using her chopsticks, she picked up a piece of her crab roll, dipped it in her wasabi and soy sauce mixture, and popped it in her mouth, the spicy flavors bursting when she bit down. The first time she ate sushi was with Dan in college. Her family rarely went out to dinner, and when they did they had their rotation of places, which consisted mostly of diners, steakhouses and the occasional Mexican restaurant. Dan took her to a little Japanese place near the campus. When the waiter brought their rolls, Whitney had stared down at them, uncertain if she was supposed to pick them up with her fingers.

"You don't know how to use chopsticks, do you?" Dan had asked, watching her.

She'd shaken her head. "Maybe I should just ask for a fork."

Dan had laughed. "No, don't do that. I'll show you." Moving from his side of the booth, he'd slid into hers, so close she caught the faint whiffs of hair gel and soap. He patiently placed her fingers on the sticks and showed her how to move them. She didn't quite master it that night, but eventually she'd gotten the hang of it. She'd shown Amelia at a young age. That way she wouldn't find herself on a date one day, unable to use them.

The girls returned, giggling, cheeks flushed. The scent of floral hand soap swept through the booth. Amelia typed something on her phone while Lauren picked up her set of chopsticks. Swallowing down her last bite, Whitney reached into her purse and closed her fingers around Amelia's gift. The night may not have gone exactly like Whitney had hoped, but she figured this gift would get things back on track. It had been months in the making and excitement pulsed through her, thinking about how Amelia was going to react.

"Oh, my God," Amelia burst out, startling Whitney. Looking up from her phone, her eyes were bright, her mouth stretched into the largest smile Whitney had seen in a while. "Dad's buying me a car!"

"What?" Whitney released the card and it fell back into her purse.

"Yeah. He said that once I pass my driving test, he'll buy me a car." She spoke so fast her words were all jumbled together. "And not even a used one, but a new one from a lot and everything."

"How?" Whitney asked.

Amelia shrugged. "I don't know. I'm sure he can fill out the paperwork online or whatever." She turned to her friend. "Can you believe it? A brand-new car!"

Whitney thought about the card in her purse. The envelope of money hidden in her underwear drawer. She'd been saving all the money from her side gigs for the past year, hoping to have enough to buy Amelia a car for her birthday. She'd saved several thousand dollars. Not enough for a new car, obviously. She'd written it all down in the card, which she clearly couldn't give Amelia now.

Smiling, she worked hard to drum up a happy energy. Amelia was happy. Really happy. And she deserved to be. So, Whitney would be happy too.

"Well, I don't have your gift tonight," Whitney said. "I thought I'd take you on a little shopping spree this Saturday, maybe get mani-pedis."

"Ooh, I can't this Saturday. I have that away meet, remember?"

"Oh, right."

"But maybe Sunday?"

"Sounds good." Whitney shoved the card farther down into her purse, while the girls went back to talking to each other, as if they were the only ones in the booth.

As if Whitney wasn't even there.

18

WHEN MILLIE SMOKED POT, she acted nothing like those kids in the video I watched in health class. In fact, when she was stoned she was more fun.

Millie was prone to bouts of sadness. It scared me sometimes how dark she could go. How cold and reserved she could become. She'd practically fold in on herself, like a turtle hiding in its shell. When she got like that, there was no room for anyone else. But when she was drunk or stoned, she turned into this giggly, fun person. Mellow, yes. But it was a happy, contented mellow. I much preferred it to the sad, introspective side of Millie.

That was why the next time Millie offered me a joint, I took her up on it. It was only a couple of weeks after the first time she'd offered. I was over at Millie's, and her mom was out. Working, I think. Or maybe on a date. I'm not really sure.

I inhaled correctly this time, having learned from my failed cigarette attempt. By the time I exhaled, I could already feel a warm, fuzzy feeling take over. It was way better than drinking.

My body softened, my limbs melting like an ice cream cone on a hot day. I felt light and airy, my head fuzzy, but not spinning. We passed the joint between the two of us until it was gone.

When we finished, Millie put on some music. Giggling for no apparent reason at all, we danced around her room. I felt like we were moving in slow motion as we swayed back and forth. Millie's smile was radiant, her fingers soft as they brushed against mine. When she threw her hands up in the air and twirled around, the sparkly rings on her fingers created a strobe effect bouncing light around the walls. It made me smile broader, laugh harder. Which in turn made Millie do the same.

The thing I had been so scared of ended up not being scary at all.

Every time we hung out after that, it revolved around drinking and getting stoned. Millie would sneak cups of her mom's tequila or vodka into her bedroom after we knew her mom had fallen asleep or gone out for the night. Then we'd sit cross-legged on the ground, plug our noses and down it. Even with my nose plugged, I frequently gagged. But, hey, at least I got it down. Then we'd turn on Millie's ceiling fan and smoke a joint, holding it out of her bedroom window.

Afterward, we'd lie in her bed eating snacks and talking for hours. I shared more with her during those nights than I'd ever shared with anyone. It was like my mellow extended to my mouth, my lips as loose as my joints. Those nights I revealed my deepest scars. Let her in on my private pain. Confessed my dreams for the future.

At the time I thought it was reciprocated.

But, now, when I look back at those nights, I remember how guarded Millie was. Careful. Don't get me wrong. She did share a lot with me. But not everything. There were always things she kept hidden. Locked away.

I'm sure there are still lots of things I don't know about her.

At times it makes me sad. Thinking of all the things she was too afraid to share.

As the weeks bled together, I did feel like Millie and I were getting closer. In fact, I kind of felt like I was turning into her. Being stoned or drunk gave me a confidence I never had before. I didn't feel embarrassed to dance with her out in public. I talked to people I didn't know. And even flirted with guys occasionally. It was like I'd found the magic potion I'd been searching for.

But as with any magic potion, it came at a price.

19

THE SKY OUTSIDE the window betrayed how late it was. The phone in Whitney's lap remained silent. "God, I wish I could go back in time and say no to her spending the night at Lauren's. I wish I'd kept her here last night, then she'd be home with me right now."

Smiling, Natalie said, "My mom used to say, 'If ifs and buts were cherries and nuts, we'd all have a Merry Christmas.'"

"What?" Whitney laughed, and then felt guilty. How could she laugh with Amelia missing?

Natalie gently touched Whitney's arm. "You can't go back in time, and it's pointless to think about what you wish you would've done. The only thing you can do now is move forward."

At Natalie's words, a memory formed.

Training wheels off. Helmet strapped on.

Amelia's little light-up shoes resting on the bike pedals. Whitney's hand gripping the seat.

"*Okay, start pedaling,*" Whitney instructed. *Amelia obeyed, and*

Whitney ran behind her, holding tightly to the pink banana seat. Amelia white-knuckled the white handlebars, the pink, yellow and white plastic fringe flapping in the breeze.

Once they got a good rhythm going, Whitney said, "Amelia, I'm going to let go, all right?"

"No, Mommy, I can't do it."

It was a Saturday and they were in the parking lot of American River College. Not a car in sight. "You can," Whitney insisted. "Just keep pedaling."

As Whitney released her grip, Amelia slowed down.

"Nope. Keep pedaling. You can do it. You just gotta keep pedaling." Amelia pumped her legs.

"There you go, sweet girl. You're moving forward." Whitney clapped, so proud of Amelia as she pedaled through the parking lot, broad smile across her face.

A knock on the door startled them both.

Natalie smiled. "It's probably Bruce."

Whitney hooked her arm around the back of the couch and scooted upward, staring expectantly at the door as Natalie answered it.

She tried to rein in her disappointment when Bruce stood in the doorway. He held a duffel bag in one hand and a pillow in the other. He wore a T-shirt with two handprints on it that read Best Dad Hands Down, sweatpants, flip-flops and a baseball hat that fit a little too snuggly on his head. To Whitney, Bruce embodied the word *dad*. He had the "dad look" and he never ran out of "dad jokes." It was almost impossible for her to picture him being anything other than a dad, even though Natalie assured Whitney that he'd been quite the catch when they'd met.

Natalie gave him a quick peck on the cheek. He stood awkwardly, his gaze sliding toward Whitney.

She understood. It was hard to know how to behave during your own crisis, let alone in someone else's. At funerals, Whitney never knew what to do. She'd stand there awkwardly as if her arms were too large for her body, mumbling apologies and empty platitudes.

"Come on in, Bruce." Standing, Whitney waved him over, hoping to ease some of his discomfort.

He stepped inside, dropping the duffel bag on the ground and handing Natalie the pillow. Then he took a few steps forward and pulled Whitney into one of his big bear hugs. "You hangin' in there, kiddo?"

His fatherly concern broke her. Tears stung her eyes and her throat burned. Blinking and breathing hard, she pulled back and wiped her hand down her face.

"I…um…I just need…" Whitney pointed down the hall. "A…a few minutes."

"Okay, hon, we'll be right here," Natalie said sweetly.

Making her way down the hallway, she could feel their eyes on her, skating over her back, boring a hole in her head. She crumbled like a Jenga tower after pulling on the wrong block. The sobs in her ears were as loud as the crash the blocks made when they hit the table. She wasn't used to all of this concern. Accusations she was used to. Distrust. Suspicion. Reprimands. Those were things she could handle. This was too much.

Smothering her mouth with her hand, she muffled the sobs against her palm. When she reached her room, she closed the door firmly behind her.

"Mommy, don't be sad." Her big eyes stared up at Whitney unblinking. "Here. Do you need a Band-Aid? Will that make it better?" Reaching up, Amelia thrust a Band-Aid into Whitney's palm. It was one of her Disney princess ones. Cinderella.

Whitney brushed a tear off her cheek and sniffed. "A Band-Aid won't fix it this time, my sweet girl."

"It's about Daddy, huh?"

Biting her lip, she nodded.

"We're not gonna live with him anymore, are we?"

Bending down, Whitney tucked a strand of hair behind Amelia's ear. "No, we're not. I'm sorry, my love."

It had been the two of them for years now. Amelia was Whitney's whole world. She had to find her.

The longer Amelia was gone, the more she felt herself unravel. Stepping farther into the room, she breathed in deeply through her nose and out her mouth the way she did trying to catch her breath after a run. It was supposed to calm her nerves, lower her heart rate. It wasn't having that effect right now.

Above Whitney's bed was a large canvas photo of her and Amelia taken several years earlier, smiling faces pressed together. They wore matching white sweaters, causing the greenery behind them to stand out. Whitney remembered following the photographer out into the middle of a giant field near the river to find the perfect backdrop. The sky was a brilliant blue that day, the temperature in the seventies. As the photographer snapped the pictures to the soundtrack of rushing water, Whitney had marveled at how blessed she was by her simple life and her tiny family. After the photoshoot, she and Amelia had gone out to dinner, then to grab ice cream. When they got home, they squished on the couch and watched some rom-com on Netflix.

Back then, the idea of Amelia running away would've seemed preposterous.

How had everything changed so drastically?

Whitney turned away from the picture. Her blinds were open, revealing a glowing crescent moon against the black sky. That's what she needed. Fresh air. A run. That would help her calm down. Clear her head.

Quickly, she changed into her running clothes and headed back to the family room. When Natalie spotted her, her eyes widened.

"Where're you going?"

"Just a quick jog around the block." Whitney brushed past

them, nearing the front door. She could practically feel the wind on her face, the pavement beneath her soles.

"Right now?" Natalie glanced toward the window, her forehead a mess of squiggly lines.

"I think it will help me relax, think more clearly." Whitney threw Bruce a smile as she reached for the doorknob. "Stay as long as you want, Bruce." Then to Natalie, she said, "I'll be right back."

"You better be." Natalie smiled, but her eyes betrayed her concern as Whitney turned the knob, and stepped into the hall.

It was Dr. Carter who first encouraged Whitney to run. He thought she needed an outlet. Something positive. He'd gone as far as to give her an entire lesson on endorphins and the effect of exercise on the brain. At the time Whitney had thought it sounded stupid. The only reason she'd tried it out was because she wanted to lose a little weight.

Dan had convinced her that she wasn't fat. And she knew he was right. Curvy. Big-boned. That's how her mom had often described her. Either way, she wasn't thin, and she wanted to be.

So, she tried it out.

Turns out, Dr. Carter was right. Running did help. Mentally and physically. It made her feel alive. Strong. When she ran, she focused on her breathing, her legs, her arms. Everything else fell away. Became secondary.

The more she ran, the more addicted she became.

Tonight was no exception. As she ran on the sidewalk, next to cars whipping past, she breathed deeply in and out through her nose. She moved her legs quickly, her feet pounding on the pavement, and she pumped her arms in time, her hands slicing through the cool air.

She rounded the corner, shedding her thoughts like a snake shed its skin. The scent of damp air, chlorine and tennis balls floated on the sharp breeze, heightening her senses.

Up ahead, looming in front of her was the gate to the community pool. She slowed her pace. Changed course. Reaching the gate, she wrapped her fingers around it, pressed her face up to the bars. A prisoner, peering out.

The bright lights shone down on the empty pool, illuminated the parking lot and the tennis courts to her left. Amelia was never a fan of tennis. Probably because playing meant she had to get out of the water, something she never wanted to do.

As Whitney stared out at the pool, she imagined Amelia's head bobbing up and down in the makeshift waves, her arms coming up in large round swoops as she carried herself to the other side. Then she saw her lying on a lounge chair, squirting white sunblock on her legs while talking a mile a minute, her hair crunchy from drying in the sun.

One of her favorite memories was when she taught Amelia to swim. At the time, Dan's parents lived near them and they had a pool. Amelia spent a lot of time at their house, and always wanted to be near the water. So, the summer she turned four, Whitney made it her mission to teach Amelia. In the afternoons, she'd head over to her in-laws', traipse in through the back door and she and Amelia would spend hours playing around in the water. The first couple of times, Amelia whined, begging for her "wa-wings." That's why the third time, Whitney was smart enough to leave the water wings at home.

"No wa-wings," she remembered saying over and over. "They're not here."

Amelia was upset that she had to be held in the water. That she couldn't go off on her own, the way she could with the floaties. But once she got past her initial frustration, she started to get the hang of it.

One afternoon, Whitney was tugging Amelia around the pool, but Amelia kept trying to unhook her fingers from her mom's.

"Mommy, let go," she begged. "I can't move my arms. Let go so I can swim."

They'd been at it for a while. She'd shown her the strokes. And Amelia wasn't wrong. She couldn't do any of the strokes with Whitney holding her arms. As scared as she was, Whitney released her grip on Amelia. She didn't move, though. She stayed right by her side, just in case.

But Amelia didn't need her. Sure, she floundered a bit. Got water up her nose. Swam in a zigzag. But she made it to the other side without any help at all.

And as Whitney watched her in amazement, her daughter's words rang out in her head:

Let go so I can swim.

SATURDAY, 11:00 P.M.

When she returned from her run, Natalie was on the couch watching TV. Whitney glanced around, wiped her damp forehead with the back of her hand.

"Bruce left?"

"Yeah, he wanted to get home. Rest. Drink a beer. You know. Guy stuff." She chuckled. "How was your run?"

"Really good." Winded, she headed into the kitchen to grab a water. Chugged it down swiftly. Then she set the empty bottle on the counter. "I'm gonna go take a quick shower and change. I'll be right back."

Afterward, emerging from the steamy bathroom, she cinched on her robe and went to her room. Heading straight to her dresser, she opened the top middle drawer, searching for her favorite pair of pajama pants. White-and-black-checkered, fuzzy material, elastic waistband. The mere thought of them gave her comfort. Her skin was still damp from the shower, and goose bumps rose on her flesh. Finding her jammie bottoms, she happily tugged them out with vigor, causing several other jammies and underwear to spill out as well, along with the envelope of money she'd been saving.

Bending down, she picked up the envelope—and found it was lighter than it should've been. Originally, there had been several thousand dollars in it, mostly in hundred dollar bills, and she'd only spent a couple of hundred on Amelia's birthday shopping spree. When she peeked inside, her stomach plummeted. Empty.

Swallowing hard, she got down on her hands and knees, dug through the clothes that fell. No money. Standing up, she foraged through the drawer. It wasn't there either.

The money she'd been saving for months was gone.

Who would've taken it? No one, not even Amelia, knew she had it.

Actually, that wasn't true. There was one person.

The late afternoon sun sprayed in through Whitney's bedroom window. Even though she was warm, her skin damp with sweat, she drew the blanket up to her chin. If a guy was going to have to see her naked body, Whitney preferred it to be in the dark. But, as a single mom, she had to take the opportunity when it was presented.

Jay rolled over, peeked at his phone. The covers on his side were bunched near his feet. He clearly didn't have the same body image issues she did. She knew, really, it didn't make much sense. He'd seen everything of hers a few minutes ago.

The front door popped open, followed by the sound of keys rattling, a backpack being tossed on the ground with a thump. Whitney's eyes widened.

"The door." She pointed.

She hadn't been expecting Amelia home from swim practice. She thought she had another half hour at least.

Jay sprang into action, racing across the room and shutting the bedroom door. Whitney hurriedly pushed her arms through the straps of her bra and tugged her shirt on.

"Mom? You home?" Amelia's voice got closer.

"Yep," Whitney hollered. "Um…be out in just a sec." Searching through the bed, she couldn't find her underwear. "Had a meeting earlier?" she shouted. "So I'm just changing real quick."

Amelia didn't answer. Probably didn't even care. Whitney heard footsteps in the kitchen, the suction of the refrigerator. When Amelia got home from swim practice, she was always ravenous. Had been since she was little.

"Jay," she whispered, since he was near her dresser. "Grab me a pair of underwear please. Top drawer. Middle."

"Sure thing." He opened the door, pulled out a lacy pair.

Of course he'd pick those ones, she thought.

Before closing the drawer, his gaze lingered in it for a moment. Then he turned, tossing her the panties. "You know, there are such things as banks, right?"

"Huh?" Standing, she pulled on the underwear, then stepped into her pants.

Face reddening, he shook his head. "Sorry, I shouldn't have said anything. It's not my business."

That's when she realized he must've seen her money envelope. She waved away his apology. "Oh, no, it's not a big deal," she whispered, walking closer to him as he wriggled into his own pants. "That's just money from my side gigs. I'm saving it to buy Amelia a car." She kissed him lightly on the mouth. "Now stay here and keep quiet. I'll sneak you out when she goes back to her room."

Then Whitney smoothed down her hair, licked her lips and stepped out into the hallway, closing the door tightly behind her.

Had Jay taken her money? She thought about the apartment that wasn't his. Did he not have his own place? Was he worse off than Whitney thought? Maybe that's what the girl meant by him being an asshole. Maybe he was mooching off them or something.

Oh, God. She pressed her hand to her forehead. *Why was I so trusting? So gullible?*

Taking off her robe, she stepped into her pajama pants, pulled them up to her waist. With her mind on edge, they didn't quite give her the comfort she'd been hoping for. After changing into one of her soft Ts, she made her way to the bed, crouched down onto it. Clicking on Jay's name, she pressed the phone to her ear. Bouncing her knees up and down to a beat only she could hear, she waited for him to answer. When it went to voice mail, frustration burned through her, a wildfire obliterating everything in sight.

Was that Jay's plan all along? To steal from her?

Thinking hard, Whitney bit her lip. No, that didn't make sense. It wasn't that much money. Besides, if all he was after was money, why date Whitney? She wasn't rich by any means.

And she supposed Amelia could've found the money. It wasn't like she'd hidden it that well.

But why had Jay lied about where he lived?

God, she couldn't understand any of this.

From day one, she'd thought Jay seemed too good to be true. Now it seemed, she was right.

20

FOUR DAYS
BEFORE DROP-OFF

"CAN I SPEND the night at Lauren's Friday?"

"Sure," Whitney responded, already fantasizing about what she'd do with a free night.

"Sweet. I'll tell Lauren." Amelia smiled, her thumbs flying over the screen on her phone. After a few seconds, she looked up. "Is it cool if I just go home with Lauren after school?"

Whitney wanted to say yes. To fight against her helicopter-mom tendencies for once. To keep that smile on Amelia's face. She rarely saw it anymore. But she couldn't bring herself to do it. Whitney knew she'd been gone a lot lately. Work had been demanding as Natalie's business continued to grow. And, also, she'd been spending a lot of time with Jay. But that was all the more reason for Whitney to be more attentive to Amelia when she was around. Not to mention the fact that she was curious about Lauren's mom.

"I'd actually rather drop you off."

Amelia groaned. "Mom, I'm not five."

"You're also not twenty-five," Whitney said.

"Is this seriously how you're gonna be even when I get my license?"

Whitney shrugged. "Maybe."

Amelia rolled her eyes. "God, I can't wait until I'm eighteen and can be on my own!" Spinning around, she stormed down the hallway, a hurricane of teenage hormones and emotion.

Whitney flinched when the bedroom door slammed. The downstairs neighbors were probably tired of hearing that sound. Whitney was definitely over it.

Amelia had always been independent.

When she was a little girl, Whitney would reach out when they were about to cross the street, close her fingers around Amelia's. But Amelia would pry them off and step away, running across the street by herself. Dan thought it was funny. Called her Little Miss Independent. Said it showed confidence. Whitney thought it showed defiance. Irresponsibility. It terrified her. She would have nightmares of Amelia getting run over by cars—visions of her little body unmoving on the pavement filling her dreams. Whenever they went somewhere, Whitney spent the entire time on edge, nervous and sweaty. Finally, Whitney gave in and bought one of those harnesses. Dan was so angry. Said there was no way she was leashing their daughter as if she was a dog. Whitney argued that it was better than having her dead on the street. They never did come to an agreement. It was one of many fights they got into about how to parent Amelia.

When Whitney's phone buzzed, she snatched it up to see Jay's name on the screen. She smiled.

"Hey." She pressed the phone to her ear.

"Hey," he parroted. "Whatcha doing?"

Whitney's heart flipped at the flirty lilt to his voice. She glanced down at the sink of dirty dishes she was about to tackle and frowned. That wasn't sexy. "Um..." Whitney racked her brain for a flirty response but came up blank. Finally, she answered with the truth. "Actually, I was just about to do some dishes."

"Hmm. I love when you talk dirty to me."

She laughed, grateful that he never made her feel stupid for her boring life. "I've got a lot more where that came from." Sinking into a nearby kitchen chair, she spoke in a sultry voice. "After the dishes, I plan to do some laundry, maybe pick up the family room and then I've got some work to do for Natalie."

"You work too hard," Jay responded.

"The life of a single mom. What are you gonna do?" She laughed.

"You could have your daughter help you. Surely, she knows how to do dishes, right?"

Whitney bristled at the statement. Why did men always feel the need to give their opinion without being asked? Judge how she did things? It was a huge part of the reason she hadn't wanted to date when Amelia was younger. Whitney finally had control over how she ran her household. No way was she giving it up. It was hard enough with Amelia's actual dad. Imagine how much worse it would be with a man who had no tie to her at all.

A defensive response lingered on her tongue, but she bit it back. Jay wasn't Dan. He wasn't trying to be rude. And it's not like he was the only one who had said this to her. Natalie was on her all the time about how lax she was with Amelia about chores. They weren't wrong. Whitney did work too hard. Exhaustion had become a way of life for her.

Sighing, she said, "Nah, she's already mad enough at me right now. I'd rather do the chores than fight with her again."

"I'm sorry." Whitney's heart melted at his concerned tone. "What were you fighting about?"

"She's spending the night at her friend Lauren's on Friday and I insisted on taking her instead of just letting her go over after school." Whitney paused, wondering if she sounded too overbearing. "She's never gone over there before," she added.

"So, you're all alone on Friday night, huh?"

Whitney's belly quivered at the memory of his gentle touch. "Yeah, I guess I am." She loved how he'd taken a dark situation and shone some light. "You wanna come over?"

"Of course I do." She smiled at his quick response. "Oh, but shoot. I can't." Whitney's heart sank. "I forgot I'm going out of town on a business trip. Rain check?"

"Yeah," she answered, trying to mask her disappointment. The only red flag she'd detected about him so far was his demanding job and traveling schedule. She'd already been married to a man like that, and it was rough.

After hanging up, she headed toward the sink. Thinking over what Jay said, she contemplated asking Amelia to do them. It would be nice to have some help around here. To be able to sit down and take a load off.

Amelia still hadn't come out of her room. Probably in there sulking and listening to music on her earbuds. She imagined how it would go if she went into Amelia's room.

"Hey, do you mind doing the dishes?"

"What?" she'd shout, rolling over, popping out one earbud.

"Can you do the dishes?"

"In a little bit." Translation: Wait for Whitney to finally give in and do it herself.

"No, I'd rather you do it now."

"Fine." Groaning and stomping would ensue. Then would come the muttering under the breath, "Oh, my God. I have so much homework to do. And I still have to study for that test."

Next would be the loudness. The banging of pans. Clinking of dishes. Slamming of cabinet doors.

For the moment it was calm and quiet. Why would she want to upset that?

It was easier to simply do it herself. Taking a deep breath, Whitney turned on the faucet. *Yes, it was better this way.*

She'd let Amelia cool off, and then she'd see if she wanted to go grab dinner or something.

Whitney had learned early to pick her battles with Amelia. She didn't want to risk losing her for good.

21

MILLIE KEPT A lot of secrets from me.

When I started finding out about them, cracks began to form in what I thought was a solidly built friendship.

The first was the truth about Mitch.

He was one of the guys who lived in the apartment below Millie's. The one we often partied with. In the beginning, I didn't notice Mitch very much. I mean, he was always there. Dark hair. Dark eyes. Black clothes. A shadow in the corner.

But he was quiet, mostly keeping to himself.

Sometimes I'd catch him watching us—Millie and me—and I would get a funny feeling in my gut. An uneasiness I didn't quite understand. I thought it was just because he was older—in his early twenties—which seemed old to me at seventeen. And I knew he was the one supplying Millie with her weed. Not only that, but I'd seen other drugs and paraphernalia in his apartment. Pills. Needles. Small glass pipes. That alone made him seem dangerous. At least, enough for me to keep my distance.

I'd like to say that Millie came clean—confessed the truth to me—but that's not how it went down.

I found out the truth on a Sunday afternoon. It was an insanely hot spring day. As we sat on the floor in Mitch's apartment, we kept joking that we were getting baked by the sun and the joint. It was just the four of us—me, Millie, Mitch and his roommate, Greg.

The AC blasted, causing my damp skin to break out in goose bumps. Heavy metal shrieked from the speakers, sharp guitars and pounding drums. Leaning my back against the couch, I stared up at the ceiling, enjoying the spacy, mellow sensation that took over. Millie nudged me, asking if I could hand her a cigarette from the pack on the coffee table in front of me. I went to grab one out, but the pack was empty.

Greg threw her one from his pack, then said he'd go up to the liquor store and get more. Millie piped up then, suggesting I go with him. When I caught the encouraging smile on her face, I thought maybe she was playing matchmaker. I'd confessed to her once that I thought Greg was cute. Even though he and Mitch were the same age, he didn't scare me the way Mitch did.

So I went.

We rode in his beat-up Buick. It didn't have air-conditioning, and the passenger window wouldn't roll down all the way. I was so sweaty that my bare thighs stuck to the seat. Luckily, the liquor store was only down the street.

When we got there, Greg left me in the car with it running— not that that helped. It only made the car hotter. I couldn't stand the heat. Sweat covered my skin, slid down my spine. I needed air, so I got out and rested my back against the passenger-side door and fanned myself, staring across the street at the Dollar Dayz Inn.

Man, I can't believe anyone would stay in that dump, I thought, my stomach churning.

Next thing I know, Greg runs out, hollering for me to get my ass in the car.

I was so scared, I had trouble opening the door. My hands were all slick and sweaty. He barely even waited for me to get my butt on the seat before peeling out of the parking lot. My door was still partially open.

He was like, "Why the fuck did you get outta the car?"

Seriously, that's what he said. No apology or anything.

I was, like, "I didn't know I wasn't supposed to."

He made some comment about me being a bad partner in crime.

That's when it hit me. What he'd done. I must have looked shocked when I asked if he stole the cigarettes, because he started laughing then. Said he'd never met anyone as innocent as me. I wasn't sure if it was a compliment or not.

I wondered if Millie knew what he planned to do. I hoped not.

When we got back to the apartment, I hurried inside ready to ask her about it. But the question died on my lips, startled by what I saw. She and Mitch on the couch, making out. I wanted to look away, but I couldn't.

His hands slid up her back, his fingers playing over her spine as if he was drawing pictures. The way we did. I felt sick. They didn't even see us. Just kept kissing, their lips plastered together in a sickening way.

It wasn't until Greg slammed the door behind us that they looked up, dazed. Lipstick trailed up Millie's cheek. Her hair was messy, tangled. Her eyes were wide. Apologetic.

I thought she would tell me it was a one-time thing. A terrible error in judgment. No way did she want to be with this guy. She was high. They were alone. I suppose I could understand that.

But that wasn't the case.

This had been going on for a while. They'd just been keeping it a secret.

Now it all made sense. How come she always had a stash of weed and cigarettes. He bought them for her because they were together.

In a relationship.

Boyfriend/girlfriend.

I felt disgusted. Betrayed.

All this time I thought she and I had something special. I thought that we had so many things only the two of us shared. But I was wrong. She'd been keeping a secret from me. A secret she had with him.

I knew then where her loyalty lay.

Not with me.

With him.

22

WHITNEY HAD NEVER given a second thought to sharing Amelia's plans with Jay. Looking back, there were times when he even asked her what Amelia was up to on a given day. It didn't seem suspicious, though, because when Amelia was gone that meant they could be alone. And that's what they both wanted.

At least that's what she thought.

Now she didn't know what to think.

In the past, Whitney dated guys she met through work: once she'd dated a dad she'd met at Amelia's school. They'd talk every afternoon while waiting for their children, and struck up a mutual attraction. But Jay showed up out of the blue.

And, actually, he'd entered her life at almost the same time Lauren had entered Amelia's.

Were the two of them connected somehow?

Whitney's mind traveled back to the night she'd left Jay's apartment early to spend time with Amelia.

Whitney opened the door to the apartment, expecting to see Amelia sitting on the couch in the exact spot she'd left her. It was what usually happened when she went out. As long as she had food, TV and her phone, there was no need for her to move.

But when she stepped inside, the couch was empty. The bowl of popcorn was half-gone, but the TV was still blaring. Whitney heard shuffling down the hallway.

After throwing her keys and purse down by the door, she followed the sound. "Amelia, I'm home!"

"Mom?" Amelia leaped into the hallway, her face flushed and her breathing slightly labored. "You're home early."

"Yeah." Good thing too. "What's goin' on?"

Lauren appeared out of nowhere. Whitney's heart seized. She narrowed in on Amelia. "You didn't ask if you could have a friend over."

"I just stopped by for a little bit. My mom was out, too, and I was bored at home alone," Lauren answered, while Amelia stared at the floor, pushing at the carpet with her big toe.

She nodded and stepped inside Amelia's room. Her mom radar was way up, her gaze inching over every surface. She sniffed the air, but it smelled like Amelia's peppermint lotion, faintly of soap and the vanilla candle she'd been burning earlier. Nothing seemed amiss. She stared deeply into both girls' eyes. Nope. Not red.

Amelia blinked. "What? Why are you looking at me like that?"

Whitney didn't bother responding. Instead, she said, "Can I talk to you in private for a minute?"

"I'll be right back," Amelia said to her friend.

Lauren nodded as if giving her permission. "Okay, Millie."

Heat rose to the surface of Whitney's skin. "What did you call her?"

"Millie," she said slowly, as if Whitney was hard of hearing.

"It's a nickname," Amelia said.

"I know that," Whitney snapped. It had just taken her by surprise. She'd never heard anyone call Amelia that before.

Whitney smoothed down her hair. Then she beckoned Amelia to follow her as she made her way down the hallway. Amelia's shoulders *were slumped, and her footsteps so slow it was like she was trekking across a sandy beach.*

When they made it into Whitney's bedroom, she put a hand on her hip and cocked her head to the side. "What's really going on?" she whispered to her daughter.

"Lauren told you. She didn't want to be alone, so she came over," Amelia deadpanned. "What's the big deal, anyway? It's not like I threw a party or something. It's one friend."

"I know, but you didn't ask," Whitney said. "And you both were acting kinda suspicious when I got home."

"God, Mom, I'm not you, okay?" Amelia groaned. "I'm not gonna make the same dumb mistakes you did. Why can't you see that?"

The words stung. But she was right. Sometimes Whitney forgot how different they were. Just because Whitney had taken a bad path at Amelia's age, didn't mean she would.

"Sorry. I guess I was just disappointed. I came home early, hoping we could spend some time together."

"C'mon, Mom, we spend all our time together."

It wasn't true. At least not lately. But that wasn't all Amelia's fault, so Whitney kept her mouth shut. She was too tired to keep arguing. It seemed like all they did was talk in circles lately, anyway.

After Amelia left the room, Whitney closed the door and started taking off her jewelry. When she went to drop the earrings on top of her dresser, a chill brushed down her back. Her stuff had been moved, rearranged. Nothing was exactly as she'd left it.

The girls giggled through the adjoining wall.

Had they been in here?

She scoured the top of her dresser again. Nothing had been taken, that she could see. But things had definitely been moved.

Why?

She tried Jay again, but this time when he didn't answer, she called McAvoy. After telling him about the missing money and her suspicions about Jay, she hung up and flung her body back down on the bed.

SATURDAY, 11:45 P.M.

She was floating in water, her body weightless. Warm. Bobbing up and down, swaying back and forth in a rhythmic pattern. Black nothingness surrounded her. Mind blank. Fuzzy.

In the distance she heard noises. The creak of a door as it opened. Something metal being raked across a pole. The shower curtain? No. That wasn't it. A clothes hanger.

Feet shuffling on carpet.

Whispered voices.

"Shh, keep it down."

Amelia?

She tried to hoist her body upward, to swim, but she was immobile, her arms and legs refusing to cooperate. Gravity won, water cocooning her. She was warm. So warm. The black nothingness beckoned her. It felt good to give in, to sink into it. To allow it to draw her farther under.

"Come on. Hurry."

"I am."

The voices again. Muffled. Far away.

Amelia!

Whitney flailed, grasping, clawing, but she gained no traction. Her fingers simply sliced through the water as she sunk farther. Holding her arms high above her head, her fingertips slid under the surface until she was completely submerged.

It was silent now, but she knew what she'd heard.

Her daughter. She was here.

A drawer slammed. More footsteps.

Whitney finally made it to the top, her head cresting the surface. The sounds were clearer now.

Her eyelids flung open.

Gasping, she shot up in bed. The light was on, the brightness shocking her. Blinking, as spots filled her vision. Rubbing her eyes, she wondered how long she'd been out.

The last thing Whitney remembered was putting on her pj's after a hot shower. She'd been so tired. She'd rested her head on the pillow and stared up at the ceiling. Her mind had been reeling, and she was attempting to make sense of everything. She hadn't planned to fall asleep.

Hearing movement on the other side of her wall, her shoulders stiffened.

Maybe the voices weren't part of her dream.

Heart leaping into her throat, she slid off the bed and raced into Amelia's room. The hallway was dark. Amelia's door was closed. It hadn't been earlier.

Without wasting another second, she twisted the knob and shoved the door open. It was pitch-dark. She couldn't see a thing.

"Amelia?" She walked inside with her arms outstretched. Fingers skating across the wall, she found the light switch, then flicked it on. Yellow light flooded the room.

Empty.

Whitney sighed. She could've sworn she'd heard voices and movement from in here. Stepping farther in, she lifted her hand to touch the bed. Her fingertips slid over the smooth fabric. That's when she noticed the comforter had shifted. It was straighter, the sides more even than before. Had she tweaked it when she was in here last? Maybe the police had.

But why fix the bedspread?

When she noticed the closet door was open, she racked her brain, trying to recall if it had been like that all day. She didn't think so. A few hangers were strewn on the ground, one right in front of the closet. That for sure hadn't been there.

Walking up to the closet, she peeked inside. Amelia had never been good at hanging up her clothes, so there weren't many in here. Most of the things she wore regularly ended up in the pile on the ground. But she did keep her jackets and bulky sweaters in the closet. Whitney couldn't tell if any were missing.

She glanced at the floor. Amelia's suitcase was gone. Whitney's stomach bottomed out.

The floor creaked from somewhere in the distance. Holding her breath, she stood still. Was it Natalie? She listened while creeping forward. As she flicked off Amelia's light and entered the hallway, she heard even breathing coming from the family room. Natalie must be asleep.

Another creak. It was coming from Whitney's room.

She tiptoed forward, one hand on the wall to guide her in the darkness. She expected to be greeted by light when she opened the door to her room. It had been on when she left it. Now it was off. A breeze blew into the room, cool air brushing over Whitney's flesh. Shuddering, she peered up at the open window.

A figure stood near Whitney's bed, backlit by moonlight.

It only took a moment for Whitney to register that it was Lauren.

"Where's my daughter?" Whitney stepped toward her.

Lauren held her ground. Something glinted in her hand. Shiny. Metallic.

Was it a knife?

"Tell me where she is," Whitney demanded.

"She doesn't want to be found," Lauren said.

How dare Lauren talk to her like that? This girl had no right to keep her from her daughter. If Lauren knew where Amelia was, she needed to speak up now.

Lauren was backing up now, making her way to the open window. Whitney couldn't let her get away. She lunged forward, both arms reaching out to grab her. But her hands only connected with air. Dazed, she blinked. Spun in circles.

Lauren was gone.

It didn't make sense. She'd been standing right here. Whitney looked back at the doorway. She couldn't have gotten past Whitney that quickly. And the window was only open slightly. Not enough to fit a person through.

Did she imagine her?

She thought of how no one knew who Lauren was.

Whitney had a strange, light-headed sensation. Lowering herself to the edge of her bed, she forced a few breaths in through her nose and out through her mouth the way Dr. Carter had taught her years ago. Her vision was swimmy as if she'd taken a few too many shots. *In through the nose. Out through the mouth.* When the dizziness remained, she squeezed her eyes shut.

When she woke again, her eyes met the ceiling. She was lying down on top of her comforter, head on her pillow. The light was on. Window closed.

Her eyes were watery, neck kinked. After hoisting herself up with her palms, she looked around. Nothing was out of place.

Was Lauren really here or had it all been a dream?

She slid off the bed and padded in her bare feet to the hallway. All the lights were on, the entire apartment lit up like a Christmas tree. She went to Amelia's room. The door was open, light still on. Her bed looked exactly like it had earlier today, comforter askew, one side hanging lower than the other. And her closet door was closed.

It must've been a dream, then.

23

THE FIRST TIME Mitch hit Millie, I told her she should dump him.

"You're being melodramatic," she said in response.

"Millie, he hit you."

"It was an accident."

"How does someone accidentally hit you?"

Flustered, she shook her head. "Well, I mean…it wasn't an accident, per se. More like a mistake." She waved away my concern with a flick of her wrist. "It was my fault, anyway."

Oh, my God. "For real?"

"No, I'm serious," she said firmly. "I went all batshit crazy on him. I kinda deserved it."

"What are you talking about?"

"He went out with the guys one night when you couldn't come over. I begged for him to let me go with them, but he said no. That it was guys' night. But then I found out later that girls were there, and I just sorta lost it."

"I don't blame you. That's really shitty."

"No, but that's the thing. I was wrong. The girls weren't with Mitch. He didn't even know they'd be there."

"Still, none of that explains why he hit you."

"I told you, it's because I was really mad and acting crazy, accusing him and stuff. And he hadn't even done anything wrong." She shrugged. "I pushed him into it. It's that simple."

"You're never gonna convince me that it was cool for him to hit you."

"Whatever." A heavy breath escaped between her lips. "It doesn't matter, anyway. It won't happen again. He promised."

"And what if it does?"

"It won't," she said, but when I raised my brows and opened my mouth to press her on it, she added, "But if it does, then I'll break up with him."

I wanted to believe her, but I didn't. She was already in too deep, I could tell.

But he didn't love her. Not the way I did.

And I had to make her see that before it was too late.

24

WHITNEY WENT TO the family room to check on Natalie. She found her curled up, fast asleep on the couch. After covering her with a throw blanket, she flicked off the family room light, shivering as darkness enveloped her. It was quiet. None of the usual noises sounded outside the thin walls of her apartment. No traffic or kids playing or people talking. It was a tangible indication of it being past the middle of the night.

Whitney would've given anything to go back in time. A year. A month. Even a week. Any time that wasn't today. Any time when Amelia was home and safe.

When Amelia was an infant, Whitney savored every second. Watched her while she slept. Took dozens of pictures and videos. Those months were so clear in her mind. Every minute. Every detail. She was in awe of the miracle that her daughter was, never taking her for granted. Amelia felt like a blessing she didn't deserve. She didn't want to squander even one second of it.

But, eventually, the busyness of life took over. Days blended together. Memories became fuzzier. Photos and videos became scarce.

Today, though, life slowed down again. Every single detail was etched in Whitney's mind with extreme clarity. Why had it taken this to get her to slow down?

She knew all the terrible things that could potentially happen to a missing sixteen-year-old but refused to let her mind go there.

Her throat was scratchy and dry. When was the last time she drank anything? Probably when Natalie made her tea. How many hours ago was that?

She went into the kitchen and grabbed a bottle of water. Food was probably a good idea, but there was no way she could force anything down. She was never one of those women who ate when she was stressed or upset. She was the opposite. When she and Dan split up, she got so thin people thought she was ill.

Bottle of water in hand, Whitney headed back to Amelia's room. Her dream had stirred some questions in her mind. Given her avenues to explore.

After stepping inside, she set her water down on the dresser and then went straight to Amelia's closet, opening the door. Several jean jackets and a few sweaters were all that was hung up. On the ground were a couple pairs of sandals, and a pair of tennis shoes. Whitney did note that her two favorite sweaters were missing. So were her Chucks, but she'd probably been wearing them on Friday. Next to the shoes sat Amelia's suitcase. Behind it, a flash of red. She shot her hand out, closed her fingers around the stiff, coarse fabric. Emotion, thick like peanut butter, lodged in her throat as she held up the small white jean jacket, streaked with red marker. Crude slashes resembling bloodied, torn skin. Whitney brought the jacket to her face, rubbed it against her skin, inhaled long and deep.

She closed her eyes, remembering.

"Amelia, what are you doing?" Whitney stood in the doorway to her daughter's room.

Eight-year-old Amelia hunched over her brand-new white jean jacket—the one her mom had saved for weeks to buy—holding a red marker between her fingers. Whitney hadn't caught her in time. The damage was done. The once pristine jacket was now covered in red marker, a messy coloring sheet.

Amelia lowered her eyes as if unable to look at her mom. Her lower lip trembled. "I told you I wanted a red jacket."

It was true. She had told Whitney that. Problem was, she'd waited until after Whitney had bought the white one. And after she'd taken the tags off. And worse, after Amelia had already worn it and stained one of the sleeves.

Anger rose within her. She didn't have the money to buy Amelia a new jacket right now. Opening her mouth, she was about to scold Amelia. But Amelia's forlorn expression stopped her. Pressing her lips together, she stepped into the room. Nothing she could say would be worse than what Amelia was already feeling. Regret painted Amelia's face.

Whitney knelt next to her daughter, reaching out to touch the edge of a sleeve. The pads of Amelia's fingers were stained in red, dotting the places where she gripped the jacket.

"It's not so bad," Whitney said. "We'll just call it shabby chic."

"What's that?" Amelia asked.

Whitney laughed lightly. "It's all the rage, trust me."

But Amelia wasn't convinced. She loosened her grip and the jacket fell to the floor. Then she chucked the pen.

"It was stupid." She crossed her arms over her chest, pouting. "I just wanted to be cool like Eve."

Whitney had heard a lot about Eve, the most popular girl in Amelia's class.

"Let me see if I can wash the pen off, okay? I have some stain remover that might work," Whitney said, hoping against all hope that she could salvage the jacket.

In the end, she couldn't. Amelia had used a permanent marker, and

while Whitney was able to get out some of it, she could never success-
fully get it all off. What started as a hard lesson for Amelia turned into
an inside joke that lasted long after the incident.

Red jacket *became their safe word. The one Amelia could use when*
she was scared or in over her head. Like at a sleepover when she wanted
to leave, or at her dad's and she needed her mom to make up an excuse
to swing by for a quick hug and chat. All she had to do was call her
mom and say anything with the word red jacket *in it.*

"Mom, can you make sure to wash my red jacket tonight?"

Or:

"I couldn't find my red jacket earlier. Do you know where it is?"

Whitney always responded with a "yes," which really meant, I've
got your back. I'm here for you…always.

She dropped the jacket. Sniffed. Wiped a palm down her face.
Continued her search.

On the shelf above her clothes were some hats, a few belts
and a stack of computer paper. Whitney pulled down the paper
and riffled through it, but the pages were all blank. Reaching
up, Whitney slid her palm over the shelf to see if she'd missed
anything. But all she succeeded in finding was dust. It coated
her hand. She wiped it on her pants.

Next, she went to Amelia's desk drawer, sliding it open. It
squeaked in protest as if it hadn't been opened in years. Papers sprung from it like an accordion being opened. She sifted
through them.

Nothing interesting.

Some old school papers. Assignment sheets. Syllabuses. A few
pages that looked like journal entries or letters but ended up
being half-written essays. Her own smiling face peeked out
from under some of the papers. She yanked out the strip of photos. They were ones she and Amelia took in the photo booth at
Marc's wedding a few months back. Smiling, her gaze slid down
all four poses—in three of them they were in costume, giant
glasses, big hats, reindeer ears, but in the last one they'd tossed

the props aside, hugged each other tight and smiled broadly. Amelia's skin was shiny, her eyes bright. It had been such a fun day. She and Amelia had danced and laughed together. They'd enjoyed themselves so much they'd been two of the last people to leave.

Desperate to sit with these memories a bit longer, Whitney clicked into her phone and went to Amelia's Instagram account. She scrolled back through, searching for the photos of them from the wedding, but couldn't find them. When she stopped, she'd gone all the way back to last summer. Confused, she swept her index finger back up. She knew Amelia had posted them. She'd seen them on her account. Amelia had been so happy with how she looked that day in her yellow sundress and gold strappy sandals. Had even said that her self-tan was "on point."

As Whitney continued scanning the photos, her stomach lurched. Not only were the photos from the wedding missing, so was every photo Amelia had ever posted of them together.

Why would they be gone?

Had Amelia taken them down or had someone else?

Music blasted from the phone, startling her. Jay's name and picture covered the screen.

Oh, thank God. "Jay?"

"Whitney," he whispered so softly she could barely hear him.

"Jay, what's going on?"

"I need you to stop calling me."

Whitney had to strain to hear him. "I'm just trying to figure out what the hell's going on. I went to your place. You don't live there."

"I know," he continued to whisper. "That's my brother's place."

"Why would you take me to your—"

"Jay?" A woman's muffled voice cut through their conversation.

"Just a minute," he said loudly. Then whispered, "I'm married, okay?"

"What? I don't—"

"Look, I'm sorry, okay? But this isn't what I bargained for. You going to my brother's place and the police contacting me."

"The police contacted you? What did you tell them?"

"That I know nothing about where Amelia is. God, I can't believe you'd even think I would." A loud exhale floated through the line. "This whole thing was a mistake. I never should've talked to you at the bar that night. Don't call me again."

The line went dead.

Whitney sunk down onto the edge of Amelia's bed, but it sloped beneath her. Pushing up with her toes, she scooted back slightly in an effort to stabilize herself. It didn't work. Inside she felt anything but stable. Her stomach shook, her chest tightened and that funny fluttery feeling that she'd had since yesterday was getting worse. She did feel slightly relieved, assuming now at least he hadn't used her to get to Amelia or steal her money. But married?

In hindsight, all the red flags were there. That apartment. His long hours and work trips—over weekends, really? Why had she refused to see them? But she knew why. It was because of how hard Amelia had been pushing her away. The distance between them felt immeasurable. She'd been so lonely. Needy. Jay filled that void, or at least a portion of it.

But Whitney should've been paying more attention to what Amelia was up to. When Amelia started pulling away, Natalie told Whitney that meant she was being a good mom. Doing her job.

Kids aren't supposed to like their parents, she'd said.

Whitney had believed her. That's why, as much as the wall between them hurt Whitney, she didn't back down. She stuck to her guns. Her job wasn't to be Amelia's friend. It was to protect her. Keep her safe.

That's what she thought she'd been doing.

Now she worried that by saying no all the time, she'd caused this. If she'd been more open, less protective, would Amelia still be here?

Her daughter had been keeping so many secrets, going behind Whitney's back. And because of that Whitney didn't even know where to look for her. She may have technically lost Amelia on Friday night, but in reality, she'd lost her months ago.

These thoughts propelled her back to Amelia's desk, her fingers greedy as they sifted through the remaining papers. Her vision blurred, the pinprick of a headache forming above her eyes. Setting down the papers in her hand, she headed back to her room to grab her reading glasses. She didn't need them all the time, usually just in the evenings when her eyes got tired or when she was on the computer for too long, working. They had blue light lenses, so that helped with the glare of the screen.

In her bedroom, she located them on her nightstand. Turning to leave, the corner of her big toe scraped against something flimsy, movable. Familiar. A piece of paper? Bending down, she felt under her bed until she located it.

An ivory sheet of paper, jagged edges. It looked like it had been torn out of a diary, the press of a pen showing through the backside of the page.

Whitney had never kept one. So, what was this doing under her bed? She was grateful for her reading glasses as she slipped them on.

When she flipped the paper over in her palm, she instantly recognized the handwriting, even though she hadn't seen it in years. Her blood ran cold as her gaze darted down to her own name, written multiple times in the diary entry.

Where had this come from, and why was it here?

She stood up, carefully pried her glasses off and tucked them into the palm of her free hand. The diary page fluttered in the other. She thought about the picture in Amelia's room. About the money missing from both Amelia's account and her drawer. And about the photos that had vanished from Amelia's Instagram page.

This entire time she'd been looking for someone to blame. Someone to pin this on. She'd been chasing after Dan, Jay and random boys. But what if the real culprit was Whitney?

What if this all had to do with her past? With what she'd done?

From down the hallway music rang out. It took her a few seconds to realize it was her phone ringing from where she'd left it in Amelia's room. Dropping the glasses and the paper, she raced toward it.

"Dan?" she answered breathlessly.

"Hey, Whit."

"Have you heard from her?"

"No," he said, his tone wary. "I actually called because I wanted to come clean about what I told the police earlier. I wanted you to hear it from me," Dan said. Whitney pitched forward. "I told them about my suspicions."

"Suspicions?" Her mouth dried out.

"About Amelia's eye color."

"Oh, my God. Are you serious?" Shaking her head, she blew out a breath. "Why?"

"Because the police need to be looking into him. He might have something to do with it."

Her chest tightened. "You didn't tell them his name, did you?" When he didn't readily answer, she let out a shaky breath. "Dan?"

"I had to."

"Why? It doesn't make any sense. He's in prison."

"Are you sure about that?"

"I don't know. I think so. Why? Do you know something I don't?"

"No," Dan said. "I don't keep tabs on him."

"Neither do I," she said, her cheeks stinging at the implication.

"Well, maybe you should."

"There's no reason to. He has nothing to do with Amelia. He's just my high school ex-boyfriend. Why are we involving him? God, what were you thinking?"

"You want everyone to think you've changed, Whit. But you haven't. Not at all. You're still the same. Always in protection mode."

"I'm not protecting him."

"I know. I'm not talking about him."

She recoiled, as if he'd slapped her. She couldn't deny it. She was protecting herself. But not just herself. She was also protecting Amelia.

Dan thought he knew everything. That he had it all figured out. But that was Dan's problem from the beginning. He'd always underestimated Whitney.

Thought he was smarter. Knew more.

He was wrong.

Dr. Carter sat across from Whitney, his eyes blinking behind his large glasses.

"I don't know what I'm supposed to talk about." Whitney picked at a hole in the thigh of her jeans, tugging at a loose string.

"These are your sessions, Whitney. You can talk about whatever you'd like."

"But they're not really. My parents are forcing these on me," she admitted. "They think I'm depressed."

"Are you?"

She didn't know how to answer that. She'd been sad, lately, yeah. But depressed? She wasn't sure she'd go that far.

"They think I can't get past my brother's death." The string came off her jeans and she wrapped it around her pinky finger.

Dr. Carter nodded, his gaze never leaving her. It was a little unnerving. "Losing a sibling is hard, especially at such a young age. He'd been sick a long time, is that right?"

"His whole life. He had cystic fibrosis."

"I bet that was hard on you."

Whitney uncoiled the string from her finger, releasing it. It fell to the ground. There was a window to her right, and she stared out of it. Dr. Carter's office overlooked his backyard. Lush, green grass, lots of flowers, a tiny garden nestled in the corner.

Dr. Carter fixated on her, present in a way her parents never were. He seemed genuinely interested in what she had to say, and she didn't want to waste his undivided attention on talking about the one person who'd been stealing the spotlight from her most of her life. Sure, she felt awful about her brother's death. It had been hard for her when he died at only eleven years old.

But it was also kind of a relief. And that was the part she could never admit to anyone.

How would that make her sound?

She had loved her brother. Of course she had. But when he died, she'd thought that finally her life wouldn't revolve around having a sick brother. But it seemed he still haunted her. Still permeated every facet of her existence. Oddly enough, in death Kevin owned her parents even more so than he had in life. They were merely ghosts of their former selves. Once Kevin was gone, she'd lost them completely.

Out the window, she caught a glimpse of the main house. She thought of the boy she'd met at the front door. Dan. He was nice. Sweet. Good-looking.

In his eyes, she'd seen pity. Concern. But, also, curiosity.

He knew she was here for therapy, and she could see his brain working overtime to figure out why.

She may have met him for only a few minutes, but it was clear he had a hero complex. It was the same vibe she was getting from his dad. They wanted to fix her. But more than that, they were interested in her. In what she had to say.

Whitney was so much more than just the girl with the sick brother. She had other things to talk about. Other things that weighed on her mind.

"I am sad about losing my brother, sure," she said, still staring out the *window, unable to meet Dr. Carter's intense stare. "But that's not all I'm sad about." She paused. Took a breath. "I met someone. Someone really awesome, who I liked a lot. But then…" She bit her lip, pondering what she should say next.*

"But then what?" he asked gently. She wondered if the soothing voice he used was the one he was born with or if he'd trained it to sound like that.

"There's this guy. He's a little older than me. I met him through a mutual friend." Bringing her hand to her mouth, she chewed on the fingernail of her index finger. It tasted like nail polish. "He was really cool. He told me he really liked me. That I was pretty. He made me feel special."

"That sounds nice," Dr. Carter said.

Bruises against pale skin. Dark purple, yellow around the edges.

She tugged on the edge of her sleeve.

"It was," she said, "at first."

"What changed?"

"I don't know." She shrugged. "It's like he was so sweet at first, always saying nice things and wanting to be with me. But then he just kinda started pushing me away."

"How so?"

"Well, like I got this haircut a few weeks ago and he told me he liked it better before," she said. "And sometimes he talks about how hot other girls are right in front of me like I'm not even there. But the worst is when he physically pushes me away."

"What do you mean?"

"One night we were hanging out with friends, smoking and drinking, and I leaned in to kiss him, but he shoved me back, turning his head away." Whitney picked at the skin around her fingernails. "Everyone saw. It was so embarrassing. I asked him about it, but he said I was acting stupid that night and he wasn't in the mood."

"Is that the only time he's treated you like that?"

"No."

"Then why do you keep seeing him?"

"I'm in love with him."

She could see the switch in his eyes then. From concern and pity to determination. He wanted to rescue her.

It was the same look her dad gave her when she'd pressed her palm into the frying pan.

And it's what she had been counting on.

"I don't know what you want me to say, Dan," she said now.

"Nothing," he said. "I just want you to finally do the right thing for once in your goddam life and find Amelia."

"Okay." She swallowed hard. "I will."

In order to keep her promise to Dan, she could no longer sit around. He thought he knew the truth, but he didn't. Not all of it, anyway. And by telling the police what he did, he only made things harder. More convoluted. She had no choice but to take matters into her own hands. They weren't here in this apartment.

She had to go back to the last place she'd seen her daughter.

Back to the place she'd left her.

25

I NEVER LIKED MITCH. Never trusted him.

But it wasn't until Millie started dating him that I realized just how dangerous he was. Despite his promise, he did hit her again.

"You're gonna leave him now, right?" I asked, reminding her of the conversation we'd had after the first punch to the face.

Her gaze bounced to the floor. My stomach sank.

"You can't be serious? Why would you want to stay with someone who hurt you?"

"It was my fault. I kinda flirted with a friend of ours. We were stoned and I guess I just wasn't thinking," she said.

"And that gives him the right to hit you?"

The smile on her face was confusing. "It's just because he likes me so much. He got jealous."

Unbelievable. She was turning his violence into a romantic gesture. I felt sick.

I knew he didn't hit her out of jealousy or passion. It was all about control for him.

I'd seen him flirt with other girls all the time. I'd even seen girls emerging from his apartment in the early mornings when I'd leave Millie's.

Not to mention that he leered at me all the time. Watching me in a creepy way, especially when we all blasted music and danced together around his living room. It's like he was getting off on it.

Millie knew all of this too. Turned a blind eye. It was like she didn't believe she was worth more. But I knew she was, and that was why I had to get her away from him. She may not have been able to fight for herself, but she'd fight for me, wouldn't she?

If Mitch hurt me, she'd have to face what kind of monster he was.

I thought she would choose me over him.

That's why I did what I did. And before you judge me, know this: I did it to help Millie. To save her. I did it out of love.

One afternoon when I was leaving Millie's I spotted Mitch standing outside his apartment smoking a cigarette.

"Hey." I walked over to him. "Can I bum a cigarette?"

Without a word, he handed me one. He wore a wifebeater tank top, baggy pants that rode low on his hips. His hair was messy like he'd just woken up. I lit up the cigarette, held it gingerly to my lips. After taking a drag, I blew it into his face.

"What the hell?" He scrunched up his nose, batting the smoke away. Big slicing motions with his arm.

My insides trembled. This would be too easy. He was already getting upset. It never did take much.

But could I go through with this?

I thought about how easy it would be to walk away now and hurry home. To safety. But, no, I had to do this. For Millie.

After taking a few more drags off my cigarette for courage, I tossed it down, ground it out with the toe of my shoe. Then looked up at Mitch.

"You know she's too good for you, right?" I said, my voice strong and steady, despite how my insides felt.

"What?" His entire face scrunched up as if in disgust.

"Millie," I said, glaring. "She deserves someone better than you." His face was reddening, but it wasn't enough. I had to ratchet it up. "In every way." My gaze traveled up and down his body. "I mean, look at you. Millie should be with someone more on her level."

Mitch threw down his cigarette but didn't bother putting it out. He stepped toward me. This is it, I thought, squeezing my eyes shut. But he didn't hit me. He started laughing. My eyes popped back open.

"Oh, yeah? And is that someone you?" he asked, his expression one of amusement.

"Huh?"

"Come on, we all see the way you look at Millie. The way you follow her around like her damn shadow. You're into her, huh?"

I swallowed hard, wishing I'd chosen a different tack. There were a million things I could've said that would piss him off. I'd seen him blow a gasket over tiny things. Spilled beer. Making fun of his favorite basketball team. Anything. Why had I chosen Millie?

"No." My voice shook. "Millie and I—we're just friends."

"Yeah, I know." He smiled. "But just admit it, you want her. You want her bad."

I backed up, my legs like jelly. "No, I—I—don't. I like boys."

"Prove it."

"What?" I froze.

Before I could stop him, his hands came around my waist. He shoved me up against the door to his apartment. The back of my head slammed into it. I bit my tongue, coating it in a metallic taste.

"I said prove it," he ground out.

Stop is what I tried to say, but the word came out so tiny it got lost on the breeze.

One of his hands traveled up to grab my breast, shocking me. Nothing about it felt good or sexual. It felt painful, cruel. I'd wanted Mitch to hurt me, but not like this. Never like this.

"God, it's like a game trying to find your tits in all that fat," he said, a cruel joke, squeezing harder.

I screamed out, flailing my arms, trying to push him away. I'd never felt so frustrated and helpless in my life.

"Stop, stop, stop!" By the time I got the word out, it sounded like a mantra.

He drew back, shook his head, laughed again. "Told ya."

My eyes widened at his cavalier response. I shoved off the wall, sidestepping him on shaky legs.

"You're not into guys," he added.

"Just stay away from me." Once I put a decent amount of distance between us, I turned to him. "Don't ever touch me again."

"Oh, trust me, I don't want to." His gaze roamed my body as if it was a mound of puke. "I only did that to prove a point. I'm not a chubby chaser."

Hot tears stung my eyes. Whirling around, I hurried away from him so he wouldn't see me crying. His laughter trailed me until I reached the street and the cars thankfully drowned it out. As I stormed down the sidewalk, I cursed Mitch with every step. By the time I made it home, I vowed to get Mitch out of our lives for good.

The minute I got home, I called Millie. My entire body was shaking with adrenaline by the time she answered. I was prepared for her to be irate with Mitch. To vehemently defend me.

But he'd already gotten to her.

She sounded stuffy when she answered. "I can't believe you would do this to me," she said before I could say a word.

"Do what?" I asked, honestly confused.

"Come on to my boyfriend."

"What? I didn't—I would never," I sputtered. "That's what he told you?"

"Yeah, he said you went downstairs to bum a cigarette and then told him he should break up with me."

"No, I didn't really say he should break up with you. I said that you're too good for him."

"What gives you the right to decide that for me?"

"No, you don't understand. I was just trying to help." I slid down the wall, pressed the phone tighter to my ear.

"Why did you meddle at all?"

We were getting off course. None of this mattered, anymore. Not after what he did.

"Millie, he…he forced himself on me. He assaulted me."

"What are you talking about?"

My gaze shifted around, grateful no one was home. "He got angry, shoved me up against the wall and touched me…you know…"

"So you told my boyfriend to break up with me and then you let him feel you up?" she snapped. "Oh, my God, what is wrong with you?"

"No, you're not hearing me!" I said, my voice rising in desperation. "I didn't let him do anything. He forced himself on me. I tried to get him to stop." The tears were back. I sniffed. "And he said really mean things about my body."

"I can't even deal with this right now," Millie said, angrily. "Just stay away from my boyfriend, okay?"

She hung up, leaving me staring down at my phone in disbelief.

I was so angry, I didn't talk to Millie all week. Even ignored her at school. I thought she'd apologize. See the error of her ways. At the very least feel bad for the way I'd been hurt. But she didn't seem to feel bad at all.

I had no other choice. I had to force her to see.

26

NATALIE WAS STILL dead asleep on the couch, face upturned, lips parted. Keeping an eye on her, Whitney tiptoed past. Careful not to make too much noise, Whitney snatched up her purse and keys. She felt like a teenager sneaking out of the house, but she knew if Natalie caught her, she'd try to stop her.

The minute the cold air hit Whitney, she shivered. She had always hated the cold. Although, she wasn't sure this weather qualified as cold. Springtime wasn't extreme here. Still, she longed to be curled up in a warm bed, not outside running around in the dark in the middle of the night.

If only that were an option.

It was quiet in the complex, blinds closed, curtains drawn, lights off, in all the apartments she passed. She made her way down the stairs, careful to take quiet steps. When she reached the bottom, she heard male voices around the corner. Kind of by the park area. The skin on the back of her neck prickled. Were the guys from apartment 204 back?

Rounding the corner, her tennis shoes pounded on the pavement. The voices got quieter, moving farther away. Desperation bloomed in her chest. She picked up the pace. When the men came into view, she hollered, "Wait!"

They both spun around, almost in perfect timing as if it was a choreographed dance routine. When they took in her face, their eyebrows leaped upward.

"Yes?" one of them said.

Whitney shrank back. There was no way these men were the ones Amelia had been hanging out with. They were Whitney's age. Maybe older.

"Nothing. Sorry," she mumbled. "I thought you were someone else."

"We could be someone else," the other man joked, jabbing his friend in the side with his elbow. His friend laughed. It was then that Whitney noticed their watery eyes, the flush of their cheeks and noses. "Tell us who you want us to be. Brad Pitt? Hugh Grant?"

Were they for real?

Her stomach tightened.

"I um…I actually should get back home…to um…my husband," she lied, tucking her ringless hand behind her back.

"Husband," the jokester said. "That's a dirty word." The two men laughed again.

It was a regular comedy fest out here.

Rolling her eyes, Whitney turned away from the strange men. Keeping her ears pricked, she hurried back where she came from. After rounding the corner again, she pressed her back against the wall and listened to the men's retreating footsteps. They were walking too slowly, and she tapped her foot against the ground with impatience.

Once it was quiet again, she stepped out of the shadows. She was anxious to get back to that house. The one that had stolen her daughter from her.

But first, she felt the pull toward apartment 204. Every apartment down here was quiet and dark, blinds closed. Apartment 204 was no exception.

She tried to peek in between the little slits in the closed blinds of the front window, but she couldn't see anything. Hugging herself, she stared at the closed door. It was like earlier. She couldn't detect any sound or movement inside.

There was another window to the left. Probably one of the bedrooms. She walked toward it. Pressing her face to the glass. Nothing. Just a wall of darkness.

Man, they kept this place locked up tight.

But there was also no noise there either.

They were either out or sleeping.

She should've known it wouldn't be that easy. What was she expecting? To find a party going on, Amelia right in plain sight? *If only.*

She started to leave, but then turned back around. Bit her lip. *Oh, screw it.*

Reaching up, she knocked on the door before she could talk herself out of it again. Holding her breath, she waited. A breeze whisked over her skin and she shivered, goose bumps rising on her skin.

No, Mom, they're geese bumps because there's more than one of them.

The memory flew through Whitney's mind fast and surprising. Tears pricked her eyes. She knocked again. Louder.

This time she didn't stop rapping until she heard something. She stood up straighter, throwing her shoulders back and lifting her chin. Her pulse was so erratic she felt its uneven beat in her neck.

The door flung open, and a middle-aged woman wearing

flannel pajamas, her short curly hair sticking up all over her head, popped her head out.

"What do you want?" she snapped. Her face was red, and mascara ringed her eyes as if she hadn't washed it off well before bedtime.

"I'm sorry," Whitney said, blinking. She hadn't prepared herself for his mom answering. "I...umm...I was just...looking for my daughter."

"My son already told the police everything he knows," she said, recognition dawning in her eyes of who Whitney must be.

"Is your son home? Maybe he can just fill me in on what he told them."

Moving back, the woman pushed the door slightly closed. "Look, I'm really sorry about your daughter, and I don't want to be rude. But my son doesn't know where she is, and I'd appreciate it if you didn't involve him in this anymore."

Whitney knew her window of opportunity was closing. And she sympathized with this mom. Really, she did. She knew she'd act the same way if their roles were reversed. But they weren't. Her daughter was the one that was missing. She didn't have the luxury of closing her door on the situation and going back to sleep. "Please. I just need to find Amelia. If there's anything at all he can tell me."

"Mom?" a voice sounded behind the woman.

Whitney's head swung back and forth, desperate to see over the mom's head. But she held her ground. The door was almost all the way closed now.

"Go back to bed," the woman said, right before the door closed completely.

But then it immediately swung back open. "No, Mom, it's fine."

Whitney's gaze skated upward at the incredibly tall, lanky boy filling the doorway. He was so tall his head almost reached the top of the doorframe. His thick curly hair fell into his face.

He ran a hand through it, brushing it back, revealing bloodshot eyes. And he was definitely the boy from the picture.

"You're Amelia's mom?" He looked Whitney up and down.

"Yeah," she said. "Do you know where she is?"

He shook his head. "I haven't heard from her all weekend." Frowning, he hung his head. His expression was one of grave concern. "I'm sorry."

"Do you have any idea where she might be?" Whitney asked, desperate.

"He already told the police everything he knows, okay?" The mom was back again, shoving at her son and attempting to close the door.

"I'd look into that friend of hers," the boy said quickly.

Whitney's heart hammered in her ears. "Lauren?"

He nodded. "Something isn't right with her."

"What do you mean by that?"

"You need to leave us alone now." The mother slammed the door in Whitney's face before she could ask what the boy's name was.

She flinched at the force of it. For a moment, she waited just in case it popped open again. But it didn't. Not this time.

Groaning, she nearly flung herself against it and started pounding again. But she stopped herself. There was no way that mom was going to let her son say anything else. Whitney thought about the boy's kind eyes and concerned expression.

Amelia wasn't here.

This boy didn't hold the answers to Amelia's whereabouts. Lauren did.

Something isn't right with her.

Whitney shivered, a memory from the first time Lauren spent the night flashing in her mind.

Whitney had been having that recurring dream where she was a high school student, lying out in the grass during lunch with her best friend. They were staring up through the branches of the tree above them, gig-

gling and chatting about classes and boys, when suddenly Whitney had this awful feeling like she forgot something. Something important. Something that made her feel panicky. As Whitney's friend droned on, she racked her brain, trying to place what it was.

She shot upward.

Amelia.

She'd forgotten about her daughter. Left her alone to come to school. What kind of mom was she?

When she mentioned it, her friend stared at her like she'd lost her mind.

"You don't have a daughter," she laughed.

"Yes, I do," she insisted.

Didn't she?

She leaped up, racing across campus toward the parking lot, desperate to get home. To find her daughter. But before she could reach the car, the parking lot faded. Darkness enveloped her. Her scalp prickled, a funny feeling descending on her.

The sensation of being watched drew her from her dream.

It was a familiar feeling. One she'd had countless times when Amelia was a little girl. She'd startle awake to find Amelia standing beside her bed.

"Mommy, I'm scared."

But this time when she opened her eyes, it wasn't Amelia in her room.

It was Lauren.

She blinked, rubbed her eyes, certain she was seeing things.

When she looked again, Lauren was gone. She exhaled. Rolled over onto her side. Then froze. Her door was open an inch or so, swaying slightly from the heating vent above. She always slept with the door closed. She slid out of bed. Padding into the hallway, she caught movement, a splash of dark hair, disappearing into Amelia's room. Whitney followed it, swung open Amelia's door. Both she and Lauren were asleep, back-to-back in Amelia's bed. Whitney stood there a moment, listening to their steady breathing.

She stepped back into the hallway, closing Amelia's door lightly be-

hind her, then ambled back into her room and stared at the spot where she'd seen Lauren. But it couldn't have been her, right?

She was asleep.

Still, she couldn't shake the feeling of being watched.

Afterward, Whitney kept telling herself that she imagined someone in her room. That she'd dreamed it. Now she wasn't so sure.

Who was this new friend of Amelia's? This girl who'd shown up out of nowhere?

And what did she want?

27

THE SATURDAY AFTER my ugly encounter with Mitch, I showed up at Millie's house late at night. She was home alone, her mom out on a date. She let me in but was clearly still angry with me. Music blasted throughout the room. Without offering me anything, she sat down on the couch, sipping a glass of her mom's vodka.

I poured my own glass and joined her. It was like liquid fire going down my throat.

"Do you honestly think I would come on to Mitch?" I asked her, wrapping my hands around my glass. The condensation seeped into my palms.

"Honestly?" she asked. "Yeah, I mean, you are kinda always butting into my life. And, no offense, but sometimes it seems like you do wanna be me."

I didn't want to *be* her, I swear. I wanted to be *near* her. Close to her. I wanted to be enough for her.

"Sometimes it seems like you're obsessed with me or something," she tacked on, staring down into her drink.

I took a gulp of vodka. Ignored the burning sensation in my throat. Swallowed it down. Liquid courage. "Those are his words, right? All week you've been ignoring me, but you're still talking to him?"

She continued staring into her drink, as if the answers to my questions were written in the center of the ice cubes.

"Do you think I'm lying about what happened? You think I made it up?"

Millie's head whipped in my direction, her eyes narrowing. "I don't know who to believe. His story is completely opposite yours."

"It's an easy choice, Mil. You believe me. Your best friend who has always been there for you. Not your asshole boyfriend who hits you!" I was done playing it cool. I was pissed.

Millie finally tore her eyes away from her drink. "That's a low blow."

"I'll tell you all about low blows," I said. "It's when you try to help your best friend out and instead you get assaulted by her boyfriend."

"Stop saying he assaulted you." She moved in closer. "You haven't told anyone else this, have you? Mitch could get in real trouble."

"Oh, my God. That's what you're worried about? Him getting in trouble?" I lashed out, angry tears springing to my eyes. "What about what he did to me?" Shaking my head, I sniffed. Blinked. "But you don't care, do you? He's the one you care about. Not me."

It hurt, even though it was what I figured would happen. My wild, seemingly carefree friend had become predictable when it came to him. Pathetic.

I took a baggie of pills out of my pocket. Dumped a few into my hand. When I first stole these, I'd hoped I wouldn't have to enact this plan. I'd hoped Millie would see reason.

"What are those?" she asked, eyeing them.

"Just leave me alone. You made your choice." I threw them into my mouth and drank them down with the remainder of the vodka. It burned and I didn't actually have enough to get all the pills down. I ended up gagging a little. Luckily, there was a half-drunk cup of water on the table—Millie's, I imagined, the smudge of her lips on the rim—and I used it to shove the pills the rest of the way down.

Millie watched, slack-jawed. "What did you just do?" She fumbled for the baggie. Only two pills left in it.

"Why do you care?"

"Seriously, what are these? What kinds of pills did you take?"

"I don't know. Some kind of diet pill Mitch gave me," I lied, already feeling a little fuzzy-headed. There was still a way to make her believe Mitch was a bad guy. A way that didn't involve me having to face him again.

"What? Mitch gave you diet pills? When?"

"Same day he called me fat." My lips trembled, remembering. "Right after he shoved me against the wall and grabbed… at me…and…" My voice trailed off, unable to relive it again. I'd already told her what a monster he was. But she didn't want to listen. That's why I had to show her. I tried to run my fingers down her arm, but they felt numb.

She set down her glass, raked her fingers through her hair. "Oh, my God. So, you are telling the truth?"

I wasn't, actually. I mean, I was about the touching and saying mean things. But I wasn't about the pills. I'd found those in my mom's medicine cabinet. They were just pain pills. I'd seen her take a couple at a time before, so I wasn't worried. I'd be fine. But Millie didn't know that, and that's what mattered.

"Why would you take so many?" Her voice sounded shrill.

Finally. There was that compassion I'd been looking for. I had her.

"The more I take, the thinner I'll get. Then maybe your boyfriend will approve of me." I lowered myself back on the couch, my limbs heavy, my head cottony. "It's not like it matters, anyway."

"You're not making any sense."

"Yess, I am. Perfect sensssse." My words were coming out a little slurred. My eyes felt weighted. The ceiling seemed to move, up and down, slowly, like ocean waves. It concerned me. I wasn't expecting to have this kind of reaction. "You chose him over me. You always choose him over me." Feeling nauseous, I rolled over just in time to puke into the carpet. Darkness crept in at the edge of my vision. My skin felt cold, clammy. I tried to grip the side of the couch, but my fingers slid off. My body followed, toppling over onto the floor. The room was spinning faster now.

I could hear Millie screaming in the distance. Felt fingertips brush over my wrist. Then everything went black.

28

SUNDAY, 4:15 A.M.
OVER THIRTY-FIVE HOURS
AFTER DROP-OFF

THERE IT WAS—the house Whitney had dropped Amelia off at. It stood in front of her. Quiet. Imposing. Lips locked, refusing to share the answers Whitney knew it had. Hiding behind its freshly manicured front lawn and rosebushes. Looking pristine and regal, so no one would suspect a thing.

Whitney knew she couldn't stop her car here, couldn't park out front where anyone driving by could see.

Circling the block, she came upon a park. So strange that she hadn't noticed it the first time she'd been here. Then again, it was hidden back behind a lot of trees, and Whitney hadn't been looking for a park then. It wasn't a traditional one. It didn't have a playground. It had a soccer field, some picnic tables, a few barbecue pits, a lone blue safety light or two. It also had a parking lot shaded by large, leafy trees. Whitney parked in the night-black back corner. After hiding her purse on the floor in the backseat and tucking her keys into her pocket, she locked her car and pulled the hood of her sweatshirt over her head. Then she hurried across the street and hoofed it up the sidewalk. She stood in front of the house a moment, gathering courage.

It felt like a lifetime ago when she'd sat in her car, watching Amelia walk up to the front door. She remembered that awful feeling. The way she'd reached down to unlatch her seat belt. The way she'd fought the urge to run after her daughter.

If only she had.

If only she'd listened to her gut. Followed her instincts.

She was positive this was the house. There was no doubt in her mind anymore.

Lauren standing in the kitchen doorway, watching her make French toast.

Something is off about her.

Whitney shuddered, stepped forward. The street was serene, dimly lit by streetlamps. Exhaling, she made her way to the front door. There was a tiny sliver of beveled glass, a pretty accent for the oak door. She squinted, trying to peer through. But all she saw was a kaleidoscope of colors. As she stepped back, spots filled her vision. Little floaters that made her momentarily disoriented.

She blinked. In the distance a car engine rumbled.

She scurried away from the door and lowered to the ground behind a cluster of bushes under the front windows. A twig scratched her hand on the way down, but it was a superficial scrape. Hadn't even drawn blood. When her butt hit the dirt, a rank smell filled her nostrils. She hoped she hadn't sat in dog crap or something.

Tires buzzed along the asphalt. She stayed hidden until it was silent again.

As she stood up, she brushed the dirt off her pants. The front windows were shuttered, and the slats were too close together to make out anything. She moved to the side of the house. It was the same in those windows.

Dammit.

After looking around, she carefully unlocked the back gate.

It creaked loudly. A dog barked. Wincing, she froze, expecting a dog to leap out at her. Instinctively squeezing her eyes shut, her entire body tensed. But nothing attacked her. Opening her eyes, she scoured the backyard.

No dog.

The barking was coming from the yard next door. Still, it was loud, and she worried it would alert someone to her being there. She stepped into the yard, closing the gate securely behind her. Then she stood still until the dog finally shut up. The yard was relatively small, only a tiny patch of grass, and a patio area with an awning. Rosebushes lined the back fence too. *They really had a thing for roses, huh?* She trekked across the perfectly manicured and freshly watered grass. The elderly couple must've had their sprinklers on a timer. The soles of her shoes were soaked right through. She could feel the dampness seeping into her socks. Her teeth chattered as she took in their outdoor table, a charcoal grill near the back door.

When she and Dan were married, they had a little yard like this. She remembered sitting out on the patio on summer evenings, sipping chardonnay while he grilled. Steak, usually. He preferred red meat. Whitney hardly ate it anymore.

Whitney had never been able to afford a yard on her own. Her apartment didn't even have one of those miniscule patio areas some of the neighbors had. She didn't think it was worth the extra money.

She turned, her gaze sweeping along the back fence. That's when she spotted the small shed in the right corner. It was the same color brown as the fence; that's why initially she hadn't seen it in the dark. It was windowless and small. Like really small. It was barely large enough to fit a person inside.

But it *was* big enough to fit a person, and that knowledge propelled Whitney forward. Adrenaline spiking, she yanked open the shed door. It swung open easily, almost like it hadn't been latched shut to begin with. She choked on the smell of dust and gasoline.

"Amelia?" she whispered as loudly as she dared.

From next door, she caught a tinkly sound, like a dog's tag being rattled as the dog ran around. She prayed that it wouldn't start barking again.

It was dark, only a sliver of light from the back porch shining inside. But she knew the sun would be coming up soon. Pausing, she wondered if this was a mistake. Didn't old people get up early? Reaching out, her fingers swiped over a lawnmower, a rake and a shovel. In the corner, she spotted a three-foot ladder folded up and propped against the wall. She bent down, finding a pair of gardening gloves, a few small shovels and a bag of fertilizer.

Abandoning the shed, she made her way over to the back patio. There was a sliding glass door leading into the house. The blinds weren't quite closed all the way, so she was able to peek inside. All the lights were off, and at first, she mostly saw her own reflection, floating in the glass, a garish head with no body. But when she moved closer, her nose brushing the icy surface, she was able to make out the shape of the couch, a couple of end tables, a lamp. Nothing out of the ordinary.

Time was running out. They could be waking up anytime now, and she was no closer to finding Amelia than when she'd left her apartment. She had to get inside. But how?

She'd had a slider exactly like this one in the house that she'd shared with Dan when they were first married. Back then, she was constantly locking herself out. She'd learned early on that the slider was her best option for getting in. That's why Dan had eventually wedged a pole in the slider. He figured if it was easy for Whitney to break in, it would be easy for anyone else.

Whitney noticed with glee that they didn't have anything wedged to keep the slider closed. And their lock was similar to the one she and Dan had had. She knew she'd be able to get the door open. The trick was going to be keeping quiet. When she'd been breaking into her own house, she hadn't had to worry about that part.

Taking a deep breath, she gripped the handle and tugged upward. When she felt the lock come loose, she shoved the slider to the left. It caught again, re-latching. She waited a few seconds, staring through the glass. No lights came on. No movement detected.

She tried again.

This time it worked, and she glided the slider open. It squeaked a little. She stood still, held her breath, waiting. Silently praying she hadn't woken anyone.

When the sound of snoring reached Whitney's ears, she heaved a sigh of relief. She took light steps into the family room, keeping her eyes trained on the path in front of her, careful not to bump into something or kick something over. After getting this far, she couldn't afford to screw anything up.

An overpowering floral scent clung to everything in the room. It caused a tickle to form in her throat. She clamped her mouth closed, forced her breath through her nose. The last thing she needed was to start coughing.

Since the blinds weren't closed all the way, light from the back porch streamed in. Whitney was grateful for that as she made her way toward the hallway. It got darker when she rounded the corner, but her eyes had adjusted enough that she could still see a little bit. She studied the row of framed pictures on the wall as she passed them. Wedding, baby, family photos. No one that looked like Lauren.

It seemed unfathomable that they had anything to do with Amelia being missing. But the girls had definitely entered the house. Amelia had been here. Deep in her gut, Whitney knew this house held the answers. And she wasn't leaving until she had them.

There was a bedroom to her left. The door was open, so she slipped inside.

A guest room. Empty. Clean. Bed made.

Across from it was a bathroom. Also, empty and clean. Smelled slightly of bleach and Windex. Little rose-shaped soaps sat out on the counter, still in their wrappers, reminding her of her childhood. Her mom had kept similar ones in her bathroom. Shaking off the nostalgia clinging to her, she returned to the hallway.

The next bedroom must've belonged to the elderly couple. Snores slipped through the door that was slightly ajar. Pressing her palm against it, Whitney pushed it open enough to fit her body through. In the dim moonlight, she scanned the walls. Her heart stopped at a figure standing across from her. She sucked in a breath before realizing it was her own reflection in a full-length mirror. The couple slept soundly in their bed, covers wrapped around their bodies. The woman was curled up in a fetal position facing the wall, while the man slept on his back, his head turned upward.

Whitney made her way to the woman's side. On the nightstand was a wad of crumpled up tissues, a pair of reading glasses, a tattered mystery novel open to the last place she'd read.

There was an ornate chair in the corner, a dress strewn over the top. A dresser was pushed up against the wall.

Again, nothing out of the ordinary.

She headed into the adjoining bathroom. Scanned the vanity, peeked into the tub. The man let out a loud snore and Whitney flinched. Carefully, she backed out of the room, keeping her gaze trained on the couple as they slept in their bed.

At the end of the hallway was an office. An office turned junk room, by the looks of it. A desk carrying an old desktop computer sat against the far wall, directly under a window. The modem had been left on, and it emitted a bright red light that shone through the room. On the other wall was a sewing machine. In the corner was a file cabinet and in the center of the room sat an ironing board. She peeked into the closet, but

it only held some boxes and fabric, sewing supplies, a stack of
printer paper.

Whitney jerked at the sound of a mattress creaking, shifting,
feet shuffling on the ground. A clearing of the throat, a loud
cough. She slipped inside the closet, but she was too claustro-
phobic to close the door all the way.

The sound of a toilet flushing came from the couple's bedroom. More coughing. More throat clearing. Footsteps in the
hallway.

Shit.

Whitney's heartbeat drew attention to itself. She swallowed
hard. Gulped in a tight breath.

The footsteps retreated. She heard a cabinet door opening and
closing. Water turning on. The clink of a cup on the counter
and then footsteps nearing her again.

She slunk back, biting her lip.

The relief she felt was palpable when the footsteps stopped,
and she heard the creak of the mattress again.

Whitney wanted to get the hell out of there, but knew she had
to be patient. Sitting in the closet, she focused on even breathing, as her heart beat out of control. Her skin broke out in a
sweat that made her shudder. Her elbow jabbed the corner of the
box next to her. Since the door was open, a sliver of red light
poured in, revealing the words written on top in black marker.

FOSTER KIDS

She looked up, tuning in. The snoring had returned. Whitney carefully lifted the lid from the box. It was filled with pictures, coloring pages, some old school papers that reminded her
of ones she'd saved of Amelia's. She picked up a few of the pictures, drew them close to her face to try to make out what she
could. They all seemed to be of children.

Had they been foster parents?

The more she discovered in this house, the less guilty they
appeared. Still, she wasn't ready to give up yet.

After crawling out of the closet, she stood up. Her knees cracked with the effort. Internally, she cursed her aging joints.

Hurrying out of the office, she made it back out into the family room. She glanced into the kitchen, at the glass on the counter, half-filled with water. Beyond it was a door which probably led to the garage. It was the only place she hadn't looked.

When she stepped inside the garage, she was blinded. It was pitch-black inside. Feeling along the wall, her finger found a light switch. It had two switches, and her heart stopped. One of them probably opened the garage door. She couldn't afford to click the wrong one.

Reaching into her pocket, she found her phone, yanked it out. Her fingers damp with nerves, she couldn't grip it well, and it slipped from her hand, crashing to the cement floor below. The loud sound reverberated through the air. Drawing in a startled breath, she froze, every muscle in her body tightening. She stayed that way for at least a minute, afraid to move.

Once she was satisfied no one was coming, she slowly lowered herself down to the ground and felt around on the floor. The pads of her fingers slid along the cold cement. When they lighted on something square, she exhaled. Closing her fingers around it, she snatched it up, feeling the screen for cracks. Thankfully because of her protective case, there weren't any. Sliding her fingers over the screen, she turned on the flashlight. It gave her the barest of light. Still, it was enough to see a short distance in front of her. Whitney walked around the garage, letting it light her path.

Not only did these people not have Amelia, they didn't lead very interesting lives either. Their garage was clean and organized. On the shelf on the far wall was toilet paper, paper towels, some gardening tools, clear boxes of Christmas decorations. Two bikes were propped up in the corner. A car sat idly in the center. Running a hand over her hair, Whitney grunted in frustration.

Where was her daughter?

She'd really believed she would find answers here. If not here, where?

Defeated, she slumped back into the house, turning the flashlight off. That overwhelming floral scent returned. She pressed her lips together, as she scanned the room. Her heart stopped. On the other side of the family room was a little hallway, an extra door. She'd missed that before. It could be nothing more than a closet, but she moved toward it swiftly anyway.

Whitney felt eyes on her. Chills skittered up her spine, prickling across her shoulder blades. Turning, her gaze swept the room. She half expected to see the elderly couple standing behind her. But no one was there.

When she swung back around, she saw vacant, glossy eyes, watching her every move.

Dolls. Dozens of them, filling a glass hutch that sat against the wall. Whitney couldn't stop staring at them as she passed. She'd always hated dolls. Even as a little girl, she'd pluck their creepy, hollow eyes out so they couldn't stare at her. These ones had all their eyes intact, and they seemed to follow her as she walked across the room.

Grateful to be out of seeing range from the hutch of dolls, she reached the second hallway. There were two rooms stemming from it. One was to her right. A bathroom. The door was open, and she peeked inside. It was pitch-dark, so she got out her phone again, and holding it tightly against her palm, she turned on the flashlight. It sprayed the yellow light throughout the tiny room. It was a half bath, and it was empty. The door directly in front of her was closed. After peeking over her shoulder, she carefully turned the knob and stepped inside.

Another guest room.

It was empty as well, but there was something about it that made her skin prickle, her heart rate pick up speed. There was a smell, different from the rest of the house. She could feel it. An energy that the other guest room didn't have. It had been occupied recently.

Breath fluttering in her chest, she stepped inside. It was just as dark in here as in the bathroom, so she closed the door behind her and turned the flashlight back on. It was a risk, but she had to take it. If there were answers to be found here, she was determined to find them.

No doubt the police had been here. Looked around. If they hadn't found anything, then this was her only shot. Her only hope.

On high alert for any noises outside of this room, she walked forward. Light bounced around, sweeping up the walls and across the carpet. The bed was neatly made, the room cleaned and vacuumed just like the other rooms.

She was about to hang her head in frustration, when she spotted something small, brown, familiar, sitting on top of the dresser. Snatching it up, she turned it over in her palm. A little hair thing that resembled an old telephone cord. Coiled and round. The same kind Amelia wore in her hair, and around her wrists. She could've sworn she'd seen one or two lining Lauren's wrists, as well.

Lots of people used these kinds of hair bands. Whitney saw them everywhere. But Whitney was positive it didn't belong to the old lady. Her hair was short, curly. Not long enough to fit into a hair band. She felt like it was a clue. That it meant something.

A sound startled her, and she dropped the hair tie.

Silence.

It was probably just the house settling.

But it was getting later, and she was certain the couple would be waking up soon. She peered down at the hair tie, feeling aggravated. So much for a smoking gun. A hair tie proved nothing. Just that someone had at one point been in this house who had long hair.

Abandoning the hair tie, she turned off the flashlight. Her hope disappeared as swiftly as the light did. When she'd first broken in, she was certain she'd find answers here. She no longer had any doubt this was the house that Amelia walked into.

But it still wasn't making any sense.

The couple seemed like good people. There was nothing in the house that seemed suspicious at all. I mean, they took in foster kids for God's sake.

She froze, thinking.

Or did they?

Recently, she'd read a news article about the police tying a man to a string of kidnappings because of pictures and mementos found in his house. Maybe the box was something more sinister than they wanted people to believe. Perhaps the label didn't reveal the truth.

Tearing out of the room, Whitney stumbled down the hallway, hurrying toward the office. As she passed the couple's bedroom, she was relieved to hear the snoring. She prayed they weren't early risers.

She scooted the box along the ground, bringing it toward the center of the room, where she could see more clearly. After grabbing a handful of the pictures, she leafed through them. A couple of baby pictures. A few school photos. God, she really hoped these had been their foster kids. She tossed the pictures back in, realizing that the answers were most likely in the paperwork. Perhaps she'd find a newspaper article. Didn't criminals like to read up on cases about themselves? If she could prove they were criminals, the police would surely take her seriously. No longer consider Amelia a runaway.

As the pictures fluttered down into the box, one of them caught her attention. Familiarity gripped her. Something about the woman in the photo. Snatching it up, she brought it closer to her face. Got a better look. It was grainy, a little blurred. Three people sitting in a hospital bed—a woman, a baby and a child, probably around six or so.

Whitney knew immediately who they were. Her own former best friend with her two daughters. She remembered the last time they'd bumped into one another, years after their estrangement.

"This is my daughter Lauren."

The little girl with her hair in two unbalanced pigtails smiled up at her.

Whitney stared hard at the picture. What was it doing here? Was this the same girl? The girl that had been in her house. Sat at her kitchen table. Ate her food. Drank her coffee. Spent the night in the room next to hers.

There's no way.

Lauren would be around twenty-four by now. Not seventeen.

Then again, Whitney remembered that the little Lauren she'd met had been small for her age. Looked younger even then. Maybe she still looked younger than her years.

Whitney didn't believe in coincidences. Not this big, anyway. There was no doubt in her mind that Lauren had been here. This photograph was proof. Why would the old couple lie about it?

Her mind was like one of those rides at the fair that spun in circles, sticking her body to the side. It spun with endless questions, round and round, never stopping. Never landing on any answers. Anger surfaced, thinking of how she'd stood on their doorstep unraveling and they stared right into her face telling bald-faced lies. They knew Lauren. She'd been in this house. In their lives.

But then she remembered how genuinely confused they were earlier. Could it be that they didn't know Lauren and Amelia had been here on Friday?

God, there were still so many things she didn't understand. Didn't know.

With every clue came a dead end.

The desperation that had been mounting since Amelia first went missing burned bright, a lit cigarette crackling down to a pile of ash.

Her gaze lowered to the picture in her hand, landing on the baby, and her stomach bottomed out.

Oh, God. If Amelia's Lauren was the same girl in this picture, then this wasn't simply a case of teenagers who ran away.

This was revenge.

29

I WOKE UP in a hospital bed the next morning. Millie had called 911 when she couldn't feel a pulse. According to the doctors, she saved my life. If she had waited, I could've died. I felt stupid. Everyone thought I'd been trying to kill myself, Millie included. But that wasn't it. I was only trying to get Millie to see me. To see that I was hurting. To see how Mitch was tearing us apart.

But mostly to see how evil he was.

I thought if she was forced to choose me, she would.

If his actions were destroying me, she'd have no choice but to let him go, right?

I figured she'd be so angry she would refuse to talk to him. Better yet, I'd hoped she'd tell her parents or even the police. If Mitch got caught giving drugs to minors he could go to jail. Then he'd surely be out of our lives for good.

But that's not how it went down.

Millie turned in my two remaining pills, and my mom recognized them as the ones missing from her medicine cabinet. And, lo and behold, I was right, they were pain pills. And sometimes my mom did take two. But never three, or more. And never with alcohol. I guess it was the perfect storm.

I'd miscalculated, and almost killed myself. Worse, it was all for nothing.

30

THE GRAININESS OF the photo and the fact that it had been taken from more than a few feet away made it impossible to see anything close-up. If it had been a digital picture, Whitney could have zoomed in.

Tucking the photo into her pocket, she secured the lid back on the box and pushed it into the closet. She wanted to march right into the couple's room and demand to know what their connection to this photo was, but that would be stupid. The only one getting in trouble in that scenario would be her.

Feeling along the wall, she made it to the edge of the hallway. When the toe of her shoe hit something, her gaze lowered to the floor. A discarded pen, a logo stamped on it. It was getting a little lighter outside, and she was able to make out the words, even from this vantage point.

Dollar Dayz Inn.

Her temperature rose. Was that right or was she seeing things? She lowered herself, picked it up. Read the words again.

Dollar Dayz Inn, just like she'd thought.

Whitney knew the place. Right off the freeway. Near where Whitney used to live.

Where Lauren grew up.

Adding the pen to the growing collection in her pocket, she stood so quickly all the blood rushed to her head. She was momentarily dizzy, so she clutched the edge of the couch until it subsided.

Then she raced out the back door. Once outside, she let out a long, slow, relieved exhale.

Cool air circled her, carrying with it the smell of damp grass, bark and flowers. She made her way across the back lawn and out to the street. A dog barked. Tires buzzed on the asphalt. A light shone from somewhere on the street. Head down, Whitney sprinted to the park.

Once inside her car, she turned on the ignition and gunned it out of the parking lot. The motel was at least twenty minutes away, and she was getting impatient.

As she sped down the street, she had the fleeting thought that maybe this was nothing more than a wild-goose chase—but then again, better chasing something than nothing.

SUNDAY, 6:00 A.M.

The motel looked even worse than Whitney remembered. She didn't think it was possible for it to become sketchier, but somehow it had. Her stomach turned at the idea that Amelia might be here. Sitting in her car, Whitney scanned the lot, her gaze resting on the motel office. Her first instinct was to go in there and ask if either Lauren or Amelia had checked in here. Now that she was pretty sure she knew Lauren's last name she could use that. But then she thought better of it.

There was no way the staff would willingly give out that information, and it might alert Lauren that she was here.

No, she'd have better luck asking around to the tenants. It was early, but she figured somebody was bound to be awake. A picture was all she needed. She didn't have one of Lauren. The one in her pocket didn't count.

But she had plenty of Amelia.

She took out her phone and pulled up her favorite one.

Phone in hand, she got out of her car, locked it tight. A couple of guys stood outside one of the rooms downstairs, smoking. Hesitating, she hovered at the edge of her car, a dark figure hidden in the shadows. They didn't look like guys she should be talking to in an empty motel parking lot. There was no one to witness if she got hurt…or worse. No one to step in and help if things went awry. Biting her lip, she peered down at the photo in her hand. There was a possibility that Amelia was somewhere in this motel. Whitney had to do whatever it took to find her. Lifting her chin, she urged her legs to walk forward in their direction.

The minute she reached them, she forced herself to talk, afraid if she waited, she'd lose her nerve. "Hey." The word she chose was casual, confident, but her wobbly voice betrayed how nervous she was.

They didn't respond with a friendly greeting of their own, just stared blankly.

It rattled her, but she wouldn't allow herself to back down. "Um…I'm looking for my daughter." Holding up her phone, it shook in her hands. With her other hand, she pointed at Amelia. "You wouldn't happen to have seen her, would you?"

"No," one of them said without even looking at the picture. His steely gaze took in the parking lot behind her as he stuck the tip of the cigarette in his mouth. The other end crackled, the blaze a bold orange, flickering against the black sky.

Whitney shivered.

The other one, squinted, moved in closer. "Um…you know, I might have. Earlier today. I think she was with that other girl." He snapped his large fingers, nudged his friend. "The one that's staying upstairs." His friend shook his head, clearly not wanting to be involved.

Whitney stood up taller, leaned in. "Was the other girl dark haired? Kinda tall? Glasses?"

"Yeah, yeah, that sounds like her," he said, drawing his cigarette to his lips.

"Oh, thank you." Whitney hugged her phone to her chest. She was so close she could feel it. Her gaze flickered to the stairs. "You said she was staying upstairs. Do you happen to know what room?"

The rude guy shook his head, muttered something unintelligible. The friendlier guy shook his head too.

It was clear that was all she was getting out of them. Still, it was something. Even more than she'd been expecting.

"Thank you," she said again, before scurrying off, grateful to be able to put distance between herself and them.

She ascended the stairs, her feet clanging against the metal steps. It was a jolting, glaring sound against the silence. The freeway was near, so during the day it was probably loud. But now only an occasional car went by. The motel lights flickered. No one was outside upstairs, and Whitney's heart sank.

There were at least a dozen rooms. How would she figure out which one Lauren was in?

Maybe it was time to call the police, to fill them in on what she knew. It was something she only contemplated a moment before realizing how dumb it was. She'd have to admit how she knew. How she'd broken into that house.

And that wasn't all she'd have to confess to. If Lauren was who she thought, she'd have to finally come clean about everything she'd done. She wasn't ready for that yet. First, she had to find Amelia, and then she'd deal with the consequences. Once she knew Amelia was safe, she'd confess to all her past sins. She'd accept any punishment she needed to.

A cool breeze whisked over her. Shuddering, she hugged herself. Glancing at each door as she passed it, she wondered if Amelia was on the other side. So close, and yet still impossibly far. She wanted to scream out Amelia's name, but knew that would be stupid. The need to do something drastic clawed at her insides like a trapped cat.

She was exhausted.

All she wanted was to find Amelia and go home. Put this whole thing behind them. But she knew it wouldn't go down like that. Even once Amelia was found, this wasn't over. Not by a long shot.

And that made Whitney even more exhausted. She could feel the tiredness seep into her bones as she continued past all the upstairs motel rooms. When she'd reached the last one, a woman stepped out. She wore flannel pajama bottoms, a ripped T-shirt. Her copper hair was pulled up into a messy bun and in her hand she held a pack of cigarettes and a lighter.

At the sight of Whitney, her eyes widened.

"What?" she snapped in a defensive tone. She drew a cigarette out of the pack and stuck it between her dry lips.

"I'm sorry. I didn't mean to startle you," Whitney said, in her most apologetic voice. "It's just…my daughter is missing." The lady's expression softened then, her eyes crinkling at the corners. Relief flowed through Whitney's chest. "I'm so worried. I think she might be staying here. And um…" She held out her phone. "I wonder if maybe you've seen her?"

The lady lit her cigarette. Then she narrowed her eyes, moving in closer. She studied the picture for a minute. Whitney held her breath.

"Yeah, actually, I have seen her."

Whitney's pulse jumpstarted. "Really?"

"Yeah, she and the other girl left like a half hour ago."

"A half hour ago? You're sure?" Her heart sank. She'd been so close.

"Yeah, cause that's what time my boyfriend left and I walked him out."

"Do you know where they went?" It was a long shot, but Whitney had to ask.

"I overheard them saying they were on their way to visit their mom. Wait. Is that you? Guess you guys had a mix-up or something."

Heat shot up Whitney's spine.

Her sister.

Their mom.

She knew exactly where they'd gone.

And it wasn't far.

31

AFTER MY OVERDOSE, I wasn't allowed to see Millie anymore.

At the time it seemed ridiculous. It's easier for me to understand now. I actually get why my parents kept us apart.

If I were in their shoes, I would do the same thing.

But in that moment, it felt like they'd destroyed my life. Taken away the thing that mattered most to me.

For the next six months or so, Millie and I found ways to interact. We'd sneak phone calls. Talk at school. If the subject of boys came up, she was vague. She never talked about Mitch.

But then she got pregnant and dropped out. That's how I knew she'd chosen him over me again.

The phone calls became scarcer and then stopped altogether.

My parents forced me to go to therapy. I know they expected me to talk about Kevin's death. That's how they justified my actions. The lying. Manipulating. Using drugs. Trying to kill myself. I was acting out because I'd lost my brother.

And maybe they were right. At least partially, anyway. Kevin's life and death had definitely affected me. His illness had permeated every aspect of our family. There wasn't a day, a moment, even, that wasn't affected by it. It consumed my parents while he was alive, and certainly after he died.

That's why I missed my life with Millie. A life that had nothing to do with Kevin. A life that was all mine.

It was the loss of Millie that I felt deep in my bones. That made me depressed. And it's what I'd planned to talk to Dr. Carter about. But when he stared at me with that expectant look on his face, pen poised over his yellow steno pad, I opened my mouth and told an entirely different story.

One that wasn't even mine.

I told him about the darkness that haunted me day and night. About the boy I fell in love with who bruised my skin and ripped at my heart. Who supplied me with drugs, and isolated me from my friends. I told the story so many times—to Dr. Carter, Dan, my parents—that eventually it stopped being Millie's and became mine.

It lived inside of me, taking on a life of its own. Fusing to my bones, attaching to my heart. Becoming real. True. Something I believed.

32

THE ROAD WAS winding, trees lining the sides, bending to meet in the middle, a canopy shading the street. It was beautiful over here in this part of town. Large custom homes with sweeping, wraparound porches. As a child, Whitney wished she'd lived over here.

As an adult, she'd come here many times.

Always to visit Lauren's mom.

Whitney wasn't surprised when she first found out Lauren's mom was here. Whitney always thought she deserved to be somewhere pretty. Elegant. She'd always hoped for the best for her, even if it had to be this way.

From a little ways off, Whitney spotted them. Lauren and Amelia standing outside on the grass. Moisture sprung to her eyes, her lips quivering. Amelia was alive. Safe. Her entire body was flooded with relief, joints and muscles instantly relaxing. Her chest expanded, and that funny fluttering feeling finally waned.

After parking along the curb, she wanted nothing more than

to tear out of the car, run to her daughter. Draw Amelia into her arms. Hold her close. Never let her go.

But that wasn't possible.

Not anymore.

Whitney had worked so hard to find her, but now that she had, she was at a loss for what to do. The tears continued to flow. If Amelia was here of her own volition, it meant that Lauren had told her the truth.

About Whitney. About Amelia, and who she really was.

Staring through the smudged glass of her car window, she watched the girls standing over their mother's grave. Sisters. Together at long last.

Lauren stared down at her mother's gravestone, feeling the swell in her chest like an ocean wave cresting and then falling. It was surreal, standing here with her sister.

Most of Lauren's childhood was a blur. Hazy at best. Muddled memories. Days blending together. Little snapshots—the places they'd lived, the yards she'd played in, her mom's voice, familiar scents, the little stuffed monkey she'd slept with. But there were a few memories that stood out. Days and moments she recalled with stark clarity. Like when she met her sister for the first time. Her mom had left her overnight. That was probably the first reason she remembered it so well. Up until that point, she'd never spent a night without her mom. It was scary, not having her there. What if she'd had a nightmare? No way would her dad comfort her. He barely looked in her direction, and she didn't think he'd ever hugged her.

That night, she'd slept coiled up in her bed, her little stuffed monkey pressed to her chest, and prayed for morning to come quickly.

When the sun had finally come up, her dad took her to the hospital. It was a crowded place with beeping machines, phones ringing, doctors in lab coats and nurses in white whisking past them. Carts being wheeled on the linoleum, women walking slowly down the hallway in hospital gowns, attached to wires and poles, people dressed in regular clothes holding flowers and cards.

Her stomach felt funny like that time she ate way too much candy the day after Halloween. But her dad didn't like when she whined or acted afraid, so she held her head high and continued to follow him.

Once she saw her mom, her fears faded. Her mom looked tired, sitting in the hospital bed wearing a white gown, her hair messy, her face pale and sweaty. But she also looked beautiful. Happy. That may have been the other reason Lauren remembered the day so well. She'd rarely seen her mom that happy before.

Her baby sister was asleep in a glass bed with wheels. When she stirred, making a tiny, squeaking noise, Lauren's mom scooped her out. She had a pink blanket wrapped tightly around her body, only her head visible. Lauren joked that she looked like a baby burrito. Her mom laughed. Her dad didn't.

Lauren was allowed to climb up on the bed with her mom so she could get a better look at the baby. It didn't look like much. A bald head. Scrunched up face. Wrinkled skin. She didn't think the baby was that cute.

Her mom told her to be careful and not to touch the baby. Said she could get sick. Lauren was getting bored. Restless. She'd been so excited to meet the baby, but now it wasn't that exciting. She didn't want to leave, though, because that meant she'd have to leave her mom. So she kept sitting there. Kept staring at the baby as she did nothing.

And that's when something magical happened.

The baby started crying, writhing around, stretching her neck from one side to the other. When the baby's neck turned all the way to the left, Lauren saw it. A birthmark, identical to the one she had on her own neck.

It made her feel special. All fuzzy inside. Almost like she and her sister already had their own little secret. Just between them.

She didn't say anything then.

But on the day of her sister's funeral, she wished she had, because when she peeked into the tiny casket, that baby's neck was white, pale, clean, no markings of any kind.

Turning her head now, Lauren took in Amelia's profile in the moonlight. A breeze kicked up, the hair brushing away from Amelia's neck, revealing the tan edge of a pear-shaped birthmark.

33

YEARS PASSED, BUT I never forgot about Millie. I stopped drinking and smoking pot. I graduated from high school, then Dan and I went away to college together. My parents were so proud of me in those days. It scared me sometimes. I'd always wanted them to see me. To notice me, the way I felt they did Kevin. But I'd mistaken pity for love. Kevin needed my parents and they were there for him, giving and giving. I thought I wanted that, too, until I had it. Their pity. Their sympathy. Their stolen worried glances.

I wasn't fragile.

I wasn't broken.

I was strong and accomplished, and not because I'd overcome so much, but because I just was. They never saw it. Not then, and not now.

To them, I'm always one bad event away from falling apart.

There were times when I was exhausted with trying to play the part. Be the person Dan and my parents thought I was.

But there wasn't an alternative. I'd lived a lie for so long, I didn't know how to live the truth.

One time, when Dan and I were visiting home from college, we ran into Millie at the grocery store. She had a toddler in her shopping cart. It was odd to see her grown-up, food shopping with a kid. I knew she was still with Mitch before she even said anything. It was clear by how gaunt she was, how skittish she seemed. Her eyes kept darting around like Mitch would show up and find out she was talking to us. There was also a slight discoloration on her cheek as if a bruise was fading.

I pulled her aside, asked if I could take her out for coffee or lunch. She hesitated momentarily, but then agreed to meet me at a coffee shop the next morning while her daughter was in preschool.

When she showed up the next morning, there was a fresh bruise on her arm. I noticed it when she brought her coffee cup to her lips, causing her sleeve to slip down her arm. Not wanting to draw attention to it, I averted my eyes.

Millie was a lot like I remembered her. Magnetic, but guarded. Careful with her words. Our conversation was shallow. The weather. Old friends of ours. The past. Anytime I tried to press her about her present, about Mitch or being a mom, she found a way to divert, redirect, distract. She had it down to a science.

Not that she needed to spell it out. It was clear to me how she was. I could see it in the paleness of her cheeks, the greasiness of her hair and the blue rings around her eyes. I saw it in the way she pulled at her sleeves. In the way her hands perpetually trembled. The continuous licking of her dry lips. And in how jumpy she was every time a grinder went off behind the coffee bar, or a person laughed or talked too loud.

Finally, I couldn't help myself.

"You don't have to stay with him, you know?"

"God, you haven't changed at all." She let out a bitter, raspy laugh. "Why can't you ever mind your own business?"

"I'm just trying to help." I caught her gaze with mine. "Then and now." She frowned. "Millie, I'm so sorry about everything that happened back then."

She shook her head, waved away my words. "That was a long time ago, Whit."

"Are things different now? Better...with Mitch?"

She glanced out the window, her eyes sad. "Yes and no, I guess. I mean, he still has a temper, but most of the time things are good." She shifted in her chair, hugged herself.

I knew it was all I'd get out of her. She wouldn't admit anything more. Not to me.

As we sat there in that coffee shop, I tried to imagine if our lives had turned out differently. If I had never tried to trick Mitch into hurting me or taken all those pills, would we have remained friends? Would her relationship with Mitch have fizzled out all on its own? Would I have won and Mitch lost?

I'll never know.

Either way, that night back then seemed to seal her fate.

I didn't see Millie again until after Dan and I were married. It was right around the time I got pregnant. We were visiting my parents for a few days before Christmas when we ran into both Millie and Mitch at the mall. It was so awkward.

We made painful small talk: How old was their little girl? Did they still live around here? What had they been up to?

And on their end: When had we gotten married? How was that going? Were we finished with school? Working?

It hurt, talking with Millie like this. Acquaintances. Former friends. Mitch eyed me suspiciously the whole conversation.

Missing her caused an ache to spread through me. So many years had passed. An ocean separating us. And yet, I wasn't ready to let her go completely. I needed to. I knew that. Dan and I were talking about having children. Buying a house. Grown-up things.

Millie wasn't part of that equation.

She was simply a portion of my past. A small blip in my history. But even as I thought that, I knew it wasn't true. She'd been a huge part of my existence. Had shaped me. Turned me into the person I was. And yeah, maybe I'd made it larger in my mind—what we had, what we'd been to each other—but maybe that's because I'd never had closure.

We'd been so close and then in one fell swoop we'd been cut from each other's lives. I thought what we needed was one more night together. One last hurrah if you will.

So that night, while Dan slept soundly in my childhood bedroom at my parents' house, I snuck out and went to Millie's. I'd been shocked to find out when we spoke at the mall that she lived with Mitch in the same exact apartment he'd once shared with Greg. How had Millie's life stayed frozen in time, when mine had blasted full speed ahead? Dan was the soundest sleeper I'd ever met. And he never got up in the night, so I wasn't worried about getting caught. As long as I got home by early morning, he'd never find out.

When I arrived at the apartment, I was glad to see it didn't look at all like I'd remembered. Millie had added her own touches. A floral painting here and there. Family portraits. Fresh flowers on the end table. A pink throw blanket on the couch. The most distinct difference, though, was that it was clean. Smelled feminine.

Mitch wasn't happy to see me, but Millie was. For a little while he hung out with us, a brooding, dark shadow in the corner, just like old times. But thankfully, he finally went to bed, and Millie and I sat up all night talking in her living room. She poured us cheap vodka and I puffed on a couple of cigarettes even though it had been ages since I'd had one. It was like old times. Even down to how guarded she was. I knew she had to be careful about what she said. Mitch could be listening to every word. I was careful, too, with the questions I asked.

When I left, I honestly thought that would be the last time I saw her. I held her tight, whispered in her ear. Something about how if she ever needed me, I'd be there.

Her eyes shone as I stepped away from the door, and I knew then that she never planned to contact me. I turned away, a lump in my throat and hurried toward my car. I'd almost reached it when Dan stepped out of the shadows. After gasping, I asked what the hell he was doing there.

Dan's gaze slid past me to the apartment I came out of and he said, "I can't believe you."

There was no convincing him I hadn't slept with Mitch. In his mind, Mitch was the ex I couldn't get over. He kept saying that he always knew my heart belonged to someone else. That he'd always felt someone else in the room, standing between us, a beating heart, a heavy breath.

He wasn't wrong about that part.

My heart had always partially belonged to someone else. Just not the person he thought.

34

LAUREN HAD ALWAYS believed in her memory of that birthmark. It was something she remembered so vividly. It was real. Tangible. Not something she'd made up. She was sure of it.

Her entire life, she'd dreamed of the little girl with milky white skin, puffy cheeks, wide eyes, the pear-shaped tan birthmark on her neck. In her dreams, the child appeared to her at various ages. An infant, a toddler, elementary school–aged. Every time, she'd want to play a game of hide-and-seek. Lauren would cover her face with her hands and count, sometimes peeking out through her splayed fingers.

The little girl would skip away, find a hiding spot.

But even the nights she cheated and peeked through her fingers, Lauren was unable to find the little girl. She'd search behind couches, inside drawers, under cabinets, in piles of blankets. Desperate, she'd scour every room, and often venture outside. Scaling walls, cutting down bushes, tearing apart plants. But in the end, all she was left with was emptiness.

Lauren would awaken to her own screams, skin dampened with cold sweat, pulse ricocheting through her veins.

In her dreams, Lauren never found her.

But in real life, she had.

It was last year right before Lauren's grandma passed away. Her grandma had been living in an old folks' home, and Lauren had gone to visit her. She'd only seen her grandma a couple of times as a young child. When she'd gone into foster care, her grandma never contacted her; as an adult, she had to assume that CPS had notified her family, and the old hag had rejected her. But for some reason, on her deathbed, her grandmother had finally reached out. Wanted to find redemption in her final moments, Lauren guessed. At first Lauren had only gone to tell her off, to make her feel bad about not taking Lauren in when she was younger. But the old woman had been so frail, so sickly, that Lauren lost her nerve. Besides, she was the only person she could talk to about her mom. And she'd been aching to learn more about the woman she'd loved so fiercely and missed so much.

Her grandma had shared a few photo albums with Lauren. They were the kind with plastic over the photos and the little spots to write in captions. Flipping through one, Lauren came upon pictures of her mom as a teenager. Her mom had always been so beautiful. In several of the pictures, she was with a friend. Next to them in cursive handwriting it read: *Millie and Whitney. BFFs.*

"Do you remember Mom's friend Whitney?" she'd asked her grandma, pointing out the picture. Her grandmother was sitting propped up in her bed, knitted blanket wrapped around her shoulders. Her eyes were glazed and watery, her mouth trembling, drool pooling at the corner as she studied the photograph.

Yes. Whitney Lewis. I'll never forget her. Her grandma's voice took on a dark quality. *She ruined your mother's life.*

As her grandma had tried to relay the story to Lauren, it was hard to follow, but one thing was clear: Lauren's interest was piqued. She'd wanted to know more about this woman who had once been her mom's best friend.

And her interest had grown further when she found her mom's journal. It was filled with stories of her mom's former best friend.

So she'd hopped on Facebook, and searched for Whitney Lewis. She was going by Whitney Carter now, but had listed Lewis as her maiden name, so she was easy enough to find. Lauren hadn't really known what she'd hoped to discover on Whitney's account. But nothing could've prepared her for the truth. She'd been stunned when she came upon a close-up, profile shot of Whitney's daughter wearing a swim cap, her neck exposed, revealing the same tan birthmark Lauren had.

Amelia yawned, her eyes glazed over as she stared down at the grave site. Lauren felt bad about having to wake Amelia up so early but she wanted to get a jumpstart on their trip. She was certain Whitney was searching for them. Possibly the police, as well.

"You ready?" Lauren asked.

Amelia nodded.

When they'd first come up with this road trip idea, Amelia had been much more excited. Today she was subdued. Almost regretful. Clearly, she was having second thoughts. And Lauren shouldn't have been surprised. Not after the DNA results came back inconclusive yesterday. Amelia wanted to believe it meant something. She'd even said as much.

Maybe your theory isn't correct, she'd said to Lauren, a hopeful lilt in her tone. *Maybe the birthmarks are a coincidence.*

But they weren't. Lauren was right. She was sure of it. The DNA test was only inconclusive because she didn't turn in a cheek swab from Whitney. She'd stolen some hair out of her brush, and taken a cup, hoping they could lift the saliva. But the company said they needed a cheek swab.

Lauren kicked herself for not leaving yesterday. She only waited for the DNA results because she wanted to give Amelia one last chance to decide if she wanted to turn her mom in or not. But she should've known waiting would be a mistake.

"Come on." She nudged Amelia playfully in the side. "If we leave now, we can be at the beach by this afternoon."

Amelia smiled. Lauren figured that would get her. Amelia had chosen Santa Cruz as their first stop. They'd already booked their motel.

"You know, my grandparents live in Santa Cruz," Amelia said, a wistful grin on her face.

Lauren's stomach tightened. "We can't visit them. Not today."

"Can I at least call my dad and let him know I'm okay?"

Lauren shook her head.

"Michael?"

"Don't you mean Phil Lopez?" she joked, and Amelia laughed. "I still can't believe your mom didn't put that together. Hard Knocks is a pretty popular band."

"If they weren't around in the '90s, my mom's never heard of them," Amelia said, smiling, as if she was proud of herself for keeping this secret from her mom.

Lauren thought about all the secrets she'd been forced to keep. Back when her dad was alive, she kept them to protect herself from his wrath. From his explosive temper and fast-flying fists. And then later on in foster care she had to hide things from the other kids, and some of the grubby-handed foster care parents.

Prior to meeting Amelia, she couldn't imagine a life where the biggest secret you kept was that your boyfriend went by the name of his favorite singer in your contacts. But ever since they'd gotten close, she'd caught a glimpse of a better life. One with a family. A sister. A trusted friend.

It was the reason she'd altered her original plan. When she first came to town, she'd been hell-bent on one thing: revenge. She wanted to make Whitney pay for what she'd stolen from Lauren. But then Lauren became friends with Amelia, and realized that she could have something better, more satisfying than revenge. She could have a family. A sister. A trusted friend.

That's why a few weeks ago, she'd come clean.

It was evening, the sun a bright orange like a flame burning out. The air had cooled, but still held some warmth to it. They sat side by side on the edge of the pool at Amelia's apartment complex. Next to them sat their discarded sandals. Their calves were submerged in the water. A few feet away, a young woman dried off her two little boys.

"Come on. Time for Mommy to make dinner," she said in a singsong voice, which was barely audible over her son's screaming tantrum. "Daddy will be home soon."

Lauren was beyond relieved when the mom was able to corral her children and get them the heck out of the pool area. His screams got gradually quieter until they disappeared altogether. She didn't envy that mom at all.

The smell of chlorine was thick, cloying. Amelia kicked her legs upward, and water sprayed in the air. Earlier Amelia had wanted to swim, but Lauren didn't bring a suit and despite Amelia's offer she knew she'd never fit into one of hers. So, they'd opted to simply stick their feet in.

Silence spun around them, the pool area empty.

An urgent feeling pressed on Lauren's chest, reminding her this was the perfect time. They were alone. No Whitney. No screaming children.

Since before she'd even met Amelia, she'd fantasized about this moment. How she'd break the news. Lauren had watched dozens of clips online of people being reunited with long-lost family members. They were cheesy, and overdramatic with a lot of tears. The kind of thing Lauren would make fun of if she'd watched with friends. Being raised the way she had been taught her to be tough. Never show weakness.

Despite that, she'd teared up watching those clips.

And as she sat by the pool with Amelia, she realized that deep down she wanted that cheesy dramatic reunion, complete with tears, sniffles and hugs.

That revelation alone almost made her keep quiet.

Growing up, her friends had often accused her of being a pessimist, to which she'd retort, *No, I'm a realist.*

She wasn't the type to get her hopes up. So, why was she doing that now?

Amelia drew her legs out of the water, placing her feet on the ground, her knees bent. Lauren's chest tightened further.

It's now or never.

"Hey!" The word burst out of Lauren's mouth at a way higher decibel than she'd anticipated. It was like turning on a car after someone else had been in it and not realizing that they'd been blasting the music. Amelia flinched, clearly startled. Lauren lowered her volume, dialing it way down. "I um…I've been…" she scratched the back of her neck, suddenly itchy all over as if she had plunged into the pool and the chlorine had stuck to her flesh "…um…wanting to show you something for a while now."

Amelia adjusted her position, turning slightly in Lauren's direction and hugging her knees to her chest. "Okaaay." She dragged out the word with a note of apprehension.

Lauren didn't blame her. It was definitely a weird segue. She didn't remember any of the people on the clips she'd watched starting their conversations this way. Maybe what she was missing was a camera crew, and a script. *Yes, that's what she needed. Lines to follow. Preferably written by someone else.*

It was too late for that. She swallowed thickly.

She tugged the hair tie off her wrist. Reaching up, she scooped her hair off her neck, fashioning it into a ponytail at the top of her head. Then she craned her neck, exposing the right side.

Amelia sucked in a breath. "Oh, my God. That's so weird. You have the same birthmark as me." She brushed her hair back, revealing hers.

"I know," Lauren said, facing her. It felt good to have her

thick hair off her neck and back. Normally, she sported a ponytail, but up until now she couldn't do that around Amelia.
When Amelia's face scrunched up in a look of confusion, Lauren continued, "'Cause we're related."

"What are you talking about?"

Lauren thought she'd ease Amelia in, but now she wished
she'd just ripped the Band-Aid off. We're related? Really? That
sounded so stupid. It could mean anything. Distant cousins, even.

"We're sisters," she blurted out.

Surprising her, Amelia laughed. "Oh, my God. I totally
thought you were serious for a minute." She stood, her legs already dry.

Lauren's were still in the water. She hoisted them out and then
scrambled to stand too. Liquid ran down her calves, pooled at
her ankles.

Amelia slipped on her sandals. "What do you wanna do tonight? Maybe watch a mo—"

"I *am* serious," Lauren interrupted, knowing if she didn't finish this conversation now she'd lose her nerve. They'd go upstairs, watch a movie, make some food and pretty soon they'd
be past the point of no return. It would be like that time she
called the new girl at school Patty for several weeks before another friend corrected her, telling her the girl's name was Addie.
By then, she felt like she was in too deep, and proceeded to call
her Patty for the rest of the year.

Amelia looked up from her shoes. "It's just a birthmark, Lauren," she practically whispered.

"No, it's not." She explained it all then. About the baby with
the matching birthmark, and how the baby who died didn't
have one. And then she told her about finding Whitney on social media and discovering Amelia. With each measured word,
Amelia created more distance between them. By the time she
finished, Amelia was several feet away, her eyes wide with disbelief. Or maybe it was terror.

Either way, her reaction was nothing like the clips Lauren had watched.

Where were the tears? The hugs? The squeals of delight?

"No." Amelia shook her head. "There's no way. You've got it all wrong."

"I don't," Lauren said firmly. "I know I'm right. You're my sister."

"Stop saying that." Amelia reached for the latch on the gate behind her. "Just leave me alone." She swung the gate open so hard, it crashed against the side. Amelia took off running.

"Dammit." Lauren shoved her feet into her sandals, stabbing her big toe into the straps in the process. "Amelia, wait!" she hollered, running after her. There was no way she could leave it like this. If she did, Amelia might tell Whitney.

And Lauren couldn't let that happen.

So, she chased her down, forced her to listen. Amelia still didn't believe Lauren that day, but she at least agreed to a DNA test. And more than that, she agreed to keep all of it between the two of them for the time being.

But one thing had been very clear to Lauren: Amelia loved Whitney, no matter what. Even if she could prove that Amelia was her sister—prove that Whitney had kidnapped her—she wasn't sure that Amelia would ever be comfortable turning her in to the police. And Lauren already loved Amelia too much to make her do it.

The road trip idea was one the girls had brainstormed together. Lauren could never let Amelia know how she'd funded the trip, though. She'd be so upset.

Lauren pulled into the apartment complex and drove around the lot. When she passed Whitney's space, she found it empty, just like she thought she would. Amelia had mentioned her mom would be on a date tonight. But Lauren needed to be sure.

Driving back out onto the street, she parked along the curb. After turning off the car, she stepped out, securing her purse on her shoulder.

She waited for a break in traffic and then ran across in her tennis shoes. It wasn't until she got to the stairs that she remembered.

Reaching into her purse, she pulled out her glasses, stuck them on her face. Then she unfastened her hair tie, allowing her hair to fall down her back and shoulders. Slipping her hair tie on her wrist, she started making her way up the stairs.

She had to stop a couple of times to regain her balance. The glasses caused her to feel slightly disoriented, her spatial awareness impaired. Usually, she tried to wear them for a little while before coming over to get used to them. Tonight, she'd been so impatient she'd almost forgotten them entirely.

Stay focused, Lauren, she chastised herself.

Once she reached the front door, she smoothed her hair down around her neck, pasted on a smile and knocked.

She heard movement inside almost immediately, but the door didn't open. To her left, Amelia's eyes peeked through the blinds. When she saw it was Lauren, the blinds clicked back in place and the front door popped open.

"Lauren! Hi. I wasn't expecting you," she said, her tone happy and a grin on her face.

"Hey." Lauren matched her smile. "My mom was out, and I remember you saying your mom was going out, so I thought I'd stop by. I hope it's okay. I probably should've called first, huh?"

"No, it's fine. I'm just chillin', anyway." Amelia ushered her inside.

A blanket was tossed on the couch, a bowl of popcorn beside it. The television was paused in the middle of what looked like a rom-com movie.

"Millie's chillin'," she said in a singsong way.

"Millie?" Amelia raised a brow.

Lauren nudged her with her elbow. "Yeah, it's a nickname for Amelia, right?"

"I guess. It's just that no one's ever really called me by a nickname before."

"Then it can be our thing," Lauren said, even though she didn't re-

ally want it to be. She didn't want to call Amelia that. She just wanted to see the look on Whitney's face when she did.

"What will I call you?" Amelia asked.

Lauren shrugged. "There's not really any good nickname for Lauren."

"Challenge accepted." Amelia smiled, her gaze flickering over to the paused TV. "I was watching The Kissing Booth, but we can watch something else if you want."

Romance movies had never been Lauren's thing, but she could tell Amelia wanted to finish watching it. And, really, she'd been the one to barge in. "No, it's fine. That sounds fun."

"Cool. Can I get you anything?"

"Nah, I'm good."

"Okay." Amelia made her way back to the couch. Scooping up the blanket, she sat down, setting it in her lap. "I can share my blanket if you want. And help yourself to some popcorn."

"Thanks." Lauren sat beside her as she unpaused the movie.

Lauren didn't take her up on the blanket offer but did take a handful of the popcorn. She didn't come here to watch a movie, but she made the most of it. Leaning back on the couch, she chewed popcorn and watched some teenage girl pine away over an older boy.

After about a half an hour, she was getting restless. She'd come here for a purpose and she wasn't sure how much time she had left. Whitney could come home at any time. "Um…I'm just gonna use the restroom," she said.

"Okay." Amelia reached for the remote. "You want me to pause it?"

"No, you go ahead and finish. I've seen it before," she lied.

"Oh, you should've told me. We could've watched something else."

"It's cool. I rewatch movies all the time." Another lie.

Amelia nodded, then turned her attention back to the TV.

Lauren scooted off the couch and made her way down the hallway. Going into the bathroom, she clicked the door closed. *What now?*

She opened the door, trying not to make any noise, and tiptoed to the edge of the hall. Amelia was engrossed in the movie.

This was her window.

Lauren crept across the hall into Whitney's room. She wasted no time, running straight to the middle drawer of the dresser. She'd found this envelope filled with cash when she was in here trying to find something to use for the DNA test.

"Lauren?" Amelia's voice rang out.

After shoving the money into her pocket, she whipped around, heart hammering in her ears.

Amelia stood in the doorway, eyebrows raised. "What's going on?"

"Um…I uh…I started my period and I don't have anything…you know."

"Oh, you should have just asked. I'll go grab you something." Amelia smiled and skipped off, leaving a sour taste in Lauren's mouth. She hated lying to Amelia.

But she hadn't had a choice. That money in the envelope, along with the money Amelia had in her bank account, was enough to keep them going for at least a month.

After that, they could decide what to do.

The truth was that, as badly as Lauren wanted Whitney to pay for what she did, she knew that if Whitney was arrested, Amelia wouldn't be able to stay with Lauren. She'd probably end up with her dad or grandparents or something. So, she planned to make the most of this time with her newfound sister. Her family.

35

AMELIA STARED DOWN at the gravestone. Weird how an entire life could be relegated to nothing more than a slab of concrete, a name crudely etched into it. Birth and death dates below. A few kind words—"Devoted wife and mother." Like that was all that mattered. Like that was all Millie did that deserved recognition.

She'd been a living, breathing person. Had been on this earth for twenty-plus years, and this was all she'd left.

Cemeteries had always freaked Amelia out. The thought of ending up here, buried deep in the soil with the worms and insects, made her skin crawl. She shivered, ran her hands up her arms. Sniffed.

Lauren threw her a sympathetic look, draped an arm over her shoulder. She felt bad then. Lauren had misread her reaction, clearly thinking she was sad. And she was kind of. This place made her feel that way, but it had nothing to do with Millie. Not personally, anyway. As much as Lauren believed Millie was

Amelia's mom, to Amelia she was nothing more than a stranger. A woman she'd never met.

It was creepy that this was the way they were being introduced.

Hello, slab of concrete. I might be your daughter. Nice to meet you.

If anyone had told her two months ago that this was where her friendship with Lauren would lead, she wouldn't have believed them. Meeting Lauren had felt random. Not calculated. They'd met in the most natural way. A party at Michael's.

Lauren had come with Craig, one of Michael's friends. Amelia had been relieved when she arrived. Up until that point, she'd been the only girl there. She'd been sitting on a bench outside by herself, nursing a beer and texting Becca.

Come over. I'm bored.

Becca's response came almost immediately: Where are you?

Michael's. He's having a party.

The seconds ticked by. Amelia waiting on the little dots. Finally, after at least a minute, they appeared. She took a sip of her beer. It was warm. Bitter. The dots disappeared. Amelia shifted on the bench. Crossed and uncrossed her legs.

Why was Becca taking so long to respond? It was so unlike her. Finally, the dots returned. Amelia exhaled.

Sorry. Can't. Busy tonight.

Her mouth was paper dry. She took another sip of the too-warm beer. Ever since she'd introduced Becca to Michael, she'd been weird. It pissed Amelia off. How many times had she tagged along with Becca to meet some guy or another? But it shouldn't come as a shock. Becca was only happy when the world revolved around her.

"Oh, thank God." A raspy, female voice interrupted her thoughts. "I thought I was the only girl here."

Amelia's head snapped upward. A tall, large girl loomed over her. Her hair was long, thick. There was a smattering of freckles across her cheeks and nose. She was fresh-faced, wearing hardly any makeup, a pair of glasses perched on her nose.

"Me too," Amelia responded, glancing around. Where was Michael, anyway? He'd gone into the apartment to get beers a while ago. Hers was almost empty. She set it down on the ground.

"Go!" a male voice shouted to Amelia's right and cheering ensued.

Oh, there was Michael. He and a couple of his friends were shot-gunning beers. Amelia cringed as foamy beer shot into his mouth, con-currently spraying him in the face. She'd only done it once. It was like drowning in a sea of bitter foam.

Sighing, she slumped back on the bench.

The strange girl plunked down next to her so hard Amelia almost shot upward.

"They're not even doing it right," she muttered. "I could take all of 'em."

Amelia laughed. When she'd told Becca she'd shotgunned a beer, she'd rolled her eyes. Told her that was stupid. Not that she was sur-prised. Amelia could never picture Becca cutting a slit into a can of beer, popping the top and shooting the liquid into her mouth, possibly get-ting it all over her face or hair. She was way too girlie for any of that.

But she could picture this girl doing it. Even though they'd just met, Amelia could tell she was completely opposite from Becca. And maybe that was why she instantly felt drawn to her.

"I'm Lauren, by the way." She brought the silver can to her lips, took a long pull.

"Amelia," she replied. "Who'd you come with?" She was curious. She'd never seen Lauren before.

"Craig."

"Which one is he?" Amelia scanned the playground area, her gaze sweeping over the cluster of guys huddled together. The cheering had died

down. Now there was only sparse laughter. Chatter. Michael wiped his face with the back of his hand.

"The guy who lost and is now puking in the bushes." She shook her head.

Amelia bit her lip, trying to stifle a giggle, but when Lauren started laughing, she joined in.

"I'm here with Michael," Amelia finally said when their laughter died down. She bobbed her head in his direction. "The guy who won."

"Ah." Lauren raised one appreciative eyebrow. "Is he your boyfriend?"

Amelia flushed. They hadn't defined their relationship. Mostly because she had to sneak around to see him. If only her mom wasn't so overprotective, then she could date like every other girl her age.

"Sort of. Is Craig yours?"

"God, no," Lauren said.

Again, Amelia laughed. It felt good, rolling around in her mouth, sweet like chocolate. She tucked her phone into the pocket of her shorts. "Wanna grab a drink with me? My beer's pretty much empty." Standing, she bent down to pick up her hollow can.

"Sure." Lauren stood with her.

As they walked off together, she left all thoughts of Becca lying on the abandoned bench.

She and Lauren exchanged phone numbers at the end of the night. And by the next day Amelia had gotten a text from Lauren asking if she wanted to hang out again. She couldn't help but notice Becca's radio silence. Determined not to let it bug her, she started hanging out more with Lauren. It felt serendipitous that she'd dropped into Amelia's life at the moment when she'd needed a friend.

But it wasn't serendipitous at all.

Fate hadn't brought them together.

Apparently, this woman had. This strange, dead woman. Frowning, Amelia turned away from the gravestone, shaking off Lauren's hand. Wind kissed her cheek, cool and damp.

"You ready?" Lauren asked. Her eyes were glazed, her nose red.

Amelia forced a nod, even though her stomach twisted. When Lauren first brought up the idea for their road trip, it had sounded fun. An adventure. She could practically taste the salty sea air mixed with a big dose of freedom. That's what she really wanted. The one thing her mom had never given her.

Freedom.

Space.

A chance to just be. To think on her own without her mom's input. To walk on the beach, without her mother breathing down her neck.

But suddenly she didn't feel free at all.

Lauren's expression was one of hope. In her eyes, Amelia saw the familiar expectations. This wasn't simply a carefree girl's trip. Lauren had an agenda.

Amelia looked out past the wrought iron gate, at the street beyond. If only she could start running and never stop. Closing her eyes, she conjured up the feel of the air on her face, the breeze slipping through her fingers, brushing back her hair. She wanted to be alone to sort through all her confusing thoughts. Sift through the information she'd been force-fed by Lauren. She imagined the truth like those flecks of gold she'd panned for when she went on that gold rush field trip in sixth grade. Right now, she was only catching the fool's gold. Shiny and brassy, deceptive. Masquerading as the real thing.

If she could be alone, quiet all the outside voices, she was certain she'd discover it.

36

THE CEMETERY WAS SMALL, covered in bright green grass and enclosed with a black barbed wire fence. Surrounding it was a street with large, sprawling homes. Some of the gravestones were intricate. Decorative statues. Some were covered in flowers, others toys or keepsakes. The girls stood almost directly in the center of the cemetery in front of a flat grave site, no headstone at all.

As Whitney approached, walking carefully so as not to alert them before she had to, she heard them talking in low whispers. But she couldn't make out their words. They stood the same, arms by their sides, shoulders slightly hunched forward. Unlike Whitney, Amelia had never had great posture. Then again, Whitney refused to nag her about it the way her own mother had done to her. In Whitney's mind, there were much more important things to harp on.

A leaf crunched under her foot. Both girls turned. It was startling how much they looked alike. Whitney wondered how she hadn't noticed it before. Then again, it wasn't something she would've ever considered. And it wasn't pervasive. Most of their features were different. But they did have the same heart-shaped lips, a similar build, almond-shaped eyes. That wasn't what struck her now, though. It was their stance, legs apart, shoulders forward. It was the way they held their mouths in a tight line, their eyebrows furrowed. They hadn't been raised together and yet they were alike in their mannerisms.

It left Whitney slightly unnerved.

She cleared her throat, ventured a step forward. "Amelia." The word came out tiny, splintered, a leaf falling to the soft grass.

"Mom," Amelia breathed out the word, her expression a mixture of relief and need. For one second she was Whitney's little girl. She even stepped forward as if she would run straight into Whitney's arms like she'd done after her first day of preschool. But then all of a sudden she halted, her face hardening. Whitney's stomach sank.

"What are you doing here?" Lauren's sharp voice rang out.

"I came to…" she paused, swallowing hard before continuing "…to get Amelia."

At that Amelia took a step backward, moved closer to Lauren. Whitney couldn't help but notice the look of triumph on Lauren's face.

The grass was wet, soaking into Whitney's thin shoes. A chill worked its way through her bones as a slight breeze kicked up around her.

Hugging herself, she spoke gently. "Amelia, you have no idea how worried I've been." Reaching out her arm, she beckoned her daughter forward. "Come on, it's time to come home."

"She's not going anywhere with you," Lauren snapped.

Frowning, Whitney turned to Lauren. "I think she can speak for herself."

Lauren's lips curled upward. She lifted her chin. "I told her the truth about you."

Whitney pinned Lauren with a challenging stare. "What exactly do you think that is?"

Whitney's response seemed to throw Lauren off-kilter a bit. Her gaze faltered, and she caught her lower lip between her teeth. "It's not what I think," she finally said. "It's what I know."

But Whitney wasn't backing down. This girl couldn't know everything. It was impossible.

She cocked an eyebrow. "Oh, yeah, what's that?"

Amelia stepped forward, her gaze catching Whitney's. "She says I'm her sister, and my real name's Bethany." Her lower lip quivered. "She says that you stole me, but that's a lie, right? I mean, it can't be true. It's crazy. Isn't it?" Her pitch got higher with each word, reminding Whitney of when she was small and begging to get her way.

"It is crazy. You're right. Of course I didn't steal you."

Amelia's head lifted, her lips twitching at the corners.

Lauren's mouth hardened into a straight line. She crossed her arms over her chest. "You're lying. I know Amelia's my sister. I have proof."

Whitney thought about the torn-out journal page, the random picture on Amelia's dresser and it hit her. Lauren must have planted them. And if she had to make an educated guess, she'd say that Lauren had gone through her dresser drawers too. "I never stole your sister. But you stole from me, didn't you? Took money from my house. My bedroom."

"Th-th-that's not what this is about," Lauren sputtered, thrown by the shift in conversation.

"What money?" Amelia asked.

Whitney was grateful to have gotten the conversation off of her for now. "I had an envelope of money in my underwear drawer. It's gone now."

"But Lauren didn't take it." Amelia shook her head, faced her sister. "Did you?"

"Not all of us are born with everything, Mills." Lauren flung

her arms upward with exasperation. "And that's nothing com-
pared to all you've taken from me. My sister. My mom."

Whitney held up a hand. "What are you talking about?"

"You're the reason my mom's dead."

Whitney felt her hackles rising. "I never hurt your mom. She
was my best friend"

"But you're the reason she's dead," Lauren said. "Do you
have any idea how awful my life has been? What it was like
being bounced around foster homes? Did you ever even think
about me?"

Whitney's stomach sank. The truth was, she hadn't. Lauren
was simply a child she'd met a couple of times. As ashamed as
she was to admit it, she hadn't factored her in at all.

"I'm so sorry, Lauren, for all that you've been through," Whitney said. "I am, but it's not because of me. You're blaming the
wrong person."

"Stop lying. I know the truth," Lauren said, but her tone
lacked the conviction it had earlier. Even Amelia appeared to
be wondering, leaning in closer.

"You know a portion. But you don't know the whole story,
Lauren." She looked into Amelia's eyes. "I know this is all really confusing, but if you give me a chance, I can explain everything to you."

"We don't have time," Lauren said. "We're on our way out
of town on a sisters' road trip. Trying to cram in time together
to make up for all the years you took from us."

"A road trip? That was your plan?" Whitney scrambled to
put the pieces together in her mind. When she'd figured out it
was Lauren who had Amelia, she'd imagined the plot was much
more sinister. Some type of revenge scheme. Going to the police
or turning Amelia against her. Then she thought about Amelia's
phone being off, the confusing items left in the house, Lauren
pointedly calling Amelia "Millie" in front of her. Her gaze shot
to Lauren. "You planted the journal entry of your mom's in my

room. The one she wrote about the night I OD'd." Lauren nodded, and she took it as permission to continue. "And the photo
of me and Millie on Amelia's dresser." Again, Lauren nodded.
"You wanted me to find all of that once you and Amelia were
out of town to hurt me. To make me think I'd lost my daughter. That she'd found out the truth and taken off."

Lauren didn't respond, but Whitney caught the twitch in the
corner of her mouth. She was trying not to smile.

"The trip isn't about you," Amelia said. "Not everything is
about you, Mom."

"Then why turn off your phone? Why the elaborate plot of
being dropped off at some elderly couple's home?" She looked
to Lauren again. She still couldn't quite figure it out. "What
were you hoping I'd do, Lauren?"

"I don't know. Feel some remorse," she said. "I've had to live
with what you did my entire life. But when I met you and Amelia, it was clear that you weren't suffering. You didn't feel bad.
You have everything you ever wanted. So, yeah, I guess I kinda
wanted to take that away. Make you feel something. Anything,
close to what I felt."

Whitney knew Lauren was hurting. She couldn't even imagine what Lauren's life had been like. On the one hand, it made
her so happy that she'd spared Amelia that life. But on the other
hand, she felt bad for what Lauren had endured.

Amelia recoiled, her eyes narrowing. "I um...I didn't know
all this. Honestly, I just couldn't deal anymore. After Lauren told
me who she was, I didn't know what to think. Who to believe.
I don't know if I am who she says I am, but I do know you've
kept things from me. You're not exactly who I thought, and—"
She looked straight at Whitney. "It's all just too much. I needed
a break."

"I get that," Whitney said to her. Then she turned to Lauren. "And I understand how you're feeling too." Lauren scoffed
at this, rolling her eyes. Whitney held up her hand. "No, I do.

And you're wrong. I have suffered. I've felt loss and sadness and, yeah, sometimes remorse. But not for the things you think. If you'd both just hear what I have to say. Listen to what really happened, you'd understand."

"No one wants to hear a sob story from a liar," Lauren sneered. But Amelia's stance relaxed a bit, her eyes peering upward.

"I…umm…kinda wanna hear what she has to say," Amelia practically whispered.

Relief flowed through Whitney's chest. She'd never wanted to tell Amelia the truth about who she was and how Whitney had gotten her. But now she had no choice.

And she was ready.

37

SO HERE WE ARE. The part of the story I've been dreading the most. I never wanted you to find out. Certainly, not this way. Not because I didn't think you deserved the truth, but because I was trying to protect you. And I fear that this will only hurt you.

But I don't have a choice, do I?

You already know most of it, and at this point you're thinking the worst anyway. I might as well come clean.

Dan wasn't there when you were born, Amelia. He was on a business trip when I went into labor. He tried his best to get home in time, but had trouble getting an earlier flight.

My mom was there for part of the time, but I sent her home early. She was being so judgmental. She and Dad had been at the house that morning when Dan and I came back from Millie's. They heard Dan's accusations, and, of course, sided with him. With my track record, no one ever believed me.

But nothing had happened—ever—between Mitch and me. Dan was the only man I'd ever been with.

I finally told him everything. What a liar I'd been. How Mitch was never mine. How I'd made it all up. My biggest fear was that he'd leave me when he knew the ugly truth. But the funny thing is he didn't even believe me.

He continued to believe the lie.

I guess I had only myself to blame for that one. My mother always said I should become an actress. Maybe she'd been right.

Your father and I stayed together, despite his accusations. He loved the moral high ground and felt forever entitled to hold this over my head. I was no longer the damsel who needed rescuing, but the witch he felt compelled to punish. You can see why our marriage was doomed.

Anyway, your timing was a surprise. You came weeks early, and he was away on a business trip. But my mom kept making little jabs at me during labor. Stuff about how she knew the real reason Dan wasn't there.

I couldn't bring you into the world with that kind of negativity. I knew the truth. I'd told the truth. And I didn't deserve those accusations.

You certainly didn't.

I gave birth the same way I always raised you. Alone. Independent. And after the birth, I felt this rush of love unlike anything I'd ever felt before. More love than I'd ever felt for my parents or Kevin, Millie or even Dan. I was responsible for a whole human life and it felt crushing, scary and exhilarating all at once.

As these thoughts were swirling through my head, the oddest thing happened.

I looked out the doorway, as a heavily pregnant woman waddled by, clearly in labor and trying to move things along by walking. She glanced up at me. Our eyes met. With a pained expression she reached her hand up slightly to wave. I smiled and waved back.

It was Millie.

By the middle of that night, Dan still hadn't arrived. Stuck on a layover in Chicago, I think. It was March, after all. He said the snow was forecast to continue through morning. At that point, I wasn't sure when he'd be back. I was exhausted. I'd been awake for hours. Labor. Pushing. The high of holding this perfect sweet new being. Feeding. Baby crying. Finally, we both fell asleep. It wasn't very long, but it was glorious.

I awoke to a noise. Someone in my room. At first, I assumed it was a nurse. But then I opened my eyes and saw Millie standing next to my hospital bed cradling a baby in her arms.

"Sorry I woke you," she said. "I just wanted to introduce you to Bethany."

I was so glad she'd sought me out. After seeing her in the doorway earlier, I'd been hoping I'd get a chance to see her. Groggy, I hoisted myself up to a seated position and waved away her apology.

I said, "Come meet my Amelia."

I'll never forget the smile on her face then.

I was certain she was remembering the same conversation I was. Back when we first became friends, I asked her if Millie was short for Amelia. We'd been lying in the grass out by the quad during lunch. Staring up through the bare branches of the tree above us, Millie got this wistful look on her face. She said something like, *Can you imagine me as an Amelia? What kind of life would I have? I'd probably wear bows in my hair and cute dresses. Have two parents who love me, and a room decorated in all pink.*

I'd laughed then, but I honestly thought it sounded amazing.

No, my real name's not Millie, she explained. *It's Tawny Milligan. But a childhood friend used to call me Millie and it just stuck.*

That night in the hospital room, Millie told me that she believed my Amelia would have that life we'd fantasized about.

It was when Millie made her way over to the bassinet that I
first noticed something was wrong. She noticed it too. Reaching
into the bassinet, I grabbed my baby out. She wasn't breathing.

I didn't want to believe it. It didn't even seem possible. How
could a healthy baby just die?

She was so still. Cold.

I looked for any signs of life, but there were none. I knew
then that there was no bringing her back. And it felt like my
heart had been ripped out. It was way worse than when we lost
Kevin or when Millie was torn from my life.

I remember I kept rocking back and forth, muttering "oh,
my God" under my breath. I wanted to scream. To yell. But
it was like my body wouldn't let me. Like that reaction was so
foreign I wouldn't know how to attempt it. Millie said I was in
shock. I'd never felt pain like I did in that moment. It was all-
consuming. Honestly, I wanted to die too. I had no idea how
I'd ever get past it.

The horror, the reality, began to set in and I began to panic
out loud. I told Millie to push the nurse's button because she
was closer.

But Millie got this strangled look on her face—a mixture of
pain, grief and then stubborn resolution—and told me to stay
calm. To stay quiet. She dragged the curtain closed around my
bed. I didn't know why. I'm not even sure I fully registered it
at that moment, I was so fixated on my baby.

And then she presented me with a crazy plan.

A plan to switch our babies.

Of course, I said no at first. I didn't want her baby. I wanted
mine.

"But yours is gone," Millie pointed out. "Nothing you can
do will bring her back."

I knew she was right, but I didn't want to believe it. I tried everything. Pressing on her little chest, breathing into her mouth the way I'd seen people do CPR on TV. But Millie stopped me and hugged me, held me. Telling me we were running out of time. Her gaze kept shooting to the door. There was a wildness in her eyes, but also a determination.

"Come on, Whit. You've always said you wanted to help me. Now's your chance," she said, her tone desperate. "Things have gotten worse with Mitch, okay? I'll never be safe from him, but she can be. You can make sure she is."

Even stricken by grief over my own child, I could see it then. Everything I'd done. The good and the bad, finally turning into something good.

I remember looking at you in Millie's arms. You were so beautiful. And I knew in that moment, I could love you. Raise you. Give you a good life. Save you.

I could still have everything I'd ever wanted.

When I looked up into Millie's eyes staring at me with desperation, I knew I couldn't say no. I never could say no to her.

So, we did it. Millie switched the tags.

I cried and kissed my baby goodbye one last time.

You became my Amelia.

I remember Millie standing in the doorway, holding my still baby in her arms, and she made me promise to always keep you safe.

I kept the promise I made to her that day. I've always kept you safe.

38

LAUREN COULD TELL Amelia was buying Whitney's story. But she didn't. There was no way her mom would give up her baby. She remembered that day in the hospital. Her mom was glowing with happiness. The love she felt for her daughter radiating off of her. No way would she just hand her over to someone else.

Then again, there were aspects of Whitney's story that rang true, like her dad's abuse.

As a child, there were times when she thought her dad was the best. Funny. Loud. Boisterous. He'd play toys with her, making up funny voices for all her characters. And he'd take her to the park and push her on the swing. But on his dark days, there was no laughing or playing with toys. He'd yell at Lauren, telling her to keep it down. Once, she'd built a huge Lego tower. It took her days to finish. And he struck it down in one second. She still remembered being on the ground on her knees, desperately trying to gather up all the pieces.

Lauren stared at Amelia's profile, watching her hair lift slightly in the breeze, revealing the edge of her birthmark. If Whitney's words were true, then her mom had chosen to save Amelia over her. She'd selflessly given one daughter a better life.

She envisioned Amelia's cozy room, the walls displaying her favorite movies. After her mom died and her dad went to prison, Lauren hadn't had her own room until she was an adult. Growing up, she shared with the other foster kids, or slept on the occasional couch. Every once in a while she got lucky and stayed at a house where she had a room all to herself, but it wasn't really hers. She couldn't decorate it, or make it her own. Beth and Henry's house was like that. They'd been her favorite foster parents. The only ones she'd kept in contact with over the years.

That's why she'd used their house as a decoy.

Both she and Amelia knew that Whitney would never be okay with dropping her daughter off at some sleazy motel. Plus, she thought that Lauren was only seventeen, not twenty-five. For years, Beth and Henry had cocktail hour out on their patio every single afternoon from four thirty to five thirty. Lauren had never known them to skip it. So, she figured that would be the perfect time for Whitney to drop Amelia off. Lauren had slipped in through her former bedroom window, like the old days sneaking home after a night out, and let Amelia in the front minutes later.

It all would've been easier if Whitney hadn't been the type of mom who insisted on dropping her daughter off, a fact that pissed Amelia off to no end. It was puzzling to Lauren, who would have loved to have a parent care about her like that.

Her mind flew back to the first time she'd spent the night at Amelia's. Whitney had peeked in on them, offering them snacks, but it was clear that the intention was mainly to be included. To know what was going on. Amelia had snapped at her, basically told her to leave.

Lauren had watched Whitney leave the room, the expression

on her face betraying how hurt she was. Before closing the door, Whitney had eyed her daughter as if willing Amelia to beckon her back in. It reminded Lauren of a dog being left outside.

Lauren had glanced at Amelia, who didn't seem to notice or care about her mother's disappointment. She hadn't known what to expect before coming here, only gathered what she'd researched herself online, perusing social media accounts. And what Amelia had told her in their conversations. From those things she'd surmised that Amelia and Whitney were close. It had been just the two of them for so long, it made sense. But she hadn't anticipated how much it would affect her, seeing this life her sister had lived. How different it was from hers.

How much better.

She liked Amelia, but at that moment she felt a little jealous.

Now as she listened to Whitney's story, she couldn't help but wish she'd been the baby that was switched. It confused her. This longing.

Before coming here, she'd been much more jaded. The world had seemed so black-and-white. Her relationship with Amelia had changed her. Now she saw so many shades of gray.

She'd wanted Whitney to pay for what she'd done. Even gone as far as planting clues to what she knew all over Whitney's apartment for her to find once the girls were long gone. She wanted there to be no question why Amelia had left. Lauren wanted to be sure Whitney would suffer. Be tormented. Possibly even drive her so mad she'd turn herself in, finally tell the world the truth about what she'd done.

But as she listened to Whitney's story, she began to wonder if she'd had it all wrong.

39

THE MONTHS AFTER I brought you home were hard. Not because I didn't love you. I did. So much. But I underestimated how much I would miss the baby I lost. How much I would grieve her. It was foolish to think one human can replace another.

Please don't misunderstand. I don't regret what I did. And the sadness I felt over losing her didn't diminish the love I had for you.

But switching the two of you didn't allow me the time I needed to mourn.

Dan assumed I was suffering from post-partum depression. But then he consulted with his dad and he started to think it was more than that. Apparently, my depression didn't fall in line with post-partum. It seemed more extreme than that to him.

I couldn't tell Dan what was really going on, so he drew his own conclusions.

Shortly after I brought you home, I heard the news that Millie had died the day after we swapped the babies. Codeine overdose.

Same way I'd almost died so many years ago. The information came from my parents of all people. They'd heard it through the rumor mill, spreading from Millie's mom and weaving its way out like a spiderweb.

A nurse had found her in the middle of the day. When they found all the drugs in her system, they assumed she'd killed herself after being told her baby had died of SIDS. One of the nurses said they'd overheard one of Millie's conversations with Mitch, observed his abusive behavior. She'd also noticed the bruising on Millie's arms. And they'd known from her medical records that she'd had an opioid addiction in the past.

As I struggled to process why Millie would kill herself, I remembered something I'd dismissed before.

In our last conversation, when Millie was trying to convince me to swap the babies, she'd said, *I'll never be free from Mitch. Not until the day I die.*

And that's when I knew. She'd been planning it all along. That's why it was so easy for her to switch our babies. She knew she wouldn't be around much longer. I wanted this revelation to bring me peace, realizing that I'd helped her find freedom.

But it only made me sadder. What if I hadn't gone along with her plan? Would she have stayed alive longer? Been able to break free of Mitch at some point? I'll never know. And that haunts me to this day.

Millie's death only added to my sadness in the days and weeks after I brought you home. Not only did I grieve for my baby, but for my childhood best friend, as well.

Things came to a head with your dad when you were around six or seven months old and your eyes changed color. As you know, your dad and I have blue eyes. You have brown.

That flipped him out, even though I tried to explain that it doesn't prove anything. I even showed him literature that debunked the eye color myth he was buying into.

But the damage had been done. I'd told too many lies. Kept too many secrets.

We didn't break up right away, though. I think he stayed with me for a while for your sake.

He never demanded a paternity test. I know it's because of how much he loves you. You stole his heart from the moment he first laid eyes on you. You're his daughter, regardless.

Even though we did our best to make our marriage work, he never trusted me again. And that's the real reason we broke up. The real reason he left me.

I'm truly sorry for that. It's one of my biggest regrets. I wanted to give you that life Millie and I had dreamed up for an Amelia. And for the most part I did. You had the dresses and bows, the pink room. But more than that, you had love. Safety. Security. All the things Millie had wanted for you. I knew I could be the mom you needed. Loving. Attentive. Encouraging.

And I like to think that I was all those things.

But I know there was one thing Millie was counting on when she asked me to raise you. Millie always wished she'd been raised by two parents. Living with a single mom had been hard for her. I know that wasn't the life she'd wanted for you.

And it's one thing I've always felt bad about. That I couldn't make things work with Dan. That I couldn't give you a home with two parents.

40

WHITNEY'S SUDDEN RECOLLECTION of her mother's last words seemed a tad convenient. Also, out of character. The Millie that Whitney remembered may have been melodramatic. Maudlin. A person who would say things like, *I'll never be free from Mitch. Not until the day I die.* But the mom Lauren knew didn't say things like that. She was strong. Practical.

Not only that, but Lauren's last conversation with her mom negated the so-called statement. Made it impossible.

The three of them sat cross-legged in the grass, facing one another, a tiny huddle. A lawnmower kicked on in the distance. All around them, people had left for work, racing out to their cars, coffees in hand, zipping out of their driveways and down the street. Probably thought the three of them were holding some sort of séance.

Lauren was tired of listening to Whitney's lies. She was ready to go. Amelia's expression worried her. It was obvious that Whitney had her—hook, line and sinker. She had to figure out what to say.

Reel her back in. Not that she'd ever really had her. She'd only been able to convince her to go on this trip by appealing to her taste for freedom, her sense of adventure. It was clear that Amelia never truly bought Lauren's story about her mom. But there was no way Lauren was giving up. Once she could get Amelia out of her mom's clutches, she was certain she could convince her. Make her see reason. Her entire life she'd been on the sidelines, watching someone else live their life with their own family.

The only living relative she even knew of was her dad. And he'd been in prison since the year after her mom died. He'd been caught trafficking drugs through his job as a delivery driver. Someone had called in an anonymous tip, and he'd been in prison ever since. He was supposed to get out once, years ago, but then he stabbed some guy in prison—he'd never been able to control his temper—and had to serve another sentence.

But Lauren's days of being alone were over. She had her sister now, and she had no intention of letting her go. Closing her eyes, she conjured up the feel of the sun on her face, salt in the air, sand in her toes.

"I know it's a lot to process," Whitney was saying to Amelia. "And right now, you probably hate me. I get that. But I hope in time you can see that everything I did was out of love. Love for Millie, and love for you. I've been a little overbearing. Strict. Maybe even slightly crazy. But now you know why.

"I never wanted you to follow in my footsteps. To make bad choices. Ones that would hurt you or others. I never wanted you to lie. Manipulate. Not the way I did. I knew all too well how bad that would turn out.

"Don't you see? Everything I did was to keep the promise I made to Millie the night you were born. My methods may have not always been great, but I did what I set out to. I kept you safe."

Lauren opened her eyes. Looked at Amelia, who swallowed hard, wringing her hands in her lap, picking at what was left of the black polish that matched Lauren's own. Her eyes were red and watery, her skin gray and pallid. Her urgency to get Amelia out of here grew.

"Say something," Whitney pled with her.

"I honestly don't know what you want me to say, Mom." Amelia pulled her lip to one side as if trying to stop herself from crying.

Lauren watched Whitney, gauging her reaction. Trying to assess what she should say. How far could she take this? How much truth could her sister handle right now? Amelia's lower lip was wobbly, and she bit down on it, her eyes sad and wet.

"I don't know," Whitney said. "Say anything. Tell me how you're feeling. Tell me you hate me. Just say something."

"I don't hate you," Amelia said, staring at her hands. "I don't know what I feel toward you. I guess I just kinda feel numb. Shocked. Sorta confused." She blew out a shaky breath. "I mean, it's like my entire life has been a lie. I don't know what I'm supposed to do with that."

"Your life hasn't been a lie, Amelia," Whitney assured her.

Lauren turned away, staring down at the dewy blades of grass. She pondered Whitney's story, wondering if any part of it were true.

"I think I just need some time...space." Amelia stood abruptly then. Lauren scrambled to follow her.

"Okay." Whitney stood too, wiping her back and legs with her palms. "I can give you that."

Amelia's eyebrows raised in surprise. "Can you?"

"Yeah." Whitney nodded. "Let's go home and you can hole up in your room for as long as you need."

"No," Amelia said. "That's not what I mean." Whitney frowned, cocked her head to the side. "I need time away. Like not at our house."

Whitney let out a startled sound, kind of a cross between a cough and laugh. "Well, where would you go?"

Amelia glanced over at Lauren, who took the bait.

"We can go on our sisters' trip," Lauren said. "The one we'd planned."

Whitney knotted her hands, bit the inside of her lip. Lauren was positive a "no" was coming. Amelia's expression betrayed that she did also.

"Please," Amelia begged. "I need this."

"Amelia, you're not old enough to go on a trip on your own."

"She won't be on her own. She'll be with her sister," Lauren pointed out.

The look Whitney gave her could only be described as a glare.

"Or I guess she could just stay with me here for a bit," Lauren added smugly. "In the motel. It's pretty safe. It's really near the police station."

Lauren noted the swell of Whitney's neck as she swallowed. *Lauren—1. Whitney—0.*

Whitney hesitated, licked her lips.

"I bet the police would be interested in seeing this." When Lauren tugged on her backpack zipper it sounded like paper being ripped cleanly in half.

"The police? What?" Amelia spoke softly beside her in a fear-laced tone. "You didn't mention anything about the police." Lifting her hand to her mouth, she gnawed on her index fingernail.

God, Amelia never would've survived Lauren's childhood.

She was way too fragile. But Lauren couldn't worry about that right now. On a mission, she ignored her. Inside, her fingers found what she'd been searching for. She yanked it out, displaying it in front of her chest.

Whitney's eyes flashed. "Is that Millie's diary?" she asked, her tone breathy, staring at the journal like it was a loaded gun.

"Yep," Lauren told her smugly, enjoying the discomfort on her face. "And I'm sorry, but after reading through this, I just don't think your story adds up." She slid her thumb against the pages, fanning them. "You're in it a lot. There's all kinds of stuff about your friendship."

"Really?" She stepped forward. "Can I see?"

Lauren drew it back, clutched it to her chest. "No."

Whitney sighed. "Lauren, your mom was always a tad melo-dramatic. The darker the better. I don't think you can read that much into her diary."

"Oh, I think I can read a lot into it," Lauren deadpanned, opening to a page and reading. "'My skin prickles, the hair on end. Fear breathes down my neck. A shadow behind me. Al-ways there. Watching. Waiting to strike.'"

"Sounds like a poem about your dad. It's like I said, she was so afraid of him. That's why I tried to do everything in my power to save Millie. It's why I went along with her plan." Her gaze bounced to Amelia who nodded as if she was eating this up.

"This poem isn't about my dad. It's about you." Lauren couldn't help the grin that emerged on her face. "Peeling off my skin, she wears it like a dress. Dipping her toes into the wa-ters of my life, she slips under, claiming it all as her own."

Whitney's jaw slackened. After a second, she forced it to close as if needing time to regain composure. She licked her lips, crossed her arms. A breath whistled through her nostrils. "I don't really even get it. It sounds made up. Just a jumble of words. Millie was like that. Dark just for the sake of being that way."

"I write dark poetry," Amelia interjected. "And it's like that. You know, symbolism. Metaphors. It's not literal." Her lips curled slightly at the corners. "I guess in that way we're alike, huh?"

Lauren shook her head. "Sure, my mom's poetry is lyrical. Symbolic. But it's rooted in truth. You didn't just want to be close to my mom, did you? You wanted to be her. You wanted her life."

Whitney blew out an exasperated breath, ran a hand over her head. "You don't know anything about our relationship."

"I know that the stories you told us today are in this diary," Lauren said. "And most of them read a little differently."

"I'm not surprised. Like I said, Millie and I often saw things differently."

"From what I read in here, you were pretty obsessed with her."

Whitney's eyes flashed. "Your mom had an inflated ego. She thought everyone was obsessed with her."

"Were you in love with my mother?" Lauren's lips curled upward, her brows raising. The flush in Whitney's cheeks told her she'd hit a nerve.

"Were you, Mom?" Amelia's eyes widened as if she was seeing a side of her mom she'd never been aware of. If Lauren didn't know better, she'd think Amelia was kind of hopeful. Lauren was mostly just saying all this to get under Whitney's skin. Ruffle some feathers. But, perhaps, there was some truth to it. A missing piece of the puzzle. One Amelia apparently wanted solved.

Whitney didn't seem to appreciate it, though. If looks could kill Lauren was sure she'd drop dead. "Millie was my best friend. Nothing more," Whitney said, throwing her hand out as if a ball had been lobbed in her direction. "This is exactly why you should give me the journal. It's personal and it's about a history you weren't involved in."

The truth hit Lauren then like a slap to the face. Hard and fast, it left her reeling. How had she not seen it before? The missing piece wasn't that Whitney was a lesbian, trying to seduce her mom. The truth was much more sinister than that.

She steeled herself against this newfound knowledge, instantly aware that she had to keep it inside for now. She had to play it delicately. No room for error.

This changed everything.

"Why would you give it to the police, anyway?" Amelia asked, eyeing the journal and picking so viciously around her fingernails, the skin was dotted with blood. "Does it say anything about Bethany?"

"Of course not. This was her diary from high school," Lauren answered.

"Then…it's not relevant to this, is it?" Amelia pointed out, once again making it clear whose side she was on.

Not Lauren's.

This entire charade had run its course. Lauren couldn't keep pushing. Sharing. It was time for her and Amelia to leave.

Still focused on the diary, Whitney tried again, reaching out her hand. "Can I please see the journal? I'll give it back. I just really want to read it."

Lauren hesitated only a second. "Fine." She thrust the diary in Whitney's direction. The relief Whitney felt was palpable as she closed her fingers around it. It gave Lauren a sick sense of satisfaction. Whitney was stupid if she thought Lauren was giving up that easily. Of course, she wouldn't hand over her only copy of her mom's diary. She had photos of the whole diary hidden in a flash drive in her suitcase.

Hope was written all over Whitney's face, and Lauren couldn't wait for the day when she could erase it. Wipe it away. This was far from over. Lauren knew the truth, and one day everyone else would too.

"So, are we cool, then?" Lauren asked, capitalizing on the moment. "To go on our trip?"

"Where exactly are you planning to stay?" Whitney asked, holding the diary close to her side, so tight her knuckles whitened, as if she was afraid it would leap out of her hand if she loosened her grasp.

"We haven't made an exact plan yet. We were gonna play it by ear," Lauren said.

Whitney's fear-laced frown grew deeper. She turned away from them a moment, running a hand through her hair. She must've gotten a text or message because she took her phone out of her pocket, peered down at it.

Lauren and Amelia exchanged a glance.

When Whitney whirled around, she sighed. "Fine."

"For real?" Lauren blurted out. It wasn't at all what she'd been expecting. Completely out of character, from what she'd seen of Whitney so far.

"But I have some rules, Amelia," Whitney said. "You have to finish out the school year. You two can take a few days, a week at most. Then you have to come back. Understand?"

Amelia's head bobbed up and down.

"I'm trusting you," Whitney added.

"I know," Amelia answered quietly, and it was then that Lauren saw what Whitney was up to. This was just another tactic to get Amelia back on her side. Too bad for Whitney, Lauren was better at manipulation. Whitney was no match for her.

Facing Lauren, Whitney said, "And you can keep the money. I won't say anything about it to the police."

"Seriously?" Amelia's tone was both shocked and grateful.

Nicely played, Whitney.

Perhaps Lauren had underestimated her.

"It was yours, anyway," Whitney said, her attention back on Amelia. "I saved it for you, hoping to buy you a car for your sixteenth birthday, but your dad beat me to it." Whitney tucked a strand of hair behind her ear. "When you get back," she said, throwing Amelia a pointed look, "and you finish out the year, maybe you two can plan some type of summer trip." She paused, and Lauren saw her chest pull in as she forced a breath. "Possibly even take that trip to your dad's."

Amelia's face fell. "Dad," she breathed out. "Will you have to tell him?"

"Yes, but it's been a long time coming," Whitney said, and Lauren could read the turmoil in her expression. It was clear this wasn't something she ever planned to do, and even though it wasn't enough, it made Lauren slightly content. She liked seeing Whitney off-kilter. Unsure. Scared.

"Do you think he'll still want me to visit?" Amelia coiled a strand of hair around her index finger. "Still want me in his life?"

"Oh, honey." Whitney took a step forward, reached her arm out to touch Amelia's. But Amelia moved away, and Whitney's fingers simply grasped at the air, as if it was something she thought she could hold. "I think he'll be very mad at me, but not at you. Not at all. He'll always be your dad, no matter what."

The sentiment made Lauren's skin crawl. Her dad would be hers no matter what, too, and that gave her no comfort. Again, she felt anger for being the one left. The one to carry this burden. This history. The family that Amelia was able to escape.

Lauren had spent so many years being angry with the person responsible for taking away her sister. There was no way this woman, this stranger, could make her believe that was Lauren's own mother.

Amelia took a step toward Lauren and then hesitated, her gaze once again finding Whitney. Lauren froze. "What will you tell the police?"

"That I found you."

"No, I mean…" Amelia looked around. "Will you have to tell them about me? Like about who I really am?"

Whitney's gaze flickered to Lauren. "I don't think it's necessary. Millie made the choice to give you to me. Like an adoption."

It was all lies.

A few nights before her mom went to the hospital, she tucked Lauren in. Rubbing her big, pregnant belly, she told Lauren that she and her sister were the only things she cared about in this world. Then she promised that she'd always protect them.

Those were not the words of a woman who would give up her child.

As Lauren and Amelia walked away from Whitney, Lauren smiled at her sister, already imagining the two of them on the beach, toes buried deep in the sand. Whitney might believe that

they'd be coming back, but Lauren had no intention of ever returning. This trip was more than a sisters' getaway. It was clear
that Amelia was already seeing cracks in Whitney's story. It
wasn't going to take much before Lauren could open her eyes
to the truth.

But even if her attempt to get Amelia on her side failed, she
would still take Whitney down. She'd get that DNA test. Gather
all the necessary evidence. In her bag, she had a tiny tape re-
corder. As much as she intended to have a good time and get
to know her sister, she wouldn't squander their time. If Amelia said something helpful to her case, she'd capture it. Use it
when she went to the police, which she fully intended to do
once she had all the proof she needed. No matter what it took,
she would make Whitney pay for what she'd done. She had to
for her mom's sake. To avenge her death. Clear up all the mis-
conceptions.

One thing she knew for sure, her mom would never have
willingly left Lauren. Not even for Bethany. Another thing that
only she knew: her mom had a plan. A way out. Information on
Mitch that she planned to use, so they could be free. She didn't
feel trapped anymore.

Death wasn't her mom's only way out, and there was no way
she would've told Whitney that.

"Time to go, Lauren." Her dad nudged her in the arm.

She scooted forward on the hospital bed, closer to her mom.

*But her mom nodded, smiled. "Go. Your sister and I will be home
tomorrow."*

"You promise?" Lauren raised her chin, stared into her mother's eyes.

"I promise."

At ten, Amelia was invited to her first sleepover. Excitement
had pulsed through her like the steady drumbeat of a pop song.
She'd barely gotten in her mom's car after school, before tearing the invitation out of her backpack and flashing it in the air.

"Casey invited me to her slumber party!" The words burst from her throat like an explosion of candy from a piñata.

Her mom had responded less enthusiastically. She pursed her lips. "I don't think I know Casey. Do I?"

"No...I...um...I don't think so." Amelia's heart faltered.

"Then it's probably not a good idea."

Amelia's heart sank. She should've known. Her mom said no to everything. Why couldn't she have a cool mom like Casey's?

"But, Mo-o-om," she whined. "Please."

"I've already made up my mind."

Usually, Amelia let these things go. She'd never known her mom to change her mind once it was made up. But the next day when all the girls were talking about the plans for the sleepover, she was infected with a major case of FOMO. That's why when they asked her if she was coming, she said, "Of course."

That night at dinner, she begged her mom to the point she thought for sure she'd be in trouble. But to her surprise, her mom gave in.

"Fine. But I need to talk to Casey's mom ahead of time and make sure she's going to be there the whole time."

Amelia's cheeks preemptively burned with the embarrassment she knew she'd feel when Casey told everyone about this. And she for sure would. There was no way any of the other parents were going to act this way.

Amelia had the most overbearing mom on the planet.

But she was willing to endure it in order to attend the sleepover. So, she gave her mom the phone number. And to her shock, no one ever made fun of her for it. Maybe Casey's mom hadn't even told her about the phone call. Or maybe Amelia was wrong, and her mom wasn't that different from other moms. Either way, she was grateful.

But her biggest challenge was still ahead of her and it was one Amelia hadn't anticipated. The evening of the sleepover, while Amelia packed up her overnight bag, nerves attacked her insides, a sudden flurry of ants coming up out of a mountain of dirt. She'd never spent the night at a friend's house. Her mind was filled with all the unknowns. Where would she sleep? What if she had a nightmare? Got scared? What if the other kids were mean to her and she was stuck there? In that moment, she'd kind of wished her mom had stood her ground, continued to tell her no.

She stopped packing, sat back on her heels, her knees tucked under her body, and she began to cry.

"What's wrong?" Her mom rushed in. As she knelt beside her, she touched her cheek, brushed a sticky strand of hair back. It felt good. Comforting.

Amelia leaned into it.

"Amelia?"

Her gaze met her mom's. "I'm scared," she admitted.

"You'll be fine," her mom assured her.

Amelia frowned, unconvinced.

Her mom tried again. "You've been looking forward to this all week. Casey's mom said you guys are going to play games and have pizza and cake. You'll have so much fun."

It did sound like fun. Amelia sniffed. "Promise?"

A slight hesitation. Her mom breathed in, smoothed back Amelia's hair again. "I'll tell you what? You go to the sleepover and if you aren't having fun, you can call me, and I'll come get you. Anytime. Even if it's three in the morning, I'll be there."

The tightness in Amelia's chest loosened a bit, but then she shook her head. She couldn't call her mommy to come get her from the sleepover. Her friends would never let her live that down. "They'll think I'm a baby."

Her mom's eyes widened as if she'd had an epiphany. She snapped her fingers. "We'll use a secret code. One between just the two of us."

"A code?" Amelia sat up, intrigued.

Biting her lip, her mom glanced around the room. When she looked into the closet, a grin spread across her face. "Red jacket."

Amelia laughed, the memory surfacing.

"It's perfect. An inside joke. Something no one else would know," her mom was talking fast now. Animatedly. "If you call me and use the phrase 'red jacket' I'll make up some family emergency and come get you. Deal?"

Amelia smiled. "Deal."

She didn't need to use the code that night, but she did end up using it a handful of times over the years. And true to the agreement, her mom was there for her. Quickly. No questions asked.

Lauren had spent the past few weeks trying to convince Amelia that her mom was evil. A criminal mastermind. A bad person.

But she didn't know her the way Amelia did.

The woman who tucked her in countless nights, singing lullabies off-key, who came up with a secret code to make her feel safe, who held her, stroking her hair when she had a nightmare and who always had her back—she was not a monster.

And there was no way Lauren could convince her otherwise.

When she and Lauren first met, she'd been annoyed with her mom's controlling tendencies. She'd been rebelling. Pulling away. And she shared a lot of her frustrations about her mom with her new friend. The girl she believed to be her age who she randomly met at a party. Lauren misread it, though, clearly thinking she could get Amelia on her side.

Truth is, deep down she was mad at her mom. She'd been hoping Whitney would deny all the accusations, offer proof that she and Amelia were flesh and blood. It's what she'd been expecting when her mom walked up to them in the cemetery today.

But she didn't do that. And her admission broke Amelia's heart.

Amelia didn't hate her, though. She couldn't. They'd been through too much.

Lauren did.

It was obvious in her expression. Her body language. Amelia was scared of what Lauren might do. Whatever she was planning, Amelia had to stop it. She believed her mom's story. It seemed entirely plausible that this drug addict married to an abusive con artist would hand over her baby to her best friend—a woman with a stable life and a husband. Besides, Lauren had shared a lot about her childhood with Amelia. It sounded horrendous.

Regardless of the circumstances, whether her mom was telling the truth or not, Whitney had saved her from that. Shouldn't she be grateful?

The thing that upset her the most was the lying. The secrets. Honesty had always been so important to her mom. She demanded it of Amelia. Turns out, Whitney had been the biggest liar of all. That was the main reason she couldn't just go home with her mom right now. When she said she needed space, she meant from everyone. But when Lauren brought up the sisters' trip again, she knew she had no choice but to go, especially after she threatened going to the police. Amelia may have spent a lot of time and energy being mad at her mom, but she wouldn't let anyone hurt her. The thought of her locked in a jail cell caused her heart to ache, her mouth to fill with bile.

And that's why she'd sent the text.

While Lauren was pleading her case for the sisters' trip, she discreetly pulled out her phone, typed two words.

Red jacket.

Pressed Send.

Then she'd turned Find My Friends back on.

Lauren may have thought that both Amelia and Whitney were giving in, but she was dead wrong. It had always been the two of them. Mother/daughter. A team. A partnership. No one was tearing them apart.

Not even her so-called sister.

Her mom had always had her back. Now it was her turn to have her mom's.

Peering over her shoulder, she caught the silhouette of her mom standing in the middle of the cemetery. Her hair flew around her face, caught in the wind. Smiling, she turned back around, warmth filling her. She had to keep Lauren close until she could figure out how to get rid of her for good. But she knew that no matter where they went, her mom wouldn't be far behind them.

Next to her, Lauren threaded her arm through Amelia's. Her face beamed as if she'd already won.

Amelia grinned back. Pretending. Maybe she was more like her mom than she'd thought.

41

WHITNEY STOOD IN the center of the cemetery, a ghost lingering over the gravestones. She watched the girls' backs as they retreated. Then she glanced down at her phone and logged in to the Find My Friends app. Amelia's picture appeared on the map, moving away from her. Relief flowed through her chest. She lowered the phone, still holding it in her palm, its existence tethering her to Amelia.

Red jacket.

If not for that text, she never would've let Amelia leave. Even though a lot had changed in the past couple of days, she trusted her daughter. She had no other choice than to believe in their strong connection.

Lauren had the power to take Whitney down. To destroy her life.

But if Amelia was on her side, there was still hope.

Staring down at Millie's name, she drew in a ragged breath. She'd come here many times, but never knew what to say. Other people would stand at their loved ones' gravesites, spilling all the words. But Whitney didn't know how to talk to a piece of granite. Dirt. Grass. Millie wasn't here. She'd just be talking to the air. All around her it was quiet and still. It seemed odd to think of Millie here. Millie, who had always been so full of life, in this place of death.

Shivering, Whitney turned away, hurrying back to her car. First things first, she fished around in her glove compartment until she found a book of matches and a rag. Sitting down on the edge of the cement sidewalk that looped the parking lot, she struck one of the matches, watching the flame dance in front of her eyes. Then she picked up the diary. When Lauren had first handed it to her, she'd been curious about the contents, wondering what Millie had written about her.

But reading it wasn't an option. Not now.

Besides, Millie was gone.

Buried. Dead. And that's where Whitney would leave her.

Holding the match to the bottom right corner of the diary, she watched the flames lick up the thick paper covers and move quickly to the pages inside. As heat licked the tip of her fingers, she dropped the journal onto the cement, allowing it to burn down. As it faded to ashes, she thought about Lauren's words.

Whitney was glad she hadn't read the journal. She hated thinking that Millie might have said mean things about her. They were best friends. They loved each other. That was what Whitney wanted to remember.

Afterward, she went to her car, pulled out her phone.

Notifications lit up the screen.

Natalie.

Dan.

Her mom.

McAvoy.

They'd all been calling. Texting. Messaging.

She called Natalie first.

"Whitney! Oh, thank God. I was so worried. Where have you been?" Natalie's words burst out the minute she answered.

"I'm so sorry." Whitney felt bad for worrying Natalie. It wasn't her intention. "I just...well, I found her."

"You did?"

"Yeah, and it was just like you thought." Whitney worked hard to drum up the enthusiasm she should feel in this situation. Amelia was safe and alive. She'd found her. But it felt like she'd also lost her all over again. "She was just milking it. Stretching out her time with her friend." Sister.

A heavy exhale floated through the line. "God, she'll probably be grounded the rest of her life, huh?"

"You know it." Whitney forced a tight laugh. She wasn't quite ready to come clean with Natalie. Maybe she never would be. If Natalie knew the truth, would she still want to be Whitney's friend? Business partner? She couldn't be sure. "So, um...you can go now. You don't want to wait for me."

"Right. You and Amelia probably need some alone time anyway," Natalie said. "Well, give her a hug for me. She may be in big trouble, but I'm really glad she's safe."

"I will. And, Natalie?"

"Yeah?"

"Thanks...for everything."

"Of course."

After hanging up, Whitney stared out the window, at the big houses and sprawling front yards. A couple walking along the sidewalk, a woman pushing a stroller on her run. Signs of life going on. Moving forward, even though her life seemed to be at a standstill. A purgatory. Waiting to see if Amelia would forgive her. If they could move past this.

She thought about the way Amelia moved away from her, out of her reach. The wariness in her eyes. The distrust. It was like the truth had created a chasm between them. One Whitney couldn't cross.

But she couldn't give up.

Red jacket.

Her daughter had thrown her a lifeline. She'd hold on to that.

And, really, it made sense. Amelia knew Whitney. Knew her heart. Knew who she was at the very core of her being. Amelia had been the only person outside of Millie who did.

When Amelia didn't come home from Lauren's, Whitney never even considered the possibility that it would be related to Millie and the swapped babies. She'd gotten complacent after Millie died, thinking the truth died with her. She'd never factored in Lauren.

Everything she'd done was for the two people she'd loved most in this life—her two Millies. All she ever wanted was to keep them close. She did everything in her power to do that.

She'd lost one Millie. There was no way around that.

But she wouldn't lose the other.

Whitney reopened the Find My Friends app, and Amelia once again popped up on the screen. They were headed down the street, around the corner. Lauren may have thought she was creating distance between them, that she was taking Amelia away from Whitney. But she wasn't. Whitney's daughter was right here in the palm of her hand.

She had a few things to take care of and then she'd follow the girls. And when Amelia was ready, she'd swoop in to rescue her the way she'd done a million times before.

The way she always would.

She almost felt bad for Lauren, believing that Amelia was blindly following her, leaving Whitney behind. Lauren had endured a lot. Whitney was an empathetic person. She understood the pain Lauren felt. She agreed with Lauren on some things. Like with Millie. Her life *had* ended too soon, and it wasn't fair. But despite what Lauren believed, it wasn't Whitney's fault everything blew apart. It was Mitch's. She'd told Millie from the beginning that he would destroy her. And he had.

Whitney thought about it often over the years. The what-ifs. The could-have-beens.

But it didn't change anything. It didn't bring Millie back. Nothing could do that. But Whitney still had a part of her in Amelia. And that was one thing she could control, keep safe. They were close. Tight. And nothing could change that.

Clutching the lifeless baby in her arms, blindly stumbling down the eerily empty hallway, tears obscuring her vision.

She sighed. Picked up her phone again. She knew she needed to call McAvoy. Tell him she'd found Amelia. But not quite yet. Dan's turn was next. She'd stalled long enough. As badly as she wanted to continue to keep this from him, she knew that wasn't an option. Now that Amelia knew, he'd one day find out. It wouldn't be fair coming from Amelia. It had to come from Whitney.

He answered on the first ring.

"Did you find her?"

"Yes," Whitney said.

"Where was she?"

Whitney scratched her scalp, licked her lips. "Well, that's actually what I need to talk to you about. Do you have some time?"

When he said he did, she started back at the beginning. Went through the entire story, the same way she'd told it to Amelia. When she got to the part about their baby, she was startled to find herself crying. Tears that she'd kept locked tightly inside finally spilled out. She'd never been able to grieve with him. To share with him. For so many years, she'd done her best to repress the memory of the baby she'd birthed. She rewrote the narrative in her mind, tricking herself to believe that the Amelia she raised was the only one she'd ever had.

It felt good to remember the baby she'd lost.

"She had so much black hair," she found herself saying, picturing it in her mind. "And the longest fingers, like yours." She remembered staring at them, touching them, running her fingertips over the wrinkled skin.

"Wait...I don't understand..." Dan murmured. "My daughter. Our daughter..." His voice, thick with emotion, trailed off. "Oh, God, it all makes sense now. The way you were acting. How sad you were. The weird things you kept saying...and sometimes...you looked at Amelia like she was a stranger." It was almost like he was talking to himself. Whitney didn't know what to say. Wasn't sure he was even looking for an answer from her. "I just... God, I don't...understand. You never said anything." Another pause. A heavy breath. "I don't get how you could lose our baby and then just take somebody else's."

Whitney sniffed, wiped her eyes. "I didn't just take her. Millie offered."

"You want me to believe that your friend gave you her baby? And none of it was your idea? She just came into your room and then came up with this crazy plan?" he asked.

Whitney hurrying down the hallway in her socked feet, clutching the baby to her chest. Rounding the corner, she slipped into the hospital room. Millie was lying in the bed, dead asleep, bruises blooming on her skin. Machines beeped. An unnatural green light illuminated the room. A baby lay in a clear plastic bassinet next to Millie's bed, her chest rising and falling. The child in Whitney's arms was still.

Whitney blinked, shaking away the unexpected, confusing memory.

"Whitney?"

"Um..." Whitney swallowed hard. "Yes. That's how it happened. You remember Millie, Dan. How messed up she was. Are you really surprised?"

"Even if that's true, how could you go through with it? All these years, passing someone else's child off as your own?"

"We've given Amelia a good life. We saved her. Do you have any idea what her life would've been like if I'd left her with Millie?"

"But she wasn't yours to take."

"Our baby was gone, Dan. There was nothing I could do to bring her back," Whitney said. "But Amelia needed a home. A family. Do you really wish I hadn't taken Millie up on her offer? Do you wish Amelia had never been a part of our lives? That she *was* Mitch's instead?"

Silence rang out. Whitney's heart pounded in her chest. So much was riding on his answer. Lauren would always be a loose cannon, ready to fire off at any moment. But she needed to know that Dan would be her rock. Someone she could count on. Someone who would defend her decision. Believe in it.

The dark eyes of Millie's baby blinking in the dark.

"No," he finally said in a voice so quiet, Whitney barely picked it up. His brokenness could be felt through the phone, like a tangible thing. Whitney had had years to mourn the baby she'd lost. For Dan, it was fresh. And no one knew better than Whitney how awful that felt.

Quietly, so as not to wake Millie, she moved fast. Her entire body trembled as if she were struck with a case of the chills as she set her own, unmoving baby into the crib beside Millie's. With damp, shaky fingers she switched their tags. Then she scooped up the living baby, savoring its warmth.

"Hello, my sweet girl," she whispered as she scurried out of the room and down the darkened hallway. "Amelia." She tried out the name, allowing it to coat her tongue. It tasted sour. Wrong. But she knew in time it would be sweet again.

The tears flowed freely now, her shoulders shaking. "I'm so sorry, Dan."

The dead can't speak. They can't give confessions. Share their version of events. No one but Whitney knew what really happened that night. So, it was up to her to tell the truth.

Millie sat in the middle of her hospital bed, crying into her open palms, her shoulders shaking. Whitney stood at the edge of the doorway, her insides knotting. She swallowed hard, but her mouth was still cotton dry.

"Millie?" she stepped inside.

When Millie's head popped up, the whites of her eyes were strawberry red, the circles around them a sickly shade of gray, as if she'd been repeatedly punched. Sticky tears coated her skin.

"It's Bethany," she choked out the words between sobs. "She's... she's gone."

"Gone?"

"Dead." The word was like a vacuum, sucking out all the air in the room.

"Oh, my God. I'm so sorry." Whitney placed an icy, trembling hand on Millie's arm. "How?"

"They're saying SIDs, but that just means they have no idea." She leaned in close. "They think I'm trash."

"What are you talking about?"

"The nurses." Her eyes were wild. "They know about my past, and it's like they're not taking me seriously at all."

"I don't think that's...that can't be." A nurse passed by the room, glanced in warily, then looked away. Whitney blinked. "I'm sorry." Dan had finally made it back to town. He'd come to take Amelia and Whitney home. They were just waiting on discharge papers. Amelia had been sleeping on his chest when Whitney left the room. She told him she needed to walk around, get blood flowing to her legs. But she couldn't be gone long.

"Why don't I go get you a soda. Pepsi still your favorite?"

"Oh, I don't need caffeine right now," Millie said.

"Orange juice, then? That might be good. Get something in your system?"

"Actually, a Pepsi sounds good."

"Okay." Whitney patted her friend's arm. "I'll be right back."

Whitney took an empty plastic cup from Millie's room, got a soda from the vending machine. In a nearby bathroom, she filled the cup with the brown liquid. Then she reached into her pocket and pulled out the bottle of codeine, Whitney's name prominent on the white sticker. A little over a year ago, she'd had a root canal and her dentist had pre-

scribed this. She only took one. It made her throw up. But she was terrible about cleaning out her purse, and this bottle had been sitting at the bottom of it ever since.

With the blunt side of a lipstick, she crushed the pills, thinking about how she was doing Millie a favor. Her friend had suffered so much. Her life was tragic, really. And there didn't seem to be any hope of it getting better. Now, with the loss of her daughter, Whitney was positive Millie would spiral even further downward. She'd never been able to save Millie before. Maybe now she could. Maybe this was the only way. She dumped the powdered pills inside the soda, then used a lip liner to stir.

"Here you go." Upon returning to Millie's room, Whitney handed her the drink.

Millie sipped it greedily.

"Look, I'm so sorry. I wish I could stay, but I...I have to go." Whitney's gaze flickered to the hallway.

"No, I understand."

"I'm so, so sorry."

Millie started crying again, and Whitney scurried out of her room, never looking back.

Whitney shook the memory away. It didn't even feel true anymore. After all these years, all that was left were her memories. Her version.

It was her story now, and she was sticking to it.

★ ★ ★ ★ ★

ACKNOWLEDGMENTS

Writing a book during a pandemic is especially challenging. While working on *Where I Left Her*, I dealt with self-doubt, crippling writer's block, and a fair amount of anxiety. If it weren't for the following people, this book never would've seen the light of day.

First, as always, my incredible literary agent, Ellen Coughtrey. Thank you for spending hours on the phone, taking apart my messy rough draft and helping me shape it into something we both could be proud of. You always have a knack for identifying the issues on the page, and drawing out the story I had initially wanted to write. To Will Roberts, Rebecca Gardner, Anna Worrall, Caspian Dennis and the entire team at Gernert, you are all so efficient, kind and helpful. I'm grateful to work with each and every one of you.

Second, my awesome editor, April Osborn. I'm grateful for your editorial skills and insight. It's always amazing to me how even little tweaks can change so much, and you have an eye for knowing what tweaks need to be made. And to Lindsey Reeder, Ashley Macdonald, Lucille Miranda, Lia Ferron and Roxanne Jones and the entire team at MIRA—thank you for all of your marketing and publicity efforts, and expertise. You are all so fun and helpful. I love working with you.

To Cal Kenny and the entire team at Sphere, thank you for your belief in me.

Megan Squires, my long-time friend and beta reader, I can't thank you enough for reading early drafts and giving honest feedback. Also: writing days with you, whether at a coffee shop or, more recently, in the barn loft, are my favorite.

Chris Sherman, thank you for your police expertise. I appreciate you taking the time to talk through procedure with me, patiently answering my questions, and reading through the police scenes for accuracy. Also, Melissa Sherman, for making it happen.

To Samantha Downing, Karen Cleveland, Sandie Jones, Samantha Bailey, Christina McDonald and Mindy Mejia, for reading *When I Was You* and sending in such kind reviews. As a fan of yours, it means so much to me.

Thank you to Abby at *Crime by the Book*, Jessica at the Towering TBR, Sonica at *The Reading Beauty* and all of the other bookstagrammers and bloggers who have shared about my books. There are too many to list but know that I'm so grateful to you. Also, to Stacy Gould at Ruby's Books, Tina Ferguson at Face in a Book, and Stephanie Rose at Books Around the Corner for your support.

To all the book clubs who have reached out to me, I'm so honored that you've chosen to read my work and include me in your gatherings.

To my friends and family, your ongoing encouragement and support keeps me going. I love you all.

Andrew, thank you for the space, time and freedom to create and pursue my dream. Eli, I'm grateful that you always lend me an ear to talk over plot issues and brainstorm ideas. And to Kayleen, I'm so glad our relationship is nothing like Whitney and Amelia's (now please let me follow your Finsta). To Luna, the newest addition to our family, thanks for being the best pandemic pet ever and for making this quarantine suck a lot less.

And most importantly, to God—everything I do is for you.